BRING DOWN the Stars

Beautiful Hearts Duet, Book 1

Emma Scott

Copyright © 2018 Emma Scott

All rights reserved.

Cover art by Melissa Panio-Petersen

Interior formatting by That Formatting Lady

No part of this eBook may be reproduced or transmitted in any form or by any means, electronic or mechanical, including photocopying, recording or by any information storage and retrieval system, without written permission from the author.

This is a work of fiction. Any names or characters, businesses or places, events or incidents, are fictitious or have been used in a fictitious manner. Any resemblance to actual persons, living or dead, or actual events is purely coincidental.

Acknowledgements

Robin Hill, if I never wrote another word, I'd still email or text you a hundred times a day and never run out of things to say. Thank you for every day. Love you so much.

Melissa Petersen, you are family and have shown that a thousand times over. You're in my heart forever.

Joanna, I found the energy and confidence to finish this book because of you. Thank you for giving me that last push over the hill. Love you.

Grey, Sarah, Angela, Joy, Suanne, and Mom for helping me chisel the raw mess of words into something I hope pays proper tribute to Edmond Rostand's masterpiece. Love you all so much.

Amy Burke Mastin, I see the house you built for her and I feel stronger. Thank you is not enough.

Joanne and Sharon, for LP. For connecting me directly to one of my deepest sources of comfort. Thank you, and with so much love.

Jade West, for knowing the rarity of a decent night's sleep; we are stronger and will get stronger every day <3

Danielle Sanchez and Kelly Brenner Simmon of InkSlinger PR. You both have been more than business associates from Day One, but have proven to be an amazing support system, above and beyond. Thank you for being there for me. <3

Kate Stewart, just knowing you are there, in the world, being Kate, brings me peace. All my love.

Kennedy Ryan, you are gift to the human race, and I thank the universe every day our paths crossed and now run together, hopefully forever (and with a beautiful curb running alongside with which we can stop and serenade the unwilling masses.) Love you.

And to the book community. I have no words. Not enough. The volume of support, care, and love you have shown me and my family has been extraordinary. I will never be able to thank you for not only being there during the sharpest agony, but through the longer, lonelier days were the ache dulls but doesn't fade. Thank you for not leaving me alone. For remembering her. For being the best collection of women supporting women—not just me, so many others. I am indebted forever. Thank you and with much love.

Playlist

Father of Mine, Everclear
Ocean Eyes, Billie Eilish
Be Mine, Ofenbach
I Feel Like I'm Drowning, Two Feet
Just Friends, Morgan Saint
Little Lion Man, Mumford and Sons
The Night We Met, Lord Huron
&Run, Sir Sly
Give Yourself a Try, The 1975

Author's Note

    This book was written in the Before. Before my life changed forever. Before I stepped into the dark forest and realized I could not go back the way I'd come. It was closed to me forever. The duet itself is a story of transformation and overcoming tremendous adversity, and it's happened more times than I can count in my writing career that art and life intertwine in mind-boggling ways. There are no coincidences. I cannot go back, only forward, and so I give you this book, from the Before, with all my hope, best intentions, and my love because the first lesson the After taught me is that love is all that's ever mattered; now, then, and forever.

Dedication

For Katy,
a gift from the universe; the kind of person Izzy would have run up to and hugged on sight

For Bill,
my love, my partner in this life; we clasped hands tightly when the forest became impossibly, agonizingly dark, and we're still holding them as we slowly emerge into the light. All my love, honey. Always.

PART I
Sinclair Prep

Prologue

"Almost Empty"
by Weston J. Turner, age 12

I was seven-years-old when my dad left us. That morning, he showered, shaved, and dressed in a suit and tie, same as always. Drank his coffee at the kitchen counter while we ate breakfast, same as always. He kissed Ma on the cheek, told my sisters and me to be good, and drove off in his Nissan Altima. Same as always.

At school, in Mr. Fitzsimmons' math class, I got a funny feeling in my stomach. By noon, my stomach churned and my skin was hot. I barely made it to the big gray trash can at the end of the row of tables in the cafeteria before puking my guts out.

The lunch supervisor sent me to the nurse, and the nurse called Dad, but he wasn't at his office. Ma had to come and get me, grousing the whole time that she'd had to take a bus from work—Dad drove our only car.

Ma and I got off the 9 bus, and walked down the street toward our house. We lived in Woburn, a little north of the city, in a shabby little house with blue siding and a white roof at the end of a cul-de-sac. On the street, with two huge suitcases in hand, was my father. He was stuffing one into the trunk of his car and the other was at his feet. He froze when he saw us.

Ma started walking fast, then running, demanding to know what my father was up to, louder and louder. She let go of my hand because I could hardly keep up, and left me on the curb while she rushed to him. They talked but I couldn't hear what they said through the fever that stuffed my head like cotton.

Ma looked more scared than I'd ever seen her. She started crying, then screaming. Dad talked in a low voice, then threw up his hand and slammed the trunk of the car. In my delirium, the sound was huge. A bomb going off. A meteor smashing us out of our home, destroying everything, leaving behind a huge crater. A hole blasted in the center of each of us.

Dad tore out of my mother's slapping, grasping hands, and climbed into the front seat to start the car. Ma screamed and screamed that he was no kind of man, and then collapsed to her knees, sobbing and telling him to go and never come back.

Dad drove the car off the curb and around the cul-de-sac. He slowed in front of me and waved once from behind his closed window. Guilt had turned his features into someone unrecognizable.

I shook my head no, and kicked the passenger door.

He kept going. I slammed my hand on the trunk. No!

He didn't stop.

For a second, I stood with my pulse rushing in my ears and my face on fire, watching the car roll away. Then I ran. I ran after him as fast as I could. I shouted at him as loud as I could, hot tears streaking down my burning skin.

Did he see me in his rearview? He must have; a seven-year-old boy screaming for his dad to come back, while running as fast as his legs could carry him. Not fast enough.

He sped up, turned the corner, and was gone.

The ground tilted out from under me. I stumbled to the asphalt, scraping my knees and palms, my breath wheezing through hard sobs.

We later found out he'd quit his job weeks ago and hadn't paid the mortgage on the house in three months. Instead, he kept the money for his escape.

Did he wonder what we'd do with only Ma's pay from cutting hair? Did he care that we'd lose our little house in Woburn? In the months to come, did he ever wonder if we cried for him? Did he consider my sisters and I blamed ourselves, because of course we did. If we were good enough, he would've stayed.

BRING DOWN the Stars

Or taken us with him.

Instead, he took his clothes and the stuff from his bathroom. Dad scraped out his closet and drawers, taking everything...except for one dress sock. Black with gold-colored thread at the toe.

I looked at that lone sock in the drawer and pictured the other one in his luggage, now traveling with him—wherever he was going. He couldn't be bothered to grab the other one.

Like us, it wasn't worth going back for.

His children were left behind like a sock in a drawer that was almost empty, and that was a million times worse than if there was nothing left at all.

The bank took the house. Ma started drinking a lot of beer at night and had to ask Uncle Phil for money to get us into an apartment in Southie.

I burnt the sock.

I was only seven but the anger in me felt so much bigger. Hotter. Like a fever that would never go away. I had to watch the sock turn to ash. That way, if Dad came back looking for it, I could tell him, "It's gone. I burnt it. There is nothing left for you here."

He'd say he was sorry, and I'd say it was too late, and I'd make him go. I'd be in charge, and when his car drove away, I wouldn't run after it.

But that was five years ago. He isn't coming back.

"You only got this shirt so keep it clean. You hear me?"

Ma cinched the maroon-and-gold striped tie up to my throat hard enough to make me wince. "You come home messed up, there's nothing I can do for you. You want to look like a poor bastard from Southie?"

"I *am* a poor bastard from Southie," I said, earning another jerk on my tie from Ma.

She wagged her finger in my face, last night's beers still lingering on her breath. "Watch your language or you'll get kicked out before you even start."

Holy irony, Batman.

My language was how I wound up winning a scholarship to the most expensive school in Boston in the first place. My essay beat 3,000 other entries to get me a full ride to the Sinclair Preparatory School for Boys, and the high school Academy. Unfortunately the ride came with no transportation, so I was getting up at five in the morning to catch the 38 bus into the city center.

I looked myself over in the mirror on the back of the door, not recognizing my own reflection. At public school, I'd worn jeans and a T-shirt every day of my life. A long-sleeved shirt on picture day. A jacket in winter. Now I stared at the maroon blazer with gold around the edges, black trousers, and white shirt with the Sinclair logo. I wondered who that guy in the mirror was trying to fool.

"Stop fidgeting," Ma said, fussing with my hair.

She'd cut it short but left some of the front long. She was a stylist down at Betty's, and she was good at her job.

"Don't you look handsome?"

I ducked from under her hand and scowled. "I look like I've been sorted into Gryffindor."

Ma sniffed. "What the hell you talking about? You look great. Just like one of them."

One of them.

I dropped my gaze to my old, worn out Chucks. They were the only thing that was the same about me, and a dead giveaway that I wasn't ever going to be 'one of them.' The other boys would have dress shoes, but shoes didn't come with the uniform, and Ma couldn't afford them this month. Maybe next. Maybe never. I was okay with never. You can't run in dress shoes.

I ran a lot. When I got mad, I ran around the old, pitted track at my public school as fast as I could, for as long as I could. I don't know why; I didn't particularly like running, but I was fast. I still had dreams about chasing Dad's car, so maybe that's why. Maybe I'm still trying to catch him. Stupid. Running on a track, you just go in circles. You always come back to where you start.

"No fighting, Weston Jacob Turner," Ma said that morning, taking my chin in her hand and turning me to face her. The curve of her acrylic nail touched the bridge of my nose where a small break hadn't healed straight. "You can't be carrying on at that fancy school like you do around here. One fight and you're out."

That's another thing I did when I got mad. I got into fights. I was mad a lot.

I jerked my chin out of her grip. "What if some other kid gives me hell first?"

"Let it go. You think the administration is going to listen to

BRING DOWN the Stars

your side over one of them trust fund babies? Those parents donate." Ma lit a cigarette, and shook her head of bleached blonde hair. She squinted through a haze of smoke and pointed her cigarette at me. "You fight with one of their kids, you're going to lose even if you win. *Especially* if you win."

It was still dark out when Ma smacked a smoky-smelling kiss on my cheek and told me to "scoot" so she could go back to bed. My sisters were both still sleeping in the other bedroom. They were both old enough to move out and get jobs, but instead they took the big room. I had the tiny room off the kitchen. Ma had the couch. She fell asleep on it surrounded by empty beer cans and the TV on every night, and kept her clothes in the hall closet.

By the time it reached downtown, the 38 bus had cleared out and I had a window seat as we rolled up to Sinclair Prep. All cement and statues—one of the old historical buildings since the time of the Revolution, not far from Trinity Church. I was twenty minutes early for first bell when I climbed the few cement steps to the heavy front door. I slipped down the quiet corridors where teachers worked to get their classrooms ready, careful to keep my Chucks from squeaking on the polished floors.

The library at the end of the main hall was silent. Cool. All gleaming brown wood—tables, chairs, floors, bookshelves. I couldn't believe this was a middle school. I had to remind myself that the library also served Sinclair Academy. Even so, you wouldn't think it was any kind of school library to see the books they had.

My fingers trailed over the spines. Grown-up books. Books I had to badger my sisters to check out for me at the public library. Books with sex and bad words and grown-up problems. I liked those better than the kiddie books. My problems didn't feel like kid problems. When your dad leaves you behind like a forgotten sock, a piece of your childhood rots away—the part where you can just be a kid without worrying so much.

I worried all the time. About Ma and how she drank a lot of beer most nights, and ranted to my sisters that all men were trash and would always end up hurting the women they were supposed to love. She didn't know I was listening, but I was.

I worried about the parade of scummy boyfriends that went in and out of our apartment over the years. Trash, just like Ma said. Maybe she was right about all men. I worried I would grow up to be

5

trash too, and would hurt any woman I might someday love, so I vowed not to love anyone.

I worried about money. Not for me, I could get by. But Ma had an ulcer from worrying about bills, and chugged almost as much Pepto as she did Michelob. They shut off the water last month for three days until Uncle Phil paid the bill.

Getting this scholarship was going to help my family. I'd get into a good college, get a good job, and maybe cut out the worrying for a little while.

In the library, I looked for one of my favorites, *Tropic of Cancer* by Henry Miller. They didn't have it. It was *very* grown-up. I'd read it twice, and certain parts of it more than twice, under the covers in my bedroom with either my notebook, or a fistful of Kleenex at the ready. Or both.

Henry Miller wrote about lice-ridden beds in Paris flats (a flat was a kind of apartment, not a woman's shoe; I looked it up) and about being hungry. Always hungry.

I was hungry a lot too.

Miller also wrote about 'crawling up' a woman in bed, and used bad words for her body parts. His writing made me want to grab my notebook and pen to write down my own words. I shouldn't love a woman, but I could write about the sex I would someday have, or admire her beauty from a safe distance. I'd write poems instead of books, where you choose only the words that mattered most, and you didn't have to say who it was about. It was just a poem, and poems can be about anyone or no one.

And anyway, writing helped. I stopped worrying when I wrote or when I jerked off.

Ha! I should've put *that* in my essay.

They found me at lunch, where I was reading Kerouac's *On the Road,* and eating spaghetti and green beans from Sinclair's gourmet cafeteria.

One hot meal a day: check.

"Look here, it's the charity case."

Jason Kingsley. I'd already heard all about him and it was barely noon. He slid onto the bench directly in front of me, while his

BRING DOWN the Stars

richie friends sat at my empty table, boxing me in.

"What did you call me?" I asked, my heart pounding a slow, heavy beat of dread.

"You're the contest winner, right?" Jason asked. "The one who wrote that essay about your dad abandoning your family?"

I slowly lowered my book, amazed my hands weren't shaking as a rush of humiliation swept through me like a wild fire, making my skin hot.

"Yep," I said. "That's me."

How the hell...?

"They posted your essay on the Sinclair website," said a redheaded guy with bad skin, who'd crowded in next to me. "Did you know that?"

"He totally did *not* know that," Jason said, watching me.

A couple of guys snickered.

Fuck everything, everywhere.

I'd forgotten that when I entered the contest, one of the stipulations was Sinclair could publish the winning essay wherever they wanted. When I submitted the damn thing, I didn't think I had a prayer of winning. It hadn't mattered.

Now it mattered.

"So your dad took off and left the sock behind?" the redhead said. "Sucks to be you."

"That does suck, Sock Boy," Jason said, plucking a green bean off my tray and chewing it. "You must feel like shit."

"Sock Boy," the redhead snickered. "Good one, Jason."

"Really? Sock Boy?" I said. "That's the best you can do?"

"I don't know," Jason said stiffly, tilting his chin up. "Maybe you're not worth more than *Sock Boy*."

Redhead picked at a zit on his chin. "You think you could do better?"

"I can think of a crap-ton better insults, just off the top of my head."

"Prove it."

"Sure. No problem."

I cracked my knuckles, thinking fast. But the insults came easy; I'd twisted that knife in my own guts a thousand times since Dad left.

"What about...Your dad abandoned your family and all you got was a lousy sock?"

7

Snickers.

Jason crossed his arms. "Lame."

I shrugged casually, while my mind revved like a racecar at the starting line. "Mmmkay. You're lucky; on Take Your Son to Work Day, you get to stay home."

The redhead kid snorted a laugh, earning a glare from Jason. I kept going, and my audience warmed to me quick. With each insult I hurled at myself, the other guys got more and more into it, covering their mouths, laughing and *oohing*, like a rap battle, where I was the attacker and victim, both.

"I hate to say you have a deadbeat dad, but if the sock fits…?"

"If you need a man-to-man talk, does your mom take out an ad on Craigslist?"

"Are you a Jehovah's Witness now? They don't celebrate Father's Day either."

The guys were in an uproar now, but Jason's jaw clenched. I leaned over the table.

"Knock knock," I said, glaring at him.

"Fuck off."

"Knock knock."

He sniffed, not meeting my eyes. "This is stupid."

I cocked my head to the rest of the table. "*Knock knock.*"

"*Who's there?*" they answered in unison.

"I don't know," I said, "but not your dad, that's for goddamn sure."

The peals of laughter seemed to strike Jason in the back as he hunched over and flinched as if the insults were directed at him, instead of me.

"You look confused, buddy," I said. "You need me to explain that one?"

"You think you're so fucking smart?" Jason said. "You just insulted yourself ten times over. But you know what?" He smiled darkly. He had the simple truth on his side, and he knew it. "It doesn't matter how clever you think you are. You're just Sock Boy, and that's all you'll ever be."

His hand snaked out and he shoved my half-full tray of food into my lap, painting my pants and white dress shirt with spaghetti sauce and milk.

"Ooops!" Jason said, jumping out of his seat. "My bad."

BRING DOWN the Stars

I shot to my feet, ignoring the cold milk in my crotch and hot spaghetti sauce on my stomach, and stared him down, nose to nose. My hands were balled so tightly into fists that my knuckles ached. Jason didn't back down and the entire cafeteria went quiet, watching.

"Go ahead," Jason seethed in a low whisper. "Take your shot. I got six witnesses who'll say it was an accident. You'll lose your precious scholarship. You wanna take that chance, Sock Boy?"

I sure as hell did. But hitting him would get me kicked out. Ratting on him was out of the question. That left letting it go like a goddamn chump.

"What's going on, guys?" asked a friendly voice.

Out of my periphery, I saw a tall guy, dark hair, big. He looked older than the rest of us.

Lots of kids talked on the first day of school, informing incoming seventh graders of their place in the Sinclair caste system. Jefferson Drake, a football-playing senior at the Academy, was the most popular kid in school. King of Sinclair. His little brother, Connor, was the prince.

I guessed this was him.

Connor stood with his hands in his pockets, casual, as if he owned the school, instead of being just another twelve-year-old kid.

Jason smirked and turned away. "Nothing," Jason said. "Sock Boy had a little accident."

"Yeah, I'll bet," Connor said, frowning at the mess on my uniform. "Why you gotta be an asshole, Kingsley?"

"I'm not. Just clumsy, I guess," Jason said, but he backed off. "See you around, Sock Boy. Shame about your shirt." He clucked his tongue. "You can always write another essay. Call it 'Laundry Day' and maybe the school will pay for a new uniform."

"Maybe your mom will," Connor said, grinning.

Jason laughed and the two bumped fists. "See you at practice, Drake."

"I hope so. You need it."

Jason flipped him two middle fingers and took his crowd away with him.

Fuck all of these guys, I thought.

I angrily brushed cold spaghetti noodles off my pants. The slacks were black and hid the stain, but my shirt looked like I'd been shot in the gut.

"Shit."

"You got a spare?" Connor asked.

"Fuck off."

He held up his hands. "Hey, just trying to help. I have extra, and my house isn't far from here. If we left now, we can be back before bell."

I narrowed my eyes at him.

"It's either that or you go the rest of the day looking like an extra in a bad horror movie."

Connor's friendly grin was seemingly a permanent fixture to his face.

"Why would you help me?"

He frowned. "Why wouldn't I?" He stuck out his hand. "I'm Connor Drake, by the way."

"Congratulations."

Connor laughed and lowered his hand. "Come on. You need to change, right?"

I clenched my teeth. "I guess."

"Let's go."

He started walking. I followed.

"You're new, right? You weren't here last year."

"No shit. I'm Wes Turner, the charity case."

Connor's dark brows came together. "Charity case... Oh, that was you? The essay winner? That explains Kingsley's nickname. Hey, don't let him get to you. He's not all bad. We've known each other since kindergarten."

"Has he been a prick that long?"

Connor laughed. "Pretty much." He lifted his chin at the security guard at the front door. "Hey, Norm. Just running home to get something for my friend, here."

Norm the Security Guard opened the door for Connor Drake, like a doorman in a fancy hotel. "Be back before bell."

"Will do."

"How did you do that?" I asked, as we stepped out of the school and into the light of a September afternoon. "Lunch is closed."

"My parents donate a lot of money," Connor said with that mega-watt grin. "*A lot* of money."

He walked us around the corner and down Dartmouth Street, which led toward a neighborhood of old, elegant row houses in tawny

BRING DOWN the Stars

sandstone and black ironwork. Connor and I walked along red brick sidewalks and passed old-fashioned street lamps. The entire block looked like one giant castle.

"Hey, congrats on the scholarship, by the way," Connor said. "I heard a lot of kids tried for that. Your essay was really good."

My shoulders hunched. "You read it too?"

"My parents can't get over it. Made me read it twice."

Fuck me sideways.

"It was all right," I muttered. I waited for Connor to give me shit about that goddamn sock. He didn't.

"It was better than all right," Connor said. "You're lucky; I can't write to save my life. And wouldn't you know it, I have Mr. Wrightman for English."

"I have Wrightman too," I ventured. "He's tough?"

"The toughest," Connor said. "He assigns a crap-ton of papers, long stories, short stories… Hell, I heard he even makes us write poems. Fucking *poems.*"

I stepped a little lighter. "Yeah, that sucks."

"Tell me about it." Connor glanced at me. "But you should do all right. Is that what you want to be when you grow up? A writer?"

The day before I might've said yes, but *Sock Boy* had shown me that I wasn't ready to deal with the repercussions. Writing was something I'd keep to myself where it couldn't hurt me again. I was worn out from being hurt. My dad taking off showed me with brutal clarity the cost of having feelings, of caring too much. I still wanted to write, but making a habit out of bleeding my heart out and having it thrown back in my face was not going to happen. Not ever again.

"I'm not sure yet." I glanced up at him. "You?"

His grin widened. "I want to open a sports bar in downtown Boston. Like *Cheers*, you know? I want to stand in the middle of it all, with a game on every TV. I love baseball. Do you like baseball?"

Before I could answer, he went on.

"I could talk baseball all day. And hockey. I want to make a place where people can hang out, talk sports or watch a game, and just have a good time."

I nodded. "Seems like you'd be good for that."

Hell, Connor Drake, even aged twelve, seemed like he was put on this earth to open a sports bar. But his grin dimmed.

"Tell my parents that. They think I should go to an Ivy League college and do something 'big and important.' Doesn't help that my brother, Jefferson, is all about *big* and *important*."

I didn't know what to say. The idea of doing something 'big and important' seemed impossible for a poor kid like me. If I could get into a good college, get a decent job to help my Ma out a little, I'd consider it a miracle.

"You're from Southie, right?"

"Right," I said.

"What's that like?"

My hackles went up. "What's *what* like? Living in a crappy apartment and needing charity to pay for a decent school?"

Connor wasn't put off by my hard tone; a trait that would endure years into our friendship. The glue that would hold it together many, many times.

He shrugged. "I don't know, maybe. Sometimes it seems like everything around here is so complicated...when it doesn't have to be. I like simple, you know?"

I scowled. "Being poor is pretty damn simple. You need money for shit and you don't have it. The end."

"Yeah, that's gotta suck," he said, and somehow, I didn't want to deck him one for sounding so blasé about what was a constant struggle in my universe.

Connor had a strange charisma; as if he were impossible to dislike. His superpower. I was the opposite; I made it really damn easy for people not to like me—I preferred it that way. And yet here I was, hanging with the most popular kid in my grade who'd told Norm the Security Guard that I was his *friend*. The disorientation grew stronger when Connor nodded his chin ahead.

"So, this is me."

I stared, slack-jawed. A four-story Victorian row house in rustic beige with black window frames. The kind of house you'd see in Boston historical brochures. A staircase led from the brick sidewalk to black double doors with ornate stained glass at the top.

"This is your *house*?" I asked.

"One of them," Connor said with a grin, again avoiding sounding like an arrogant douchebag.

I stared up at his house, drinking it in because my brain couldn't comprehend that people could actually live in houses that belonged in brochures. Connor wasn't just rich, he was billionaire-

BRING DOWN the Stars

rich. I wondered if his parents were famous. He looked famous himself—like the guy they'd cast in a movie about a popular star baseball player, who takes the poor kid under his wing. The kind of guy who was too happy to be a bully or prick, and who coasted through life on a never-ending wave of his parents' money.

Turned out, I was right about all of it, and the poor kid Connor Drake took under his wing was me.

The Drakes' cleaning lady washed my uniform and gave me one of Connor's old shirts. After school, we went back and played his Xbox that was hooked up to his state-of-the-art sound system while sitting in dual black leather beanbag chairs.

Connor asked me to stay for dinner, and I met his parents, Victoria and Alan Drake.

Mr. Drake owned a hundred different companies under the Drake name, and Mrs. Drake was a state senator. Boston royalty, or as close to it, as you could get.

The Drakes fed me the kind of elaborate dinner I'd only seen in movies about rich people. In their immense dining room, under a heavy crystal chandelier, I felt some of the pressure they put on Connor: to work hard and get better grades, to go to college, instead of opening a sports bar like he wanted. They wanted a friendship between their son and me—the scrappy street kid who'd show Connor how far hard work and smarts could get you. They wouldn't shut up about my essay; how impressed they were, how I'd turned a bad situation into something positive.

I thought Connor would hate me after his parents talked me up so much, but for some crazy-ass reason, he liked me. Our friendship was instant, as if we'd known each other in a past life and were just picking up where we left off. And despite his parents' pressure, he was happy. I'd never met anyone who was happy. The tight coil of tension that twisted my gut since my dad left, eased a little when I was around him. I wasn't jumping for joy every minute, but sometimes I stopped worrying, and that was enough.

Connor saved me from a Sinclair-lifetime of dodging fights and being called Sock Boy. His buddies left me alone, and by the time we started at the Academy, they were my friends too, if only by the sheer power of his effortless charm.

The Drakes treated me like a son and even extended their generosity to my mother and sisters over the years. My family's loud talk and Southie accents never sounded more pronounced than they did bouncing off the Drakes' dining room walls, but the Drakes treated them with kindness and respect. To my mortified humiliation, they paid the bills Ma shamelessly admitted she couldn't pay. They gave generous gifts at birthdays and holidays, never asking for a thing in return.

Still, I felt an unspoken pressure to take care of Connor, to make sure he 'made something' of his life aside from running a sports bar. I never tried to talk him out of his sports bar dream, but I kept him afloat at Sinclair by helping him with the essays and papers in Wrightman's class.

By the end of the first year, I was writing them for him. Connor wasn't dumb, but he didn't like to think too hard or dig too deep. Contentment was his default mode. He lived to laugh and have fun and when I wrote his papers, I tried to channel his happiness over the rough, fraying wires of my own anger and pain.

I always remembered to misspell a word or two.

Throughout high school, I broke every Sinclair record for track and field. Running got me a two-year NCAA scholarship to Amherst University in western Massachusetts.

A liberal arts college wasn't what the Drakes had in mind for Connor, but he hadn't shown an interest in any college until I got into Amherst. Connor—who could have gone anywhere in the country thanks to his parents' checkbook—wanted to stick with me, and that touched me more than I could ever say.

I promised his parents to help him out and make sure he did his work, knowing I'd be writing his college papers too.

The Drakes paid the rent on a sweet, off-campus apartment for us, which allowed me to stretch my scholarship over three years instead of two. They would've paid my entire tuition if I let them, but the free rent was hard enough on my stubborn pride. I was determined to make it on my own—to show my asshole dad I didn't need his help. But every kindness the Drakes bestowed was a weight on my shoulders. A growing debt.

And where I came from, debts must always be repaid.

PART II
Amherst

CHAPTER One

Autumn

He cheated on you.

    The same thought greeted me first thing in the morning, riding on the current of my clock's blaring alarm and slugging me in the heart. I snaked out my hand to shut off the alarm. The painful whispers weren't so easily silenced.

    You gave him your heart and he threw it in the garbage.

"Stop it," I whispered to the dark room.

    The clock read four in the morning. I was trained for early rising. Growing up on the Caldwell Farm in Nebraska, 'sleeping in' meant staying in bed until eight, and only on your birthday. Three months ago, I would've popped out of bed, humming a tune and ready to tackle the day. But that was before I walked into my boyfriend Mark's bedroom and found him naked and voracious with another woman.

    Mark stole my ability to fall asleep at night, and get out of bed in the morning. These days, when the alarm went off, I only wanted to sink back into bed and sleep for a hundred years. Or curl up under the covers with my worn-out copy of Emily Dickinson poems and cry. Cry until the vision of Mark and that girl was washed out of my eyes forever.

BRING DOWN the Stars

"It's the first day of classes," I muttered to the ceiling. "He's not allowed to ruin this for me."

I blinked the sleep out of my eyes, then sat up and stretched, shaking off the tiredness. The heartache clung harder and wouldn't let go.

I showered, then put on a pretty sundress in cream with small pink flowers all over it, and a matching cardigan. The dress was a designer label I'd found at Marshall's for fifteen dollars. Designer labels didn't mean anything to me, but looking nice at all times did.

If you want to be successful, dress as if you already are.

I'd read that in a magazine once. That advice went hand in hand with a Yale study I read about that showed people who dressed nicely or professionally were taken more seriously. I had serious goals, and any preconceived notions about me—a poor farm girl from Nebraska—would only get in the way.

I tied up my long, coppery red hair in a bun to keep it out of my way for work. A little mascara and lip-gloss was all I ever wore for makeup. As I dabbed sunscreen on the light smattering of freckles across my nose, my phone chimed with a text.

Here's to a wonderful start to your junior year! We're all proud of you. Love, Mom, Dad, and Travis

I typed back, **Thank you. Love you all and miss you already. Xoxo**

I blinked back sudden tears. I'd returned from my summer in Nebraska only a week ago, but the urge to go back was an emotional hunger stronger than the physical one rumbling in my stomach. I wanted to go home and nurse my heartache surrounded by people who loved me.

I headed downstairs for coffee. The apartment was quiet and dark. My roommate wouldn't be up for hours. Ruby always scheduled all her classes no earlier than eleven a.m. But she didn't have to work like I did.

I sat at the counter with my First Day of Class To-Do List and a cup of coffee. I was big on lists. I'd read that making lists helped calm anxiety about all the stuff you have to do. Another article said that writing down goals helped them come true. I had journals full of goals and lists. Getting over Mark was #1 on today's agenda.

"Everyone suffers terrible break-ups," I muttered to my empty kitchen. "You have too much work to do this year to let Mark Watts

17

drag you down."

Saying his name out loud was a bad idea. I gulped the last of my coffee, swallowed it down hard and grabbed my backpack. I took a last look at myself in the mirror. Shadows under my red-rimmed eyes but otherwise okay. Maybe the same advice about looking professional applied here too.

Don't act like you're heartbroken and you won't be.

The sun was creeping over the eastern horizon when I stepped out of the campus apartment and unlocked my bike from the rack. The burnt orange and purple light spreading over Amherst reminded me of sunrises on the farm. When I was little, I'd sit on my dad's shoulders and watch the light turn wheat fields to liquid gold, or spill over the sea of green corn in spring.

"Do you know why the dawn is so beautiful, Autumn?" Dad asked. "Because every day is another chance for something amazing. You just have to be ready for it."

Maybe that's why I dressed as nicely as my tiny budget would allow, and got up early, even on Sundays, and made lists of my goals, and worked my butt off with the hopes of doing some good in the world. When something amazing came my way, not only would I be ready, I'd have helped make it happen.

I wasn't about to let Mark's betrayal—or anything else—get in the way of that.

I put on a smile as I stepped into the bakery at a few minutes to five. The scent of warm bread, sugar, and coffee wrapped pleasantly around me, along with a baritone voice singing an operatic aria.

"Good morning, Edmond," I called, stowing my bag behind the counter. I took my apron from a front peg on the wall and tied it around my waist.

The singing grew louder and the large frame of Edmond de Guiche burst through the back door, his hands folded over his heart as his aria took a turn for the dramatic.

Edmond only sang about love. Lost love, true love, unrequited love. The big Frenchman with the elegant mustache was like an opera character himself, dispensing lines of poetry or bursts of song to his customers with every pastry, convinced love and food went hand in hand.

"Ma chère," he said, when the last notes faded. He wrapped his thick arms around me in an embrace I desperately needed. Edmond's

BRING DOWN the Stars

hugs felt as good as getting a full night's sleep.

"So good to see you again," he said, holding me at arm's length. "How was your summer? How is your family?"

"They're fine," I said, crossing two fingers to hide the white lie. The farm wasn't doing so well. Dad said none of the farms in our county were, but we shouldn't worry. *Yet.* Of course, I'd spent the summer watching him and Mom do nothing but worry, while I worked waiting tables at Cracker Barrel.

"I missed you," I told Edmond, and that wasn't a lie at all.

"I missed you, ma petite chère," he said. "This place is dimmer without your beauteous light."

Tears sprang to my eyes again. Crying twice in one morning was unacceptable. I turned away quickly to work on prepping the coffee machines.

"Always the romantic, Edmond."

"Always," he said. "Are you ready to begin a new year at the big school?"

"I think so. This year is tough because—"

He cut me off by tipping my chin up with one finger. His large brown eyes were heavy with concern. "I see a new sadness here."

"It's nothing."

Edmond frowned.

I sighed. No sense in hiding it. Mark and I had been inseparable for two years. He'd dragged himself out of bed many a morning to have a coffee at the Panache Blanc while I worked, just so he could be close to me. Edmond knew him well.

No, he didn't. Turns out, no one knew Mark well. Least of all me.

"I broke up with Mark," I said.

"Quel bordel!" Edmond bellowed.

"I'm fine. I'd rather not talk about it—"

"Why? What happened?" He waved his flour-covered hands. "I know, you will not want to discuss, but he is a fool, that is plain. *Pfft.*"

He made me feel the fool.

I smoothed my skirt. "Done is done. I'm going to move past it."

Edmond wrinkled his nose. "A tough cookie, as you Americans say. Bon. I have no cookies for my tough cookie but..." He took a cranberry scone from the tray he'd just pulled from the oven, put it on

19

a plate and handed it to me.

"Oh no, I don't need…"

"You do. I insist." Edmond called to the back. "Eh! Philippe!"

His backroom assistant, a wiry eighteen-year-old named Phil Glassman, poked his head out from the back room with a vague grunt. His eyelids were still at half-mast. Poor Phil—a year and a half working here and he still couldn't get used to the early hours.

"Philippe, you prepare the coffee," Edmond said. "Autumn will start after she eats."

"I'm fine," I said, knowing there was no arguing with Edmond when it came to matters of the heart. Food, wine, and song were his cure-alls, and I had to admit the scone smelled amazing. I could use the comfort food.

Edmond ushered me to the back room, plopping me down on a chair. "Eat, ma chère. Eat and taste the sweetness in life, not the bitter, oui? You are too good for mortal men, but true love will find you. This I know."

He patted my cheek and barked at Phil again as they prepared for the morning rush. I ate the scone and tried to take his words to heart. It helped. Not so much the food as the love baked into it.

There might be jobs in Amherst where I could make more money, but none of them had Edmond.

After the early morning rush, I hung up my apron, waved at Edmond and biked back to campus. My first class of the day was Intro to Economics with Environmental Applications, a course both in line with my humanitarian career goals and that satisfied a general ed requirement. Win-win.

I always sat in the front row of my classes, taking notes until my fingers cramped. I envied the students who captured the lecture on their smart phones. My phone was more than a few incarnations behind the latest model, and I didn't want to wear it out.

After class, a text came in from Ruby:

Lunch on the quad?

Usual spot, I typed back.

I'll be the super hot one in the yoga pants.

BRING DOWN the Stars

I grinned. Whereas I never left the house without looking as put-together as possible, Ruby Hammond could hardly be bothered to wear matching shoes.

The sun was brilliant that September morning. I loved the Amherst campus with its miles of rolling green grass stretched along Federal-style buildings of red brick. Trees dotted the green where students basked in the late summer sun, talking and reuniting after the summer break.

Whether you were in kindergarten or college, the first day of school seemed to hold a special feeling of possibility. Like one of my dad's mornings, where amazing things could happen.

Ruby and I had claimed a wrought iron street lamp in front of the Admin building as 'our place.' She was waiting for me, stretched out on the grass, wearing the promised yoga pants and a wrinkled baseball-style shirt. Her dark hair was tied up in a messy bun and she shielded her eyes with a caramel-colored hand.

We'd been paired up randomly as freshman roommates, and despite our differences, we hit it off at once. I kept our place clean, and in exchange, she kept me laughing when my studies threatened to bury me.

"Here we go again," Ruby said, greeting me with a smile. "Same Bat-time, same Bat-place. Same same-same. Are we in a rut?"

I folded my dress under me as I knelt beside her. "It's the first day of class. We can't be in a rut already." My smile slipped. "And not everything is the same."

Ruby frowned, and dug into her bag for her lunch. "You're right. That cheating asshole is out of the picture. Can't say I'm sorry."

"I can," I said, smoothing my skirt.

"Hey," Ruby said, touching my hand. "I'm no good at saying the right thing to make you feel better. This we know. But in a month, my thoughtless commentary will be just what you want to hear."

"I know. I wish I could fast-forward."

"Fucker," Ruby muttered, and leaned back on her elbows to survey the activity on the quad. "On the bright side, Amherst has no shortage of fine-ass men to distract you from your problems." She jerked her chin to a group of guys tossing around a football. "Mmhmm. No shortage at all."

I rolled my eyes and drew out my own lunch—a salad with dried cranberries and feta cheese, and a bottle of iced tea. "Pass."

"Girl—"

"Ruby, please," I said. "It's only been three months."

"I'm not suggesting anything serious. I'm talking purely sexual encounters of the meaningless kind." She smiled gently. "I know, I know. Not your thing. I just hate seeing you hurt. Mark's a damn fool and you can quote me."

I took a bite of salad and let my gaze follow Ruby's to the guys throwing a football. My eyes kept landing on a tall boy with broad shoulders and a wide, charming smile. Even at a distance, something about that flashing smile was comforting. Like one of Edmond's scones. A smile that made it seem like all was right in the world.

My astute best friend caught me staring. "On the off-chance you're wondering, that's Connor Drake. Junior hottie. Baseball player, *player*-player, and all-around beer pong champ two years running."

"I don't think I've seen him before."

"No, of course not," Ruby said with an eye roll. "I've only mentioned him, like, a dozen times since we started here. Then again, kind of hard to notice other guys when you've been sucking face with Mark."

"Not to mention, *working hard at my classes*," I said pointedly.

"True." She swiveled her gaze from Connor to me. "You like?"

I shrugged. "I like his smile. And his eyes. He seems…friendly. Easy-going. Happy."

"In other words, he's a babeshow."

I gave my best friend a playful shove. "What? I'm not allowed to look?"

Just then, Connor laughed loudly at something one of the other guys said as he effortlessly caught an errant throw one-handed. The same pure joy in his laugh as in his smile.

"You should do more than look," Ruby said. "He's all kinds of hot."

I shook my head. "If he's a player, then I'm not interested. And I'm done with relationships, anyway."

"You sit on a throne of lies," Ruby intoned in a deep voice. "You're an incurable romantic. It's in your blood."

"I know. But Mark made a fool of me, Ruby. He made me believe in something that wasn't there. Like everything we had was a lie or a joke. Or that *I* was the joke. The butt of a terrible joke he called *us*. Feeling like this sucks and I'm not going to get hurt like that

BRING DOWN the Stars

again."

On cue, the pain squeezed my heart. Mark Watts hadn't been my first serious boyfriend, but I'd fallen more deeply for him than anyone else. After two years, I'd begun to envision a future together. We were young, but we both wanted the same things from life: to travel, to find a worthy cause and champion it, to spend a life of activism, helping.

Or so I thought.

"I'll never understand why he couldn't have been honest with me," I said, my gaze following Connor Drake. "Don't want to marry me? Fine. We're only twenty-one. But don't tell me all kinds of romantic, intense things that make me feel like you want to build a future life together, and then cheat on me."

"You can date without getting emotionally involved," Ruby said around a bite of her peanut butter and jelly sandwich. "You can have fun with a guy without getting attached for life."

Connor stood with his friends now, talking and laughing. His laugh was booming and infectious. The other guys loved him; giving him their full attention, keeping him the center of their universe.

"I always get attached," I said. "I can't help myself. I don't want casual, I want electricity. I want someone I can talk to for ages, someone who sets my blood on fire. And not just physically, you know?"

Ruby pursed her lips. "Gee, don't expect much, do you?"

"Only everything," I said. "And why not? That's exactly what I have to give." I sighed and rested my chin on my drawn-up knees. "I have one year to figure out an emphasis for my post-grad Harvard project. Maybe the universe is telling me to try being single for a change."

"Mmhmm," Ruby said. "Is the universe also telling you to keep your eyes glued to Connor Drake? Because if that's the case: mission accomplished."

I laughed and leaned into her. "He really is hot. And that smile…"

"Go talk to him. This could be a good experiment for you. Talk to him, ask him out. See if you can keep it casual." Her eyes narrowed. "I triple-dog dare you!"

"What are you, ten?" I asked, and watched her take another bite of her PB&J and wash it down with a swig of Yoo-hoo. "Maybe you are ten..."

"Kid food is the best food," she said. "And you're ignoring my challenge."

I shook my head, stood up, and brushed the grass from my skirt. "Nah, it's too soon. Players aren't my type. He probably just wants to get laid, and that's fine, but it's not for me."

"How do you know what Connor wants if you never talk to him?"

I shrugged, shouldered my bag. "Guess I won't. He'll remain a mystery. Something to admire from afar while I keep to my studies. On that note..."

"The library? Already?"

"I have forty minutes before my next class. Are you coming?"

Ruby shook her head and pulled a small bag of Fritos from her brown paper bag. "Italian majors don't do any work until we've eaten. It's in the syllabus."

I laughed. "See you at home."

"See you. But since you won't give Connor the time of day, I might see if I can take the poor guy home with me. So you better knock first."

I gave Connor Drake a final, parting glance. This time, he caught me.

Our eyes met and I felt a little thrill shoot up and down my spine before settling in my stomach. He gave me a mega-watt smile—his teeth were blindingly white—and raised his hand in a half-wave. As if we were old friends.

My cheeks warmed. I gave a quick, spastic wave before hurrying away, keeping my head down.

As I headed to the library, my romantic imagination couldn't help but wonder if Connor was thinking of me the way I was thinking of him. If he linked me to his beautiful day on the quad, just as his effortless smile linked him to mine.

That feeling, I thought. *That's what I love. The first connection. A little uncertain moment that builds into something strong and real.*

Except that I thought I'd had that with Mark. While I was busy building our future, he was knocking it out, brick by brick, until the whole thing came crashing down.

I glanced over my shoulder a final time at Connor Drake. He was laughing with his friends again, wearing that beaming, sunshine

BRING DOWN the Stars

smile. I wondered what it would be like to bask in that smile, and then brushed the thought aside.

Gorgeous men with winning smiles were no longer on my list.

CHAPTER Two

Autumn

I took the cement stairs into the library and entered the cool, hushed confines of the main reading room. None of the long mahogany desks with green-shaded lamps were empty. One of the university clubs had taken over two-thirds of the space. The rest of the tables were filled with students like me, trying to get a head start on their course load.

    I finally found an empty seat at the end of a table, opposite a blond guy engrossed in reading. His open backpack spilled books and papers into what I hoped could be my table territory.

    "Excuse me," I whispered. "Can I…?"

    He looked up, his expression vaguely hostile. Piercing blue-green eyes set in a stunningly handsome, if angular, face met mine. High cheekbones, sharp chin and long straight nose but for a small break along the bridge. He looked chiseled out of smooth stone at first glance, then his features softened for a moment as his gaze swept over me. Something like recognition lit up his eyes, and I could see the gears of his brain turning as he studied, analyzed, and then came to a conclusion. Not a good one, I guessed, because his expression hardened again.

    "Yeah, sure," he muttered. He stood up, leaning his tall, slender frame over the table to corral the books back into his pack.

BRING DOWN the Stars

"Thanks," I said, thinking if he wasn't a basketball player or a runner, he was a model.

All right, girl, get a grip.

I sat, cracked my textbook and settled in to read. I wasn't through two pages when the words blurred to nonsensical gibberish and my skin prickled with the sensation of being watched.

I glanced up, straight into the ocean eyes of the guy across from me. A million thoughts swirled in their soft depths before they quickly glanced down. He slouched lower in his chair, disappearing behind his book—the collected poems of Walt Whitman. Part of me wanted to melt. Good Lord, a hot guy reading poetry? I was only human.

And this is how you wound up with a broken heart in the first place.

I must've been frowning at the book because the guy held it up and said, "Not a fan?"

I blinked back to reality. "No," I said. "I mean, yes. I love Whitman. And poetry in general. I just… Never mind."

He regarded me a long moment, then slowly closed Whitman and picked up *Atlas Shrugged* from his short stack of books.

"Ugh, that's even worse," I muttered without thinking, and then shook my head. "God, sorry, I left my filter at home. Don't listen to me."

His lip curled. "Is there anything in my collection you approve of?"

A hot, smart asshole, I thought. *Game on.*

"Sorry," I said. "I'm not in a good mood today and it's making me forget my manners. I'll leave you to read your capitalist propaganda in peace."

The guy's eyebrows shot up, disappearing under the blond hair that fell across his brow. "Not a fan of Rand either?" He smirked knowingly. "No, of course you aren't."

My blood heated at his flippant tone. "What's that supposed to mean?"

The guy nodded at my textbook—*Global Responsibility and the Third-World Hunger Epidemic*—and shrugged, as if that answered everything.

"Oh." I frowned. "Well… yes. I mean, Rand's point of view is purely capitalist and mine isn't. Not by a long shot."

The student sitting to my right exchanged glances with the girl sitting across from him. Then both packed up their books and left.

"We're being disruptive," I said to my across-table neighbor. "We need to stop talking now."

He leaned back in his chair, his eyes intent on me. "So, what's your point of view?"

"My what?"

"You said your point of view isn't capitalist." He raised a brow. "So what is it?"

"Humanist, I suppose, since you asked. I think everyone; regardless of race, creed, income-level, or sex, should be granted the same shot as anyone else." I raised a brow at him. "But you don't?"

"Are you asking me or telling me?" he said with a slight chuckle. "Since we're tossing labels around, I'm a realist." He held up his book. "And not a fan of Rand either."

"You're not?" I leaned back too, crossing my arms. "Are you just messing with me or what?"

"Maybe," he said. "What do you care what I think anyway?"

My mouth fell slack. "I don't. Thanks for reminding me."

"No problem."

"Wow, you're rude."

"That's the word on the street."

"I can see why." I lifted my own book up to signal *conversation over,* but my eyes wouldn't focus. I could feel the hum of his presence like a field of electrical wires, getting under my skin and infiltrating my thoughts. The buzz went beyond distraction. It felt like a challenge had been laid down.

And I never walked away from a challenge.

I lowered my book to see the guy's glance hide behind his book again.

"Well?" I demanded.

"Well what?"

Why are you watching me?

"Why are you reading Ayn Rand if you don't like her either?"

"Required reading for an English Lit minor."

"And your major? Let me guess, pre-law."

"God, no," he said.

I raised my eyebrows, but he offered nothing more. "Are you going to make me run through Amherst's list of majors until I guess which one is yours?"

"Yes," he said. "Alphabetically, please."

A laugh burst out of me against my will, and the guy almost smiled. Every one of his hard angles softened.

"Economics," he said. "But I don't know what I'm doing with it."

"That feels like the most honest thing you've said to me so far," I said.

"And that's important to you?"

"Yes," I said, my laughter dying away as I remembered Mark and that girl, naked in his bed… "Honesty is *very* important."

He lifted one shoulder.

"You don't agree?" I asked.

"Being honest is sometimes mistaken for being rude."

"You must be *really* honest," I said.

Again, he almost smiled. "Must be."

Satisfied that I'd held my own against this beautiful, but hostile member of the opposite sex, I went back to my book…for eight entire seconds before my skin started prickling again. The electric hum of his attention was impossible to ignore.

When I looked up this time, he didn't look away but cleared his throat.

"I'm Weston Turner."

CHAPTER Three

Weston

This wasn't the first time I'd seen this girl. She was in my Econ class this morning. Her hair caught my eye; a copperyred tendril had escaped the bun she wore and curled against the porcelain skin of her neck. Now, she sat across from me.

Leaning on her elbow, chin on her hand and a little smile on her lips, she replied, "Autumn Caldwell."

My thoughts took off the same way I did at the starting gun of a race.

Her name was Autumn.

Of course it was. As if her parents knew she'd grow up to be a living embodiment of the season. Coppery hair, like an October forest of turning leaves. Hazel eyes that were mostly rich brown, but flecked with gold, green and amber, and weighted with sadness. A petite girl—I guessed five-foot-nothing to my six-one—passionate and unafraid. I liked toying with people to get them riled up, and she'd seemed an easy mark. But instead of walking away, she'd met me head on. I liked that.

I liked her.

And I didn't like anyone.

A silence caught and held between us, our eyes locked. Then

she shifted in her chair.

"I'm not dating right now," she said, subtle as a fifty-pound bowling ball dumped onto my crotch.

"Okay," I said slowly.

"Shit, sorry," she said, the color in her cheeks deepening. "I don't mean to be presumptuous. I just meant that it's nice to meet you, but I need to focus on my classes. I have a lot of work to do. Double-major and a scholarship to maintain." She waved her hands. "God, I'm rambling…"

I squirmed inside. At first glance, in her expensive-looking dress and carefully-matched cardigan, I'd pegged her as a stiff and prissy trust fund baby.

Wrong, Turner. Just sit here in your wrongness and be wrong.

"I'm on a scholarship too," I said.

"Oh?" Her smile was tinged with relief that we were on the same team, financially speaking. "For what?"

"NCAA. Track and field," I said. "Your double major is in…?"

"Social anthropology and political science."

"Social anthropology," I said. "The major of choice among all humanists."

She rolled her eyes, the sadness replaced by a confident spark that made the gold stand out. "Going for a master's in smartass, are we?"

"I've heard that once or twice."

"I'll bet." Autumn tucked a lock of hair behind her ear. "Social anthropology is the study of modern human societies and their development. I want to have a master's degree that focuses on a humanitarian aspect."

"Sounds ambitious," I said. *And good,* I thought. *Noble. Sincere.* Nothing I'd ever be accused of.

"Maybe it's idealistic," Autumn said, her finger trailing over the edge of her book. "Technically, the master's degree doesn't actually exist with that kind of narrow angle, so I'm going to create a project to submit to Harvard Grad School. Build my own degree."

"What area of emphasis?"

"I don't know yet. So many causes need attention. Like how population impacts global health and the environment. Or maybe disability rights. Or how racism affects people on socio-economic levels. Something like that." She shrugged and reached for her book.

"I only know I want to help."

I only knew I didn't want to be done talking to her.

"You were in my class this morning," I said.

She looked up, her hazel eyes luminous. "Econ with Environmental Applications?"

I nodded.

"I didn't see you."

"I was in the back. You sat up front."

"Did you like the class?"

I shrugged. "It's required for my major."

"You don't sound enthusiastic about it."

"Do I need to be?"

"If it's going to be your life's work, one would think you'd be at least mildly interested. Passionate, even."

"I don't know if it's my life's work. And passionate, no. Letting feelings get involved in important life decisions is a surefire way to make a mess of everything."

My tone was turning sour. Writing should've been my life's work, but I had to relegate it to a back burner. It didn't matter how I *felt* about writing when I *needed* to help support my family. Besides, after the *Sock Boy* fiasco, I wasn't in a big hurry to share anything again. Aside from classwork, I kept my personal musings in a journal and I kept that journal in a locked drawer.

Autumn crossed her arms over her chest. "You don't think feelings are important?"

"Feelings," I said, "are like tonsils. Mostly useless, and occasionally a source of pain and discomfort."

She laughed. "So, what's the alternative? Have them removed?"

"If only."

Which, from the stunned look on her face, was exactly the wrong thing to say to a girl like Autumn Caldwell.

She sat back in her seat, arms still crossed. "Well, I think being passionate about life is exactly why we're here. To experience life in all its facets, including the painful. Isn't that where great art comes from? Beauty and pain?"

I nodded slowly. "I guess that's true."

"Beauty and pain," she said, almost to herself. "I don't think you can separate the two."

BRING DOWN the Stars

"Maybe pain exists to make us appreciate the beauty," I said.

Autumn glanced up at me, her eyes soft. Inviting me closer.

I wanted to be close to this girl, but I was counter-programmed against letting anyone in; a little souvenir from Dad abandoning us and then having my innermost thoughts on the matter splattered all over Boston. They didn't call me the Amherst Asshole on the track for nothing. I had a literal mean streak, outrunning everyone and leaving them in *my* rearview.

I coughed the softness out of my voice. "Or maybe pain is just pain, and we romanticize the hell out of it to make it survivable."

Autumn leaned back. "I like your first theory better. Then again, my roommate is always telling me I'm a hopeless romantic. Well, I was anyway."

"Was?"

Autumn smiled sadly.

I waved my hands. "Never mind. Sorry. I'm…"

Better on paper.

Autumn heaved a sigh worthy of Juliet on her balcony and her delicate fingers toyed with her pen. "What good is romance, anyway? A bunch of pretty words don't mean anything unless there's something real behind them."

The sadness in her eyes I'd seen earlier returned, and I wondered if it had a name. Some asshole who'd pissed on her sunny romantic ideals and left her with clouds and rain.

She needs someone good. Someone who'll make her smile and laugh. A decent guy with a big heart…

"Hey," said a deep voice. "We meet again."

Connor stood by the table, hands on his hips, King of the World and All He Surveyed. Autumn's eyes widened to see him, and she swallowed. I followed the movement down her delicate throat, to the hollow just above her collar, where her pulse jumped. He smiled down at her, and she smiled up at him, recognition in both their expressions.

He met her first.

"Knew I'd find you here," Connor said, chucking me on the shoulder, his gaze still on Autumn. "Didn't expect this surprise." He held out his hand. "Connor Drake."

"Autumn Caldwell," she said, her cheeks turning pink as her small hand was engulfed in his large one. The sadness in her eyes was

33

long gone.

"I thought you said you already met," I said, my voice lifeless as a drone.

"Not really," Autumn said. "Just a hello-wave outside. How do you two know each other?"

"Roommates," Connor said. "And friends since middle school."

"How sweet." She began gathering her books. "Both from around here?"

"Boston," Connor said, watching her pack up. "Leaving already? Was Wes giving you a hard time?"

Autumn flashed me a smile. "I held my own."

"Good for you," Connor said. "Wes likes to pretend to be an asshole but deep down he's... Actually, no, he's just an asshole."

I clenched my jaw. "Fuck off, Drake."

"No, we were having a very interesting conversation," Autumn said. "But I really have to go."

"Gotcha," Connor said. "But hey, this Saturday a bunch of us are getting together at Yancy's Saloon. You know it?"

Autumn raised a brow. "Best pear ale in town."

"I'm a whiskey and beer guy myself, but I'll take your word on the pear ale." Connor winked. "So you'll come hang out? Shoot a little pool and chill before the semester gets crazy?"

I crossed my arms over my chest to watch this convo, vanishing from their world.

"Maybe," she said.

"Great," Connor said. "See you there."

She laughed. "I said, *maybe*." She shouldered her bag and started off, then stopped and turned back to look at me. "Bye, Weston. Nice talking to you."

I nodded stiffly. "Yep."

Because that's what all great writers say to a beautiful girl they want to impress. Yep.

As I watched her walk away, Conner slugged me in the arm. "She's a stunner, isn't she?"

"Mm."

He slid into the chair Autumn had just vacated. "Not like other girls I usually go for."

He's 'going for' her. My stomach felt heavy.

BRING DOWN the Stars

"No, not like other girls," I said slowly. "At all."

"Sounds like a warning," Connor said with a short laugh.

"I'm just saying I got the impression she's not a one-night stand type of girl. She's..."

Special.

"Different, right?" Connor said. "Classy and sort of elegant. I like it. Wait, did I interrupt something? Are you into her?"

Yes.

"No," I heard myself say. "I think she's into you."

He leaned forward, a higher pitch to his voice. "Yeah?"

I could count on one hand the number of times Connor needed reassurance. You had to know what to look for. That higher tilt to his voice. A little uncertainty in his mega-smile. It was so rare, Connor wanting or needing anything his money, charm or looks couldn't give him. Sometimes I felt as if college essays were all I had to offer our friendship, when the reality was I'd do anything for my friend.

"I'll totally back off if you are. Bro Code, and all," Connor was saying with a grin. "Even if I *did* see her first."

I remembered the way Autumn's face lit up when Connor took her hand, all the sadness melting away.

"She'll be there Saturday," I said. "To see you."

"You think?"

"I know."

"Awesome." He got to his feet. "Come on, let's get out of here. If you want to get laid this semester, hanging out in the library is not the way to do it."

Tell me about it.

I gathered my stuff and we headed outside.

"Maybe Autumn will bring her roommate or a hot friend," Connor said, slinging his arm around my shoulder. "There's hope for you, yet."

I brushed him off. "Have I ever needed your help getting laid?"

"Here?" Connor's other hand gestured around the quad. "No. During the Sock Boy years, you needed all the help you could get."

"Fuck you," I said.

But it had no bite to it. I owed him the earth for what he did during the Sock Boy years. He was my best friend and I loved him like a brother. He wasn't much in the romance department but he didn't need to be. He made girls feel good just by being around him. Seems

35

like he made Autumn feel good, distracting her from her sadness, and he was into her.

    That's all that mattered.

CHAPTER *Four*

Autumn

"You have a date," Ruby said in a song-song voice. "With Connor Drake."

I rolled my eyes at her through the bathroom mirror. She lay on her stomach on my bed, crossed ankles swinging.

"It's not a date," I said for the millionth time. "Some people are going to Yancy's, and so are we. That's all."

"*Some people* including Connor."

"Yes."

"And he invited you."

"We probably would've gone anyway."

"My ass." Ruby snorted. "In two years, I've never been able to drag you out on the first weekend after class starts."

I shot her a stink-eye through the mirror. "We don't need his invitation to go to a place we hang out at regularly."

"Semi-regularly and God, you are so stubborn. And picky." Ruby raised her eyebrows. "If this isn't a date, why are you obsessing over what to wear?"

I fussed with my dress, the third one I'd tried on. It was navy blue with white flowers, flowing prettily around the knees with cute buttons up the front. A designer label I'd found squashed on a rack in a thrift store.

"I want to look nice," I said, "but not like I'm dressing nice for *him*."

"God forbid," Ruby muttered.

I sagged and turned around to face my roommate. "This is a bad idea."

Ruby sighed. "We're going to hang out at Yancy's and Connor might be there, just like you said. No pressure. Just try to have some fun."

I nodded. "You're right. I'm being silly. I'm not used to…casual."

"Clearly." Ruby rolled off the bed and joined me at the mirror. She looked effortlessly pretty in a black skirt and black blouse. She hadn't straightened her hair, but let it spring from behind a colorful band.

She slung her arm around my shoulders. "Have a drink or two, get to know him. That's it."

"That's it," I said. "Two drinks, max. I'm on a budget and you know how I get when I drink too much."

"I do," Ruby said. "You get *fun*."

I elbowed my friend then grabbed her arm. "What if Mark is there? With *her*?"

"All the more reason to hang with Connor." She pursed her lips. "No offense, but Mark's a little boy compared to Mr. Drake."

I started to defend Mark but my cheeks warmed. "No comment."

Ruby laughed. "Atta girl."

We went outside to wait for the Uber. The September night was cool, and I pulled on a dark cardigan, while Ruby slipped on a jean jacket. I never wore jeans—after eighteen years of jeans on the farm, I'd vowed never to wear denim again.

"What's Connor's roommate's name again?" Ruby asked. "Wesley?"

"Weston," I said.

"What's he like?"

"Econ major. Intelligent. But prickly."

"How so?"

"Cynical. He compared feelings to tonsils."

"Ouch." Ruby laughed. "Is he hot?"

BRING DOWN the Stars

The unhesitant thought, *he's gorgeous,* caught me off guard. "I guess so," I said. "Tall. Blond. Blue eyes. He's a track and field runner."

"Track and field…" Ruby's eyes widened. "Oh wait, *Wes Turner*? Oh my God, where's my head? Of course. The Amherst Asshole."

I stared. "The *what*?"

"You really have been on another planet, haven't you? That's Wes's nickname on the track, on account of his *sunny* disposition," she said with a laugh. "He's a real dick to his opponents, apparently."

"Oh," I said. "That's too bad. We had a nice talk."

Except that Weston hadn't been too friendly. Not at first.

But we warmed up to each other, eventually.

"He has a rep for being quite skilled in the bedroom department, too." Ruby grinned. "This night just got a whole lot more interesting."

I glanced at my friend under the streetlamp. She was beautiful, smart, and the boy-crazy act was only one manifestation of her bottomless well of self-confidence that I envied.

If Weston tried to mess with her like he did me, she'd snap right back. They might hit it off.

The thought was oddly unsettling.

The Uber took us down Pleasant Drive to the little town of Amherst. Yancy's Saloon was only a block away from Panache Blanc.

"I'm not staying out too late," I told Ruby as we exited the car. "I have to work my double shift tomorrow."

"Tell that to Connor when he takes you home tonight," Ruby said.

"No one's taking me home but you."

Ruby did her best—which meant terrible—Jack Nicholson impersonation. "I tell you buddy, I'd be the luckiest gal alive if that did it for me."

We pushed through the swinging doors into a fog of beer and greasy pub food. Wood furnishings and warm yellow lights. Purple and white Amherst banners plastered on the walls. "Be Mine" by Ofenbach played over the sound system. I recognized it instantly. We didn't get much alternative music back home, and I'd fallen in love with it at Amherst. Like denim, my mother's oldies and Dad's blues were things I left at the farm.

The music barely masked the crack of pool tables from the gaming area, where Ruby was now pointing. Connor Drake stood in a circle of friends, head thrown back in laughter.

"There he is," Ruby said. "Let's go say hi."

"I want a drink first," I said, steering her to the long bar.

"Let him buy," Ruby said. "God knows he's good for it."

I stopped. "What do you mean?"

"I mean his dad owns like a zillion companies and his mom's a senator."

My nose wrinkled. "How…? Do you keep dossiers on every guy here?"

"Doesn't everyone?" She laughed and nudged my arm. "No dear, I pay attention to my surroundings, not just the insides of textbooks." She studied my frown. "Don't tell me Connor being rich is disappointing to your delicate farm girl sensibilities?"

"No, it's not that…"

It's just one less thing we have in common. On the heels of that thought was the memory of Weston saying he was at Amherst on scholarship too.

"Anyway." I squared my shoulders. "All the more reason I should buy my own drinks. If he's wealthy, people probably assume he'll pay for everything."

"Maybe," Ruby said. "But he's not like *wealthy,* in that he drives a nice car and wears nice clothes. I mean he's *wealthy* like a thousand dollars could fall out of his pocket and he wouldn't notice."

Ruby would know. She wasn't Drake-wealthy, but her Jamaican mother was a professional singer and her Dutch father was a high-powered lawyer in Boston. Ruby liked to say she'd won the "Hammond Scholarship." Her parents paid for school, so she didn't have to work while completing a degree in Italian.

She held up her hands at my dry look. "Just saying. But let me get the first round. To celebrate the momentous occasion of your first post-Mark outing."

I shook my head, a wave of affection for my friend making me smile.

At the bar, Ruby ordered a 7-and-7 for herself and a pear cider for me. She held up her glass. "To keeping it casual and having fun."

"Amen," I said, clinking my glass to hers.

"And to possibly getting laid."

BRING DOWN the Stars

"For you, yes. For me...too soon."

Ruby narrowed her eyes and set her drink down. "On that note, can I ask you something? How was Mark in the bedroom department?"

I spilled some pear cider over my lips as I sputtered. "*Ruby.*"

"Because you were with him for two years and we never talked about it. Ever. Any fireworks...?"

"I... What does that have to do with anything?"

"Everything," Ruby said. "You're a junior in college now. You're supposed to be living it up and sleeping around and having a good time, and you were missing all that." She put her hand on my arm. "I'm not happy that Mark cheated on you—it's a super shitty thing to do—but I am happy you're free."

"Free?" I pulled my arm away. "He broke my heart, Ruby. I loved him."

"Did you?" She held up her hands again. "I'm honestly not trying to start shit. I just never got the sense that he set your blood on fire. Your words, not mine."

I hunched my shoulders and faced forward over the bar. "Nobody's perfect," I said. "I'm not. Mark wasn't either. But we had good conversations and he understood what I was trying to do with my degree."

Ruby pursed her lips and took a sip from her drink. "I don't like to see you hurt. But I can't help but feel like this is an opportunity for you. You work so hard. You deserve some fireworks."

I started to protest but Ruby's words sunk in. I *did* work hard at my double-major. But I'd also worked hard on Mark and me. I told myself the electrifying romance phase couldn't last forever, especially after two years. But we *had* fallen into a rut of banal conversations and routine sex; a rut that he had broken—spectacularly—with another girl.

I glanced over to the pool tables. Connor Drake stood with some friends, chalking his pool cue. A huge smile broke over his face as he greeted a newcomer with a hearty handclasp and hug, welcoming the friend into his circle.

Seems like a nice place to be.

"Go," Ruby said. "Just walk over, say hello, flirt a little and see what happens. Okay?"

"Okay," I said. "There's just one problem."

41

"What's that?"

"I'm a terrible flirt."

"That, my friend"—Ruby handed me my glass—"is what the alcohol is for."

I shot her a look and downed the rest of the pint—more than over halfway full.

Ruby laughed as I plonked the empty glass on the bar. "Hallelujah, girl." She finished off hers and signaled to the bartender for another.

Pear cider isn't the strongest drink in the world, but my slight weight and short height felt the effects immediately. The pleasant buzz gave me the confidence to walk over to the pool tables and step into an established clique of sporty guys and their girlfriends.

I knew, instinctively, that Connor wouldn't act differently toward me in front of the girls or brush me off in front of his bros. And I was right. The second he saw me, he stopped mid-conversation, and his broad smile widened even further.

"Hey, Wes," Connor called, keeping his eyes on mine as the words went sideways. "Look who's here."

I followed the tilt of his chin to the three dartboards mounted on the bar's back wall. Weston turned around, the dart poised in his hand. His eyes widened slightly as he saw me.

So did mine.

Ruby leaned in. "The Amherst Asshole, in the flesh."

I nodded. Ruby smiled.

"Not bad."

His handsomeness was equally as potent as Connor's, yet cut from a completely different cloth. Where Connor was broad and built, Weston was tall and lean-muscled. Connor wore a white shirt that hugged his shoulders, and his dark hair was shorter and spiked. Weston wore black and his gold hair fell over his eyes in the front. Still looking at me, he tossed it out of the way with a jerk of his head.

Connor strode up to us. "Hey, you made it."

"We did," I said. "This is my roommate, Ruby. Ruby Hammond, this is Connor Drake."

It felt strange introducing them since Ruby was more acquainted with Connor's reputation than I was. Connor greeted her with a friendly smile, then turned immediately back to me.

"Your next drink's on me, I insist." He looked back over his shoulder. "Wes, get over here and say hi. Let's get a game going."

Weston turned back to his dartboard and lanced the little arrow straight at the bullseye, then moved to join us.

"Hi," I said.

"Hey."

"This is my roommate, Ruby."

His blue-green gaze flickered to her and back. "Hey."

"A pleasure," Ruby said with a smirk.

"Until we get some shots into him, my good buddy Wes doesn't speak unless spoken to," Connor said with a laugh.

He introduced us to bunch of his friends, all of them baseball or basketball players. Ruby knew a few of them and was immediately absorbed into a circle of talk.

"Let's rack 'em up," Connor said to Weston. "Decker, you in?"

A dark-haired guy leaning against the wall raised his beer bottle in salute.

Connor turned to me. "Do you play?"

"I've played a few times," I said, with a smile I hoped was flirtatious. I sipped the last of my ale and traded him my pint glass for his pool cue. "Can I break?"

Connor raised his brows. "Be my guest."

I bent over the table, slid the cue back and forth over my hand, then took my shot. The crack reverberated through the tavern as the cue ball smashed into the triangle of balls, scattering them across the green felt. Two striped balls sunk in the corner and side pockets.

Connor pointed at me and deadpanned, "She's on my team."

Decker whistled low in his teeth. "A ringer."

"Got that right." Connor turned to me, moved close. His voice was low and deep, and his cologne—clean, masculine, and expensive—wafted over me, making my nerve endings tingle. Somehow, he made the entire bar disappear until it was just he and I.

"You've played a few times, huh?"

"I'm from a small town in Nebraska," I said. "My dad used to take my brother and me into town every weekend to shoot pool."

"So you're a shark," Connor said. "I like it. Unexpected. Makes me want to find out more about you."

It was probably a cheesy line to someone less inebriated, but I was tipsy from chugging two pints. Having Connor Drake's full attention was another kind of buzz. He was beautiful up close, with large green eyes under heavy, dark brows, and a broad mouth that looked like it might be as good at kissing as it was at smiling.

"There's a lot to know about me," I said, screwing chalk onto the end of my cue.

"Is that so?" Connor's smile softened. He raised his hand, and for a second I thought he was going to touch my face, but he hesitated. "You have an eyelash stuck to your cheek."

I brushed my face where he was indicating, my skin warm under my fingers. That he'd wanted to touch me but didn't, was more of a turn-on than if he had touched me.

"Thanks," I said.

"No problem," he said, and then his mega-watt smile was back, and I was basking in it. "Autumn Caldwell from Nebraska," he said, "let's shoot some pool."

CHAPTER Five

Weston

I watched Autumn bend her petite frame over the pool table and break like a pro. Connor moved close to her and they shared a few quiet words. It looked as if he was going to touch her cheek but didn't. A classic Connor Drake move. Matt Decker, the only other guy in all of Amherst I considered a friend, noticed too.

He leaned in to me, using his pool cue as a mic, and spoke in a low voice, like a golf commentator.

"Connor's got all the right moves tonight, don't you think, Wes?"

"Indeed he does, Matt," I whispered back. "He's on fire. The signature Drake-Fake-Eyelash-Take. Perfectly executed. Let's go to the instant replay."

"Flawless, Wes. What technique. And the red-headed judge awards a perfect ten."

Decker chuckled, while I averted my eyes and took a long pull off my beer.

I talked to her first.

Pathetic. She wasn't a territory. I hadn't planted my flag in her.

Judging by the way things are going with her and Connor, you aren't going to plant anything in her anytime soon.

The crude thought was a flimsy cover for the truth: I hadn't stopped thinking about Autumn Caldwell all week. I liked talking to her, and if I'd been better at it, I'd be the one sharing a pool stick with her. Standing over her while she looked up at me with those incredible hazel eyes. Instead, I'd mentally surrendered her to Connor without a fight.

"Wes," Connor said. "You and Decker done whispering sweet nothings to each other?" He swung a casual arm around Autumn's delicate shoulders. "My secret weapon and I are going to clean your clocks."

"We'll see, Drake." Decker turned to me. "You in?"

The last fucking thing I wanted was to play pool with Autumn and Connor. But my competitive streak, born on the streets of southside Boston and honed on the track, revved up like it did before a race.

"Yeah, let's go."

Matt Decker was a decent pool player, and I could always hold my own against Connor. But Autumn turned out to be a true phenom. Every ball she or Connor sunk was another opportunity for him to high-five her, give her a hug, or say something that made her smile.

Soon enough, they were down to the eight ball, while Matt and I had three left on the green. I lined up my shot, while at the other end of the table, Connor stood close to Autumn. Closer than I thought necessary for a non-date, date. I forced my gaze to the table, but just as I took my shot, Autumn laughed. My stick scraped felt and glanced off the side of the cue ball, sending the ball into the side pocket.

"Duuuude," Decker groaned.

"Damn, Wes," Connor said. "I haven't seen you scratch like that since summer camp, eighth-grade."

"Fuck off," I muttered under my breath, and pulled another of our balls onto the table.

"It was my fault," Autumn said. "My dad taught us to keep quiet while an opponent is taking a shot." She smiled beautifully at me. Genuinely. "Forgive me?"

Yes. Anything. Always.

Jesus fucking Christ, this girl had me wrapped around her goddamn pinky.

"It's fine," I muttered like an idiot and took a long pull off my beer.

BRING DOWN the Stars

"You two have known each other since eighth grade?" Autumn asked.

"Since middle school," Connor said, studying the table.

"Oh that's right. You told me in the library. And now you're in college together. That's sweet."

"Hear that, Turner?" Connor bent over the table, his eyes intent on his shot. "The first and last time someone's going use the word sweet to describe you. Including your own mother."

"*Your* mother called me sweet last night, Drake."

"Boom." Decker gave me a no-look fist bump.

"That hurts, my friend," Connor said, taking aim over his stick. "Hurts so bad I might miss this shot…"

His stick lanced out, hit the ball with a *crack* that sent the eight ball streaking into a corner pocket. Game over.

He held out his hands, grinning triumphantly. "Or maybe not."

Decker mumbled a curse. I didn't give a shit about losing the game, except that now I had to watch Connor celebrate the victory with Autumn.

His palm slapped hers in a high five, and with another Signature Drake Move, he held onto her hand and pulled her in for a bear hug. There was nothing sexual about it—he put her down immediately and backed off—except I knew he was getting in as many platonic, friendly touches as possible.

I wouldn't touch you so quickly, I thought. *I'd wait. Draw it out. Build up the moment so that when it happens—when each of us feels the other's skin for the first time—it'll be something sublime. Something earned.*

I took another long pull off my beer as if I could drown the frustration and mystery that was my infatuation with this girl. One library conversation, one round of pool, a few smiles and now she was lodged in my psyche and wouldn't let go. Except that I felt like I knew more of her than that; a strange recognition or déjà vu that didn't fucking make any sense.

Fuck this shit.

I slammed my empty bottle onto the bar, fished some money out of my pocket, and gave it to Decker for more alcohol.

"This round's on me, for the scratch. Go."

He smirked. "Sir, yes, sir."

I went back to darts while Connor and Autumn racked up the

47

pool balls again. Ruby and a few others joined them, and I tried to tune out the laughter and easy talk.

My foul mood made me a better dart player, and winning always made things better. Over the next twenty minutes, I beat my next two opponents easily; earning back the money I'd given Matt, and enough to come back to Yancy's next weekend. My opponents skulked away and I shot solo.

I took aim, fired, hit the twenty.

"How did you get so good?" came Autumn's soft voice from behind me.

I froze, another dart poised by my ear, and my eyes slowly swiveled over to her. She blinked back over the rim of her pint, her face flushed.

"I pretend the dartboard is the face of my enemy," I said.

She laughed and sat herself on a stool, setting her drink down on a ledge. "Is that so? And who are you skewering tonight?"

Me.

"Do you want a game?" I asked. "Are you a secret dart pro, too?"

"Oh no," she said and raised her glass. "This is my third. Or fourth? I can't be trusted with sharp, pointy objects."

"You seem to do alright wielding a long stick." I glanced at her sideways then shot another dart. Eighteen. "So…taking a break from pool?"

And from my best friend?

Her hair glinted red and gold under the lamp as she nodded. "I had to quit while I was ahead. Before I started shooting badly and ruining my mystique."

"Your Nebraska pool shark mystique."

"It's a little more exciting than my Nebraska farm girl mystique."

"You grew up on a farm?"

"Born and raised. My father grows corn and wheat."

My stupid mind conjured her standing in a field of wheat, her fingertips brushing the stalks, her coppery red hair glinting in the sun. A simple dress billowed around her knees in a breeze that made the wheat bend and sway around her like a sea of shallow waters…

"How was that?" I asked. "I mean, what was it like?"

"I loved it," she said, her hazel eyes liquid. "I love the land.

BRING DOWN the Stars

Love watching my father work to make things grow."

She was tipsy with booze and it softened her further. Her speech slowed down and her Midwestern drawl crept back in.

"But it wasn't enough for me. I always did really well in school and had always planned on getting out do something important. I was voted Most Likely to Save the World." She smiled shyly. "A slight exaggeration…"

I shrugged. "Better than Miss Congeniality."

"What were you voted in high school?"

"Mr. Congeniality."

She laughed. "Liar."

"I wasn't voted anything."

She cocked her head. "No? Shame. I would have nominated you for Best Eyes."

I flinched mid-throw and the dart careened off the metal edge of the board.

Autumn covered her mouth with her hand. "See, alcohol is like a truth serum for me." She frowned suddenly, thinking. "What's that song…'Ocean Eyes'?"

I picked up my fallen dart and gathered the rest from the board. "Haven't heard it."

She hummed a few notes. "Ocean eyes and diamond mind. It's a great song. More than just one verse and chorus a hundred times over. Her lyrics are like poetry. You know? They have something real to say."

"You like poetry?"

Please say no.

"I love it." She pressed her hands into the stool she sat on, her legs swinging a little. "I love Dickinson and Keats, and e e cummings. I love how a few words, carefully chosen, can elicit deep reactions. Or evoke a certain mood, or make you feel something real, you know?"

Yes, I know. I know, exactly, Autumn.

She gave her head a shake. "Sorry, I wandered into the stars there for a moment. What were we talking about before? Oh, right. Why I left the farm."

"You're going to save the world." I tossed a dart. Nineteen.

"Right," she said. "I wanted to get out of Nebraska and take whatever aptitude I had and apply it toward something big."

"So many causes need attention, and you only know you want

49

to help."

Her delicate brows came together. "How did you…?"

"You told me in the library."

She laughed and raised her glass. "Booze. Eraser of filters *and* memory."

I let my eyes rake her up and down while she was occupied with her pint. She was so slender; small, delicate. Her body was lithe as a dancer's and I knew it would take nothing to lift her, pin her against the wall while I kissed the pear-flavored tinge on her lips and tongue…

Then write you a poem about how you felt against me, and how sweet you tasted…

"…Boston?"

I jerked my mind out of the fantasy. "What?"

"I asked if you were a Massachusetts native. Your accent sounds like Boston."

"Yeah." I flung a dart, hard. Ten. "I was raised in Woburn, just outside Boston. My mom moved us to Southie when I was seven."

"Just your mom?"

I glanced behind us, to where Connor, Ruby, and some people were talking and laughing.

"I'm sorry," Autumn said. "That's a little personal—"

"Yeah, just my mom."

The question of my dad dangled in the air. The answer hesitated on the tip of my tongue. I *wanted* to tell her. But Friday night at Yancy's didn't feel like the time or place to tell the sad, pitiful tale of Sock Boy.

"Is my accent that obvious?" I said.

"Ummmm…" She looked away, chewing on a corner of a sheepish grin. "Scale of one to Matt Damon-in-*Good Will Hunting*?"

I laughed. "Sure."

"I'd say eight. Not quite Matt Damon. But keep working on it."

"Hell no, I'd rather ditch it."

"Don't you dare," she said. "It's cute."

My accent is cute and she likes my eyes.

I wished we were alone. And sober. Not that half-in-the-bag Autumn wasn't enjoyable, but I wanted to talk to the girl I'd met in the library, the one who was having a hard time choosing which broken piece of the world to fix first.

BRING DOWN the Stars

Autumn drained her glass and swayed a little on her stool. "Jeez, I'm a cheap date."

"You want something to eat?" I asked. "I'll get us—get you something. If you want."

"Not that I'm on a date," she said, as if she hadn't heard me. "I'm just having some fun. Ruby's always telling me I need to get out more." She bit her lip. "That makes me sound like a recluse or like all I do is study doesn't it? I don't just study. I mean, I *do* study a lot but also I just got out of a relationship, so I am most definitely not interested in starting up something else."

With Connor? Or…anyone?

Autumn covered her eyes with her hand. "Oh my God, I'm over-sharing like a madwoman, and I'm sure you don't want to hear any of this. I was supposed to keep it to two drinks…"

She slipped off the stool and stumbled. I was too far away, but oh thank the fucking heavens above, Connor was there to catch her.

"Whoa, there," he said with a grin. "You okay?"

Autumn clung to his arm for a second, then her cheeks reddened and she pulled away to preserve her pride.

"I'm fine," she said, smoothing her skirt. "I should go. It's late." She looked around. "Where's Ruby?"

"Present." Ruby slipped in between Connor and Autumn, linking arms. "Time to call it a night."

"I'll walk you out and get you an Uber," Connor said, reaching for his phone.

"No, thanks," Autumn said. "We got this."

"*I* got this," Ruby said.

"Well, hold up," Connor said. He dimmed his smile to make it private, as if he and Autumn were alone in the crowded bar. "Am I going to see you again?"

Autumn's jaw moved up and down. "I don't know. I have a lot of work this semester."

"Oh, hey, I've got it," Connor said, louder. "Come to Wes's track meet next Saturday."

I blinked. "Do what now?"

Autumn's glance danced between us. "Next Saturday?"

"It'll be fun," Connor said. "We can cheer our boy on and hang out. Just chill."

"It's just a prelim," I said. "Not a big deal."

Please come.
Please don't.

I gritted my teeth; it didn't matter either way. I was screwed equally in both scenarios.

"Maybe," Autumn said. "We'll see if I've regained my sobriety by then." She smiled at Connor. "Thanks for the cider. And the pool." She looked to me. "Bye, Weston."

"Yep," I said, and watched her walk out, her arm still linked in Ruby's.

As soon as she was out of earshot, Connor whipped around to me. "Holy shit, she's perfect."

"Perfect for what?"

"To *date*, you moron. She's a humanitarian. Did you know that?"

"Yes." I took up the handful of darts and took aim. "I knew that."

Connor sat on the stool Autumn had just occupied. "She's beautiful, smart. Probably comes from a good family."

"She's from a farm in Nebraska," I said and tossed a dart. Four.

"Yeah, but some of those farms are like empires," Connor said. "If her family has a business—"

"She doesn't have any money," I said. "She's here on scholarship."

"Oh." Connor thought for a second, then shrugged. "Even better. She's salt of the earth. Can you just see me bringing her home to meet my parents? They'll eat that shit up."

I glanced around at him. "What are you talking about?"

"They're on my ass, Wes." Connor absently took up Autumn's half-full pint of cider. "They think I'm just fucking around out here, not getting serious about anything."

"Because you *are* fucking around out here, not getting serious about anything."

"I know, I know. But I picked a damn major I'll never use."

Connor had picked Economics too, ostensibly so I could help him with the course load, but mostly because it was the only one his parents approved of.

"So drop out," I said. "Open your sports bar."

"You know they won't release my trust fund until I graduate. And even then, I have my doubts…"

BRING DOWN the Stars

"We've had this conversation a hundred times," I said. "Forget the trust. Take out a loan and do it yourself."

"Sure. Because walking away from six million dollars is that easy."

I shrugged. "I don't see how Autumn helps your case. If you're only using her to impress your parents…" I tossed a dart. Eighteen. "That's messed up."

"I wouldn't. But she's not like anyone I've dated before." He sipped her cider and made a face. "Holy shit, this pear-water got her drunk? That's cute as hell." He chuckled. "I really like her."

I froze. "You do?"

"Sure. Who wouldn't?"

I clenched my teeth. *Who wouldn't?*

My dart flew.

Bullseye.

CHAPTER Six

Weston

"Goddamn," Connor grumbled as he came out of his bedroom in flannel pants and an undershirt the following Friday morning. He tossed his cell phone onto the designer couch his parents had bought us. "It's too damn early in the morning for their bullshit."

I looked up from where I knelt by the front door, tying my running shoes. "Whose bullshit?"

Connor yawned, scrubbed his hands through his dark hair. "Dear Mom and Dad have decided that they want monthly reports on how I'm doing in my Econ classes."

"What for?" I tied my other shoe, then bounced up and down on the balls of my feet to warm up.

"To make sure I'm not fucking it up. What else?" Connor yawned again and squinted tiredly at me. "Christ, Wes, it's not even light out."

"Ten miles, rain or shine," I said.

"I know, but I'm usually not awake to witness it. I'm exhausted just looking at you."

"I think *jealous* is the word…"

He snorted a laugh. "Seriously, though. I'm screwed. I suck at math."

BRING DOWN the Stars

I leaned on the console table near the door, arms crossed, giving him my full attention. "Exactly what did they say?"

"They said I needed to *demonstrate responsibility*. And to prove that I can apply what I learn in Econ, and that I didn't choose it as my major only because you did."

"Busted."

He laughed. "Shut up."

"So do the work," I said. "When you've got the degree, you'll be able use it to run your sports bar."

Connor's normally mega-watt smile was bitter. "On top of that little ultimatum, they gave me an earful about how Jefferson's going to graduate Harvard with honors. As if I'd forgotten that since the *last time* they told me. *And* he's dating some socialite from Connecticut. Looks like they'll probably get engaged."

"Poor bastard."

My gut told me Connor would be better off without his parents' money. I was grateful for all the times they bailed my mom out of trouble, and Connor and I lived like goddamn kings in the off-campus apartment the Drakes paid for. But it felt like unpaid debt.

I moved to him and clapped a hand on his shoulder. "Do you want to stay at Amherst?"

"Of course I do," he said, his grin returning. "You'd be lost without me."

I smirked. "Do your best. I'll help you out if you need it."

"Just like old times?" he asked. "Except not as many papers to write."

"True. But I'm pretty good at math."

"You're pretty good at everything."

"No argument there." I went to the door.

"Hey, Wes?"

I turned. "Yep."

"Thanks."

A smartass remark was on the tip of my tongue, but I swallowed it down. My best friend slouched on the couch, pressed down by the weight of his parents' expectations.

"No problem, man," I said.

"Enjoy your torture." Connor stretched out on the couch, slung his arm over his eyes. "Which reminds me, I hope Autumn shows up at your meet tomorrow."

My hand gripped the doorknob. "Oh. Right."

Connor's worry melted away into a sleepy smile. "Can't stop thinking about that girl."

Take a number.

Without another word, I stepped out into a chilly September morning. The dawn was just beginning to glow in the east. I shivered a little in my black long-sleeve shirt and fitted running shorts that came down to my knees. The coppery sunlight spread as I started my run along the outskirts of the campus.

Running was like meditation. It cleared my mind and burned through some of the anger and pain that still haunted me. If I wasn't in the mood for music, I paced myself with a mantra:

Fuck him.

Forget him.

He's gone.

But since meeting Autumn, my feet hit the pavement to a new chant while the streets slipped underneath me.

Get over it.

Forget her.

Move on.

It made no fucking sense that I couldn't stop thinking about this girl. Amherst was filled with smart, pretty women, many of whom I'd known in the Biblical sense. Yet Autumn Caldwell's beautiful smile and sweetness suffused my every waking moment. Something good and whole in her spoke to something rotted and broken in me.

Get over it.

Forget her.

Move on.

I blended the words into the rhythm of my feet hitting the pavement. Slipped them between the huffing of my breath.

It didn't work that day. Autumn Caldwell was alive in my thoughts and I couldn't run away from her.

Later that afternoon, I sat in my favorite course: Poetry, Essay, and Lyrical Writing. I hid behind my Econ major with an English Lit minor, where I could take the classes I truly cared about.

BRING DOWN the Stars

At the end of his lesson on form, Professor Ondiwuje assigned us a poem.

"Object of Devotion," he said from the front of the lecture hall. He was in his mid-thirties, with smooth, dark skin and eyes that were sharp with intelligence and observation. Dreadlocks spilled over the lapels of his gray suit.

"I want you to expand your creativity. The object can be a person, of course. Or a dream. A goal. A physical item. The latest iPhone…"

A current of laughter rolled lightly through the class of sixty students.

"Dig deep, and leave nothing on the table," he said. "Because in art, there are no limits. If you have only one takeaway from my class at the end of the year, let it be that poetry—the words by which we give shape to our thoughts—is as limitless as our thoughts themselves."

The small auditorium rippled with enthusiasm.

"Mr. Turner," Professor Ondiwuje called over the shuffling of students leaving after class. "Can I see you a moment?"

I shouldered my backpack and took the side stairs down to his desk. Trying to keep my cool. Michael Ondiwuje was quite possibly the only man on the planet I looked up to. He had won the William Carlos Williams Award for poetry award at the age of twenty-four. A well-worn, dog-eared, highlighted and underlined copy of his collection, *The Last Song of Africa*, resided on my bookshelf.

The professor sat on the edge of his desk, rifling through some papers.

"I read the essay and the poem you submitted two weeks ago," he said. "They were both very good. Excellent, even."

"Thank you, sir," I said, every cell in my body screaming, *Holy shit. Michael Ondiwuje just said my work was excellent.*

The professor raised his eyes from the papers to meet mine. Studying me. Taking me in. "English Lit is your minor, yes?" he finally asked.

"That's right."

"What do you plan to do with an Economics major?"

"I don't know. Work on Wall Street."

"That's what you wish to do?"

"It would be better for my family situation," I said slowly, "if I had a good job and steady income."

He nodded. "I get that, but I can't let talent like yours slink out the back of my class without saying something."

I shifted my bag. "Okay."

"When I read your work, I sense a young man with deep fires burning within and a cold wall around him."

Professor O's stare was relentless but I didn't look away. My head moved in a faint nod.

"A guy with poetry in his blood," the professor went on. "But he keeps his blood from spilling where anyone can see. He sits in the back. Doesn't talk. All the while, words pile up inside. And to a mind and heart like his, all that emotion is hard to take. It's too much. Dangerous. It hurts." His eyes bored into mine. "Doesn't it?"

No one had ever talked to me this way. As if he were trying to pry open my chest, and get at what I kept locked up. The words and thoughts I kept to myself. My instinct was to walk away. Or run. But a deep well of longing stirred inside me to stand in the presence of someone who had crafted a life out of writing. A reality I could reach out and touch too, if I wanted.

I shifted my bag again.

Professor O's smile returned. "I see you, Mr. Turner. And I want to hear you. For this Object of Devotion assignment, give me your blood and guts and fire. Give me everything."

"Everything?" I smiled nervously. "That's all, huh?"

He touched a hand to my shoulder. "I know you have it in you."

After classes, I went back to the apartment to drive my piece of shit car to the Panache Blanc bakery-café in for my pre-race routine: carb-load with a big sandwich the night before.

My car was a fifteen-year-old silver Dodge Stratus I'd bought when I graduated high school with some of my tuition money. The Drakes had tried to buy me something better, but I'd refused. It was old, it took three tries to get it to turn over in summer, ten or more in winter, but it was mine.

At our apartment, it was parked next to Connor's brand-new,

BRING DOWN the Stars

chick magnet, eight-billion-horsepower Dodge Hellcat.

A Tale of Two Dodges, I thought, as I climbed into my old sedan and turned the key. After three tries and a belch of smoke, the engine came sputtering to life.

At the Panache Blanc, I sat at a corner table with a sprout and cucumber on wheat and a side of fruit, contemplating an empty notebook and the give-me-everything poem I was supposed to write in it.

Professor Ondiwuje had X-rayed my damn soul, missing nothing. He knew I wrote my feelings instead of speaking them. Speaking out loud felt like weakness. I'd loved my dad. I'd told him in my own voice, and screamed it after him as he drove away. He took that love and tossed it away like garbage. Never again would I let myself feel that naked and exposed. Not out loud, anyway. Writing was different.

It hurts, doesn't it?

Too fucking much. Which meant I had plenty of blood, guts and fire to write about.

I put my pen to paper. *Let's do this, motherfucker…*

Five minutes later, I had doodled an impressive Bruins logo.

I turned the page and let my mind wander. Lines about coppery red hair and eyes like gemstones started appearing on the page.

"Hell, no. We are *not* going there."

I scribbled those out and tried again. My pen doodled and then a sentence emerged.

Her eyes were the season, personified…

I tore the page out and balled it up.

For the next hour, customers came and went around me. A slow, lazy weeknight. Edmond, the big Frenchman who sang opera and recited sonnets on the regular, wasn't there, but Phil lounged over the counter, scrolling his phone.

I finished off half the sandwich, and took up my pen again.

Pick a fucking subject that's not her. Running. Write about running.

Safe. Easy. I could describe the adrenaline that coiled in my muscles right before the starting gun fired. Or what it felt like to fly over a hurdle. Or that last leg of the baton race with my lungs on fire and my legs driving to the finish line…

Where Autumn waited for me to wrap her arms around my

neck, not caring if I was all sweaty, and she'd kiss me…

"Christ…"

I was about to call it a night when my Object of Devotion walked in the door. With her red hair and green dress, she looked like a handful of rubies and emeralds. My stupid heart took off at a gallop and then nearly stopped short when her exquisite face lit up to see me.

"Hey," she said. "Fancy meeting you here."

"Yeah," I said, my eyes drinking her in as fast as they could before looking away. "Small world."

"Small world? I've been working here for two years and I've never seen you." She started to sit in the chair across from me, then froze. "Oh. Are you busy? I'm just here to pick up my schedule. I won't bother you."

"You're not bothering me." I moved my shit from her half of the table so she had room. "I didn't know you worked here."

Autumn sat sideways in the chair, her purse in her lap. "Most mornings, and a double shift on Sunday." She glanced at my plate with the half-eaten sandwich. "Carb-loading for your meet tomorrow?"

"Yep."

"I remember Connor mentioned it at Yancy's." Autumn's cheeks turned pink. "God, I was a mess that night. I didn't say anything terrible, did I?"

You said I had ocean eyes.

"Nah, you're safe."

"Thank God. When I drink I have no filter *and* amnesia," she said with a laugh. "The worst combination."

Which meant she probably didn't remember saying I had ocean eyes. Or much of our conversation about poetry and music. Erased by booze, and all that was left was laughing and playing pool with Connor.

Disappointment bit at me, but I brushed it away. *Better that way. For her.*

Her glance landed on my doodle-filled paper. "Working hard or hardly working?"

"I have a…paper due." I flipped the notebook to a clean page. "Advanced Macroeconomics."

"That's right, you're an Econ major. Do you have an emphasis?"

"Not yet," I said, and struggled to fill the silence; to give her something so she didn't have to drive the conversation. But the girl left me damn tongue-tied while my brain was firing off a thousand thoughts a minute.

The paper due is about you, with an emphasis on how beautiful you look in every light. In sunlight, in a bar, in a dim cafe. The object of my devotion. I've only been in your presence for a handful of minutes, and the only fucking thing I want to write about is you.

"…tomorrow?"

I blinked. "Sorry, what?"

"How many races do you have tomorrow?"

"Three."

"Three in one day?" she said. "Is that hard?"

"They're spread out so I have time to recover. Two are short—the sixty-meter and one-hundred-ten-meter hurdles. Then one baton relay."

"How long have you been running track?"

"Since I was a kid."

"And Connor's been cheering you on the whole time?"

"He comes to every meet," I said. "Hasn't missed one. He's had my back for a long time, actually. Since prep school, when other kids gave me shit for…lots of things. Not having any money."

Connor did all that for me because he's my best friend and he'd never screw me over. Not over a girl, not for any reason.

"He's a good guy, isn't he?"

"One of the best," I said.

Autumn blushed prettily at this and propped her chin on her hand. "What was prep school like?"

"You ask a lot of questions."

Her shoulders rose in a shrug. "Can't help it. Like Einstein says, *I have no special talents. I'm just passionately curious.*"

"I doubt that."

"You doubt my Einstein?"

"I doubt you have no special talents."

Autumn's smile softened. "That remains to be seen, playing a mean round of pool aside. So. Prep school. Was it as uptight as it sounds?"

"Worse. Bunch of wealthy kids in uniforms. I felt like I'd wandered onto a movie set by accident."

"How did you…?"

"Afford it? I got in on a scholarship for that too."

Autumn reached over and tapped my hand, like a mini high-five. "Good for you. Track?"

I nodded and took a sip of my coffee. Autumn had no clue about Sock Boy and with any luck, he'd stay safely locked in the drawer where he belonged.

"You've been running a long time, then," she said.

Chasing, not running. I'll be chasing that fucking car until I die.

"Yep," I said. "Speaking of which...?"

"Am I coming tomorrow?" She sighed. "I'd like to, but..."

I leaned forward slightly. "But...?"

"But this is awkward. You're his best friend. I just..." Autumn bit her lip. "I don't know if I should be talking about this with you."

"Talking about what?"

She tapped her fingers on her chin. "The other night was fun. Ruby, my roommate, tells me fun is what I need. But I don't know that I should be pursuing anything with someone right now. Especially knowing how I get."

"How you get?" I raised my brows. "Should I start looking for you in the bushes outside our place?"

She balled up a napkin and tossed it at me. "Yes. I've set up camp already. You should remember to turn your lights off when you leave the house, by the way. Saves energy."

I grinned. "I'll try to remember that."

Autumn grinned back, then sighed it away. She leaned her arms on the table, and her chin on her arms. "But for real, you're going to think I'm such a girl."

"You don't leave me much choice."

She laughed but didn't look away; held my gaze steadily. "I want romance. I want holding hands and love letters. Fireworks. I want all that and I'm not going to settle. But that's a lot to expect, so I'm going to try my hardest to not expect anything and just roll with it." She narrowed her eyes at me. "You're going to take all this covert knowledge straight back to Connor, aren't you?"

I smiled though it felt like knives in my cheeks. "I wouldn't be a good friend if I didn't."

"Which is precisely why you're the wrong person I should be talking to about him."

BRING DOWN the Stars

No truer words...

"He likes you," I said, pushing the sentence past my teeth. "I mean, he'd like to get to know you better."

Her eyes brightened, showing sparkles of gold in the hazel irises. "He would?"

"Yeah, he would. All expectations aside, Connor's a good guy. Easy-going. Likes to laugh and make other people laugh. But he's not a clown. He's got a lot to offer."

"You're quite the wingman, aren't you?"

Yes, because he'd do the same for me. Without hesitation.

With a war of emotions in my stomach, I asked, "Does this mean you're coming to the meet tomorrow?"

"Yeah, I am. One, because I want to see you race. Two..."

"Because if you go and Connor's there, it wouldn't suck."

"It wouldn't suck, and I'll just leave it at that," she said, but her blush was back as she stood up and shouldered her bag. "Is it bad luck to say 'good luck' in track and field?"

"The worst. You just cursed me. Thanks a lot."

She grinned. "Sorry. Break a leg."

"Now I'm fucked. Get out of here."

Autumn laughed and plucked a sprout off my plate. She tucked it in the corner of her mouth like a wheat stalk, and I had a sudden, desperate wish to see her on her farm; this wildflower that dressed in expensive-looking dresses, but who wore scuffed shoes and carried a bag that had been probably been new ten years ago.

"Bye, Weston," she said with a little wave.

"Bye, Autumn."

I watched her greet Phil, then go in the back and come out with a folded paper. She gave me another little wave and a smile, then stepped out into the dying light of day.

She's into Connor.

This was no longer debatable. A fact as black and white as ink on paper.

It hurts. Doesn't it?

I put my pen to the blank sheet in front of me and began to write.

CHAPTER Seven

Autumn

"Let me get this straight." Ruby said. "We're here to support Wes, in order to hang out with Connor?"

"*And* to make a sober appearance," I said. "I need to make up for getting so drunk last weekend."

"You weren't *that* drunk. You weren't pee-on-a-pile-of-clean-laundry-thinking-it's-a-toilet-drunk." Ruby shook her head. "God, remember that poor girl at Marty's party last year?"

I giggled. "I think she transferred out of state the next day."

"Smart move." Ruby adjusted her designer sunglasses as we walked in the brilliant sunshine toward the track at Richard F. Garber field. Instead of her usual slouchy, weekday wear, she wore jeans and a cream-colored V-neck blouse that revealed just the right amount of caramel skin.

By contrast, I felt a little prim in a baby blue sundress that buttoned up to my neck. But I burned easily and was already wearing enough one million SPF sunscreen to over-power my perfume.

"Anyway," I said. "I was sloppy at Yancy's. I need to make a better impression."

"On Wes or Connor?"

I shot her a look, which she shot right back.

BRING DOWN the Stars

"I ran into Weston at the bakery last night," I said.

"Oh?"

"We hung out a little while."

"And?"

"And I like him. I like talking to him."

"You two did look pretty chummy at Yancy's."

"Not my type," I said. "He's a little…too dark for me."

"He looks pretty golden from where I'm sitting," Ruby said, lowering her sunglasses and squinting over the field.

I followed her gaze and found Weston in his white and purple Amherst gear, warming up with his teammates. The opponents from Tufts, Wesleyan, and Williams were scattered in their own groups farther away.

The Amherst teammates talked and laughed, except for Weston, who stood apart, stripping out of his warm-up pants and jacket. Underneath, he wore a white running tank and purple shorts, revealing the long, lean lines of his body. His muscles flexed under bronzed skin, perfectly outlined by the tight contours of his running uniform.

God, he's beautiful.

"You sure you're not here for that?" Ruby asked. "Because I am *so* here for that."

"Jeez, Rube," I said, not looking away.

"I'm talking about the whole team, not just Wes. Damn, I just became a track and field groupie." She flapped her hand at the men stretching long limbs. "*Look* at them. And soon they'll be running and leaping and sweating…"

I laughed, grateful for the cool breeze that wafted over my cheeks as my gaze ate up Weston.

"Yep, he's a looker, that Wes," Ruby said. "But you're right—he's got a pretty good scowl going on. Or maybe he just has a bad case of Resting Asshole Face."

"That's not a thing. And he's a good guy. But he's—"

"Not Connor." She grinned. "Speak of the devil. This should be fun."

I turned to follow her gaze. Connor was taking the bleacher steps two at a time to meet us. He wore jeans, a T-shirt, and lightweight jacket that all looked like they'd come straight off from a GQ runway.

65

"You made it!" Connor's wide-open, carefree smile lit up his entire face. "And wow, you look amazing."

owing not to make a touchy-feely fool of myself again, I offered my hand. "Nice to see you."

Connor's hand swallowed mine, and then he pulled me in for a hug.

I lived for a good hug. One that made me feel safe or comforted. Edmond de Guiche had been my longtime hug dealer, but as I was enveloped in Connor's strong arms, suffused with his cologne and the warm scent of his skin…

Not fair, I thought, as my body started to melt against his broad chest.

He released me and stepped back to give Ruby a shoulder squeeze. "So glad you came. Have we seen our champ out there?" Connor shaded his eyes, scanning the field. "Ah. There he is." He clapped his hands together a few times, then cupped them over his mouth and yelled, *"You're my boy, Blue!"*

Weston's head came up and he scanned the crowds. He found Connor, gave him the finger, and then his eyes found me. I offered a little wave. Weston held my gaze a moment then went back to his stretches.

"The old Turner charm," Connor said, laughing.

"How come he doesn't hang with his team?" I asked.

"Weston doesn't work or play well with others."

I frowned.

"Don't feel sorry for him," Connor said. "Wait 'til you see him run."

A warm feeling spread through my chest at Connor's obvious affection—and proud smile—for his friend.

The Amherst coach huddled up his team. Weston stood at the periphery, hands on his hips, listening but not participating when the team broke with a loud, *"Gooo Mammoths!"*

The first race was the sixty-meter dash. Weston lined up with eight other racers, one of them an Amherst teammate. I found myself at the edge of the bleacher, biting my lower lip as the runners crouched at their places, working their fingers onto the track. In unison, they straightened their legs, hands still on the ground. The air tightened in that few seconds before the gun went off. When it did, the tension cracked. The runners took off and we cheered them on.

BRING DOWN the Stars

Nine men raced alongside each other, a mass of long legs. Weston pulled out in front immediately, and within seconds the race was over. His teammates clapped hands and swatted butts, but only one said something to Weston. He nodded in return, hands on hips and breathing hard but not heavily. I imagined if Connor were on the field, Weston would end up with a bear hug whether he wanted it or not.

The scoreboard lit up with names and times.

Turner, W. AMHERST ……………… 6.97

The second place finisher had a time of 7.14.

"Holy crap," I said.

Connor beamed. "The world record is 6.39. My boy is *fast*." He cupped his hands over his mouth again. "Way to go, T!"

Weston didn't smile, but he didn't give Connor the finger again either.

Connor turned to me. "Want something to drink? Lemonade?"

"That'd be great, thanks," I said.

He leaned around. "Ruby?"

"Please."

I reached for my little pocketbook. "Here, let me…"

"I got it," he said. "Sit tight. We have some time before Wes races again." He started to rise, then sat again. "Before I let one more second go by, I want to say you look really pretty today."

A warmth spread through my chest. "Thank you."

He stepped over us to the stairs and headed down, waving at someone to his right, pausing to talk to someone on the left. This part of the bleachers weren't even half full for these prelim races—maybe sixty spectators—but Connor seemed to know everyone.

Ruby leaned into me. "I need to tell you something, Auts."

"What?"

"You are *sooo* pretty today."

I shoved her off. "Shut up."

"That boy has moves on top of moves."

"You think it's all an act?"

"No, but he's like one of those track guys—he's put in a lot of training, honing his craft."

"He's sweet," I said.

"He's definitely the most popular guy here." Ruby jerked her chin down to the field. "Can't say the same for Wes."

Weston was off by himself again, sipping from a water cup and watching the next event—the eight-hundred-meters.

"So maybe he's an introvert," I said. "No crime in that."

"Says the reformed introvert. By the way, I'm so proud of you. I mean, *two* social events in two weekends. That's a record right there."

I laughed and leaned back on my elbows, turning my face to the sun, trusting my layers of sunblock. A cool breeze took the edge of the heat. Connor came back with lemonade and popcorn. We talked easily, laughed a lot and overall, the day couldn't have been more perfect.

The track crew finished setting up for the one-hundred-ten-meter hurdles and Weston lined up with nine other racers.

Connor leaned in close to me, his outstretched arm pointing to Weston in the outside lane, closest to us. The scent of his cologne filled my nose and his stubble brushed my cheek

"Watch him," Connor said, his voice low and gruff. "Most hurdlers take four steps before each hurdle, but a few can take only three. Wes takes three, which gives him an even bigger advantage."

I turned my head slightly. Connor's chin nearly touched mine, and our eyes met. This close, the green facets were stark and clear. His gaze moved from my eyes to my mouth. My heart pounded at his pure masculine perfection and my heartache for Mark suddenly seemed to belong to another person.

The moment broke apart by the announcer telling the racers to take their marks. Connor smiled faintly and we both turned our attention to the field.

"Let's go, Wes!" he bellowed.

The racers lined up, crouched, and took off with the gun.

"You see it?" Connor said excitedly. "He takes three steps…"

I tried to count but Weston was so fast. His legs a windmill blur before unfolding to take the hurdle. Left leg stretched, the right tucked under him, landing each time with perfect grace into the next three steps. He never once broke rhythm. Other hurdlers knocked the fences down, but Weston cleared every one and won the race. I didn't have to look at the time to know it was at least a half-second faster than the second-place finisher.

Ruby, Connor and I cheered, and then Connor leaned into me again.

"Three steps. He's unbeatable."

BRING DOWN the Stars

His smile was infectious and the way his eyes held mine…

Slow down. You just had your heart broken and you're already climbing back onto the ledge, contemplating another jump.

I gave myself a shake. This was precisely why I should have stayed home. I couldn't do casual. With his popularity and arsenal of moves, Connor probably didn't want any kind of serious relationship.

And my romantic heart didn't want anything less.

I returned Connor's smile and faced forward. The rest of the afternoon, I did my best to keep our conversation floating along surface topics: music, majors, and college life. But with every one of Connor's smiles, every laugh, every casual touch, I felt the pull that whispered for me to take the jump—that the fall was exhilarating. But I remembered all too well how hard and unforgiving the ground could be.

Chapter Eight

Weston

My third and final race was 4x400-meter baton relay. Coach Braun always had me run anchor for the simple fact - I won races. Which also happened to be the only reason my teammates were still talking to me. Fine by me. I wasn't there to make friends. I was there to win.

The 4x400 began, and as the baton was passed once, then twice, I took my place on the track for the last leg. We had about twenty seconds before our teammates rounded the curve for the final stretch, and a cloud of nervous tension hung over us. We all craned our necks to look over our shoulders, arms stretched back for the baton, reaching and ready, praying to the gods we wouldn't drop it.

"Hey," I said to the Tufts runner in the lane on my right, a guy I'd run against for two years. "Hey, Jacobs."

Todd Jacobs—lanky and dark-haired—glanced at me quickly, scowled. "Fantastic. Another season with the Amherst Asshole. Just what I always wanted."

"Do you like my uniform?" I asked.

The third-leg runners were rounding the curve. The anchors started taking half steps. Jacobs' gaze darted to me, then back to his approaching teammate.

"Huh?"

BRING DOWN the Stars

"I said, do you like my uniform?"

"Ignore him," said Hayes Jones, a runner from Wesleyan on my left, his dark eyes on the track behind him. "He's just trying to rile you."

"What about you, Jones?" I asked. "Do *you* like my uniform?"

"Fuck off, Turner."

We were all jogging now, arms reaching as our teammates closed in, their own arms out long.

"It's a great uniform," I said, running faster now as my teammate, Doug Bonham, stretched to hand off the baton. "Hold on, I'll show you what it looks like from behind."

I felt the baton hit my palm, wrapped my fingers around it and took off. Within seconds, I'd left Hayes, Jacobs, and the other runners in my rearview.

As I ran, I called upon reserves of energy in my legs and reignited the smoldering embers of pain in my memory. Anger at my asshole father. Anger at myself for not being able to leave him in my dust too. Anger that I still cared… I would turn it all into a fucking victory if it killed me.

That anger burned hot, and I pushed my body hard. Muscles screaming, lungs burning, stomach tightening in a thousand knots. I ran as if the rest of the racers were on my ass and not ten meters behind me, and crossed the finish line a good four seconds ahead of anyone else.

Win confirmed, I dropped the baton, slow-jogged to the nearest trashcan, and puked on the mound of empty paper water cups inside.

My post-race ritual: the carb-unload.

"Nice win, Wes," Coach Braun said when I straightened and wiped my mouth with the back of my hand. He pressed a cup of water at me and patted my shoulder. "You good?"

I nodded, still catching my breath. He opened his mouth to say something, maybe offer some advice, but opted for a clap on the back and leaving me alone. He'd learned in my freshman year that I showed up when he needed me to show up and I ran what he told me to run. But no one was allowed in my head.

The other racers paced to cool down, hands on hips and catching their breath as we waited for the times to post.

"You know what, Turner?" Hayes panted, his hands on his knees. "I'd admire you…if you weren't such a prick."

"Some day," Jacobs said, between sucking breaths. "He's going…to get his. I just hope I'm around to see it."

I shrugged them off. I'd won. That's all that mattered. And as I did after every won race, I waited for joy or elation to hit me.

It didn't.

It never did.

Instead, I indulged my other post-race ritual, one I'd had since Sinclair Prep. While the other runners were intent on the scoreboard, my eyes scanned the bleachers for *him*.

Pathetic and futile and yet I couldn't help it.

Give it up, Sock Boy. He's not here, and he never will be.

My wandering gaze found Autumn sitting with Connor. His dark head and her flaming red hair close together. Just talking? Or was he sneaking a kiss? I doubted it. Connor was pretty good at reading women, and probably knew Autumn wouldn't tolerate a move like that without an official first date.

A smile ghosted my lips. *You can steal all the high-fives and hugs you want, but you have to earn a kiss from her.*

The meet ended, and Amherst—thanks to me—destroyed the other teams. But even without my points, we had a deep roster of talent. The Mammoths were going to have a good year.

I walked past where the Tufts crew packed up their duffels. "See you next month, Jacobs," I said with a wave.

"Suck it, Turner," he snapped back.

Friends and family trickled onto the field now, and I braced myself as Connor and Autumn approached.

She came. Sure, so she could see Connor. Because she wanted to see him. But still, she came.

Connor and I clasped hands and he tried to give me a hug.

"Get off," I said. "I stink and I'm not done puking."

Connor laughed and ruffled my hair instead. "You kicked ass. But you and your puking. Maybe an antacid before the race?"

"I'll keep that in mind," I muttered.

"That relay was incredible," Autumn said, her eyes and smile wide. "All three races were incredible. You were amazing to watch. Congrats."

She moved toward me and I took a step back, conscious of my breath. Her smile faltered. Hurt flickered across her eyes and I scrambled to think of a gracious reply to her compliment but came up empty.

Strike one.

Autumn retreated, and she said to no one in particular, "Look at Ruby."

Ruby was over by the Wesleyan team, chatting up Hayes Jones. Both of them laughing with familiarity, as if they'd met in kindergarten.

"She's really good at that," Autumn said. "Meeting new people? I get butterflies at the thought of walking up to a stranger and starting a conversation."

"But walking up to strangers in libraries and trashing their capitalist propaganda is no problem," I said.

"I did not— shut up." Laughing, she started to give me a shove. I was soaked with sweat and stepped back again, out of range. Her laughter died off, leaving that same hurt in its wake.

Strike two, idiot.

Autumn glanced at her watch, then looked up at Connor. "So…I had great time. I'm glad I came. Thanks for the lemonade."

"That was nothing," he said. "How about dinner?"

I flinched. *Christ, not like that, dummy. You can't ask her on a first date like she's any old nail and you're the sledgehammer.*

Autumn adjusted her bag. "Oh, thank you, but I—"

"There's a great Thai place down the road," Connor said. "Ever been to Boko 6?"

Of course she had. There were only ten restaurants in town. I walked away, hands on my hips as if I were still winded, but really, I needed to get away from Connor's ham-fisted invitation. Autumn needed a light touch and romance. A few seconds ago I couldn't manage a "thank you," but I suddenly knew exactly how *I'd* ask her to go out with me.

Have you been to the Emily Dickinson Museum? Maybe we could check it out, then try to cheer ourselves up over coffee after.

Would you like to have dinner with at the Rostand? Or just drinks. Even if it's only for a glass of water, I need you to see the sunset from the top deck.

Have you been to the Orchard Hill Observatory? We could bring a picnic up there at dusk and watch the stars come out…

But it looked as if Connor was doing just fine after all. He had his phone out and appeared to be plugging in Autumn's number.

Strike three. I'm out.

I must not have been recovered from the race, because the urge to puke came over me again.

Ruby joined them, stuffing her own phone in her back pocket. A few more words exchanged, and then the girls headed off across the field. But after a few steps, Autumn turned back and waved at me.

"Bye, Weston. Congratulations on your wins."

"Yep," I said, and Connor joined me to watch them go. In the falling twilight, Autumn's hair was gold and fire, falling down her back in long curls. I stared until Connor elbowed my side.

"Digits secured," he said. "But man, that girl makes you work for it. I'm not even guaranteed a date."

I glanced at him as we walked to where my duffel lay on the grass in my team's huddle. "No?"

"She keeps telling me how busy she is, and has a double-major, and who knows what else," Connor said. "She gave me her number but then said, 'We'll see.' What does that mean?"

"It means, dumbass, she's going to wait to see what you do with it. What you say when you ask her out. *How* you ask."

Connor frowned. "I already asked her out."

"And she didn't say yes." I pulled on my track pants and sweatshirt. "She's not a Netflix-and-chill. She wants romance."

He narrowed his eyes at me. "How do you know?"

"She told me. But I think she likes you," I added.

"She does?" His eager smile melted into a grin. "Yeah, I think she does."

"She *might*," I said. "But you should know…"

"Should know what?"

I scrubbed my chin. "I think she's been burned recently, so take it easy, okay?"

"Did she tell you that, too?"

"No. Just a hunch."

Connor slapped me in the middle of the back. "Look at you, giving me woman advice. I think your racing wins are going straight to your head."

"Yeah," I muttered. "That must be it."

I rummaged through my bag for my phone and found a voice message from Ma sent this morning.

Hey baby boy, I just wanted to wish you luck today at your

BRING DOWN the Stars

races. You take all that God-given talent and go kick some ass, okay?

A turned my face away from Connor to conceal a small smile. Miranda Turner had her own way with words.

I heard her puff a cigarette and exhale.

Oh, and did I tell you? Your genius sister, Kimberly, dropped her phone in the toilet. How many times I tell her to get off that damn thing while she's in the mirror putting on her makeup. Too much makeup, by the way. She's getting bad skin, but does she listen to me? God forbid. So that's a few hundred bucks I don't have. Down the toilet. Literally.

She cackled her loud, infectious laugh, which degenerated into a barking cough.

But honestly, things is tight enough and I know Paul would help but I'm trying not to start down that road already, you know? Oh jeez, I haven't told you about Paul! I met him at the salon while he was waiting for his sister to get done, and we hit it off. His name is Paul Winfield and he's not like nobody I been with. Just you wait 'til you meet him. Come back home, baby, first chance you get, okay? You can meet him and maybe talk some sense into your sister's empty head.

Love you. Felicia sends her love too. Be good, but not too good, and give that sweet Connor a kiss on the cheek for me, you hear? Okay, love you, baby boy. Bye.

I turned back around, dropped the phone in my bag and hoisted it onto my shoulder. "Sorry. Miranda had some things to say."

"How is she?"

"Okay," I said, as we headed off the track. "Money's tight, as usual. She's seeing some new guy, as usual."

"Could be good," Connor said, scrolling his phone as we walked.

"If he's like any of her other boyfriends, he's going to bum what he can off her and she's got nothing to bum." I gazed around at the sprawling grounds of Amherst, green and gold in the dusky light, while my mother was cramped in that tiny apartment in Southie. "I should get a job."

"You have no time for a job. That's why you have a scholarship."

"I could squeeze it in," I said, mentally trying to figure out where. Hoping for an early graduation, I'd loaded up my schedule with as many classes as my counselor would let me take. Between course work and track, my days were packed. "I could work a nightshift somewhere."

"And be too tired to study or run," Connor said, putting his phone away. "Dude, why not try for the big show? The Olympics? You're so fucking fast. You'd get in, easy."

"Because training for the Olympics isn't cheap and it's a full-time job. I'd need a coach. And there're no guarantees. One snapped ligament and my career is over. I wouldn't be any good to Ma."

"My parents are always there, you know," Connor said in a low voice.

I swallowed down the bitterness, because I knew. "Anyway, Ma wants me to come to Boston and meet this new guy, Paul, but I'm not in a fucking hurry to meet the latest bum who's probably leeching off her, just like every other guy she hooks up with."

"If they're still together at Thanksgiving, you can meet him then."

"That works."

Every year, the Drakes invited my sisters and my mother—with her cigarettes and too-loud laugh—to Thanksgiving dinner at their gigantic row house. Every year, my mother drank too much, no matter how many times I told her to take it easy. They'd call a car for her—a sedan, not an Uber—to take her home, with Mrs. Drake making sure Ma had a week's worth of leftovers with her and an invitation to Christmas Eve dinner a few weeks later.

The Drakes were good people.

"It would be awesome if things were good with me and Autumn by then," Connor said. "And I know what you're going to say, but I like her. She's beautiful. And super smart."

"Did you guys talk a lot at the meet?" I asked.

"Sure," he said with a one-shoulder shrug, which meant he was full of shit. They hadn't gone below surface topics.

"Maybe you should get to know her a little bit better before you start weaving her into your grand plans to please your parents."

"I'm not planning anything, except for a first date. I've never hung out with a girl more than twice and not gotten to first base." He grinned. "I like a challenge."

I rolled my eyes, ready to tell him that Autumn was a human being, not a challenge, but he held up a silencing palm.

"I'm *kidding*," he said. "Autumn is…I don't know. Different.

BRING DOWN the Stars

She's kind of shy, but she stands her ground. I like that about her."

"Yeah, I like that too," I said quietly.

"What was that?"

"Nothing."

Later that night, Connor lay sprawled on the couch with SportsCenter blaring, scrolling his phone. I sat at the kitchen table, tapping my pen against an empty page in my notebook and contemplating running as my Object of Devotion. I couldn't muster the blood and guts to put it to paper. I liked running. It served a purpose, but did I want to make it my life?

"Oh shit," Connor cried from behind me.

"What is it?"

"I accidentally texted her."

"Who?" I said, knowing damn well who.

"Autumn. I was fucking messing around and I hit that stupid predictive text thing, then panicked and hit send."

"So what?"

"I don't text or call a girl until *at least* three days have passed."

I set down my pen and turned around. "Are you serious?"

"Of course I'm serious. It looks desperate to text her the *same day*."

I hid a smile. "What did you text?"

"Just 'yes'." His eyes widened. "Shit. She's texting me back."

Connor jumped up from the couch and came to where I sat, standing next to my chair as we both watched his phone.

Yes...? :)

Connor typed, **Hey**.

I smirked. "Really?"

"Yeah, so?"

A pause, then a new text bubbled up. **What's up?**

"Now she's annoyed," I said. "Or impatient."

Connor looked to me. "What do I say?"

"Why are you asking me?"

"You're good at this shit. How many papers did you write for me at Sinclair?"

"This is *not* the same thing."

"Ballpark." Connor made a face. "Dude, she's waiting."

I frowned, thought for a moment. "Tell her the truth."

"Hell no—"

"Tell her the truth but make it better. Tell her you were messing with your phone while thinking about her. Tell her that you wanted to talk to her so badly, your subconscious made it happen."

"Oh, that's good."

Connor's fingers flew, and then he hit send.

There was a pause and no answer.

Connor frowned. "What's this mean?"

"It's good. I mean she's thinking about what you said."

The rolling dots of Autumn's reply came in.

The old 'accidental text' move? I feel like I've seen that before... ;-)

"She's not letting you off the hook so easily," I said, smiling despite myself. "Don't deny. Tell her she's one hundred percent right. You'll make any excuse to talk to her."

"That's perfect, man." Connor typed and hit send.

I like your honesty, came the reply.

"Hey, it's working." Connor beamed. "Now what?"

It was working, and I didn't like what *it* was.

"I don't know, man," I said, waving a hand. "Type something. Whatever you're thinking."

"I want her to go out with me."

"Then ask."

With a horrible fascination, I watched Connor type, **So, dinner?**

"Jesus, dude," I said.

"What? That's exactly what you told me to do."

"Not like that," I said. "I told you she needs romance."

I don't know, she wrote. **I have so much work to do already.**

"Fuck," Connor said. He nudged me with his phone. "Wes, man, you do it."

I blinked. "Do what now?"

"Ask her out for me. The right way."

I stared.

"Look, this girl is special. I'm not too proud to admit I need back-up getting things rolling with her." He grinned that winning smile. "C'mon. Just this once."

"But…"

Connor shoved his phone into my hand. "Come on, man. Do what you do. Write something witty and poetic. Something that'll impress her enough to get me another text. Another…anything." He clapped me on the shoulder. "Write something that knocks her on her ass and gets me in the door. That's all I ask."

I looked at Connor's phone in my hand and Autumn Caldwell's text, waiting for an answer. I felt my best friend's expectations literally breathing down my neck as he leaned over me.

Ignoring the small ache in my heart, I thought about what I would've said to Autumn had it been my phone in my hand, and began to type.

CHAPTER Nine

Autumn

"I'm ready," I said, smoothing the flared skirt of my black halter dress. "At least, I think I am. Is black too formal for a first date?"

Ruby, sprawled on the couch, looked up from her magazine. "Girl, you look amazing. That dress is perfect for the Rostand. Connor is going to lose his mind."

"He can keep his mind and use it for stimulating conversation." I sucked in a breath and smoothed my skirt again. "I'm nervous. Why am I nervous?"

"Because you haven't had a first date in ages. You aimed high with Mr. Drake."

"I'm not aiming for anything," I said. "No expectations. I'm just going to see what happens."

"Uh huh," Ruby said. "How many times have you read that text of his?"

"Oh, hush. I haven't read it in days."

Because I had it memorized.

You're the Halley's Comet of girls. The kind that doesn't come around but maybe once in a life. I don't want to spend the rest of mine wondering what might've been if I hadn't tried, one last time, to take you someplace where every man will stare at you and wish they were

BRING DOWN the Stars

me.

My cheeks warmed and Ruby raised a brow.

"Okay, fine," I said. "I'm hoping for romance. For electricity. The same kind I felt while reading that text. What if there isn't any?"

"What if there is?"

"Maybe this was a bad idea."

Ruby wagged her eyebrows. "Bad ideas are my favorite kind."

I jumped as the door buzzer buzzed.

Ruby checked her phone. "Not even six yet. A little early for dinner, isn't it?"

"He wants me to see the sunset from the Rostand's top deck."

"Wow," she said. "I wouldn't have pegged him for a romantic, but I've been proven wrong twice now." She shook her head, laughing. "You are *such* a goner."

"No expectations," I said. I went on muttering it under my breath like a mantra as I went to hit the button on the intercom. "I'll be right down," I called.

"Have fun," Ruby said. "Text me if you're bringing him back here. I'll crash at Deb and Julie's. Or maybe I'll give Hayes a call. How far a drive is it from here to Wesleyan?"

Since meeting at Weston's track meet, Ruby and Hayes had been texting and calling each other all week.

"It's about an hour," I said.

"Definitely within my range."

"I'm not bringing Connor back here," I said, throwing on a black cardigan. "Just dinner."

"After dinner comes dessert."

I shot her a look as I grabbed my purse.

"Come on." She rifled through her magazine. "You're trading fuddy-duddy Mark Watts for Connor-flipping-Drake. This is like watching a brand new rom-com after staring at PBS for two years."

"I'm so glad my love life is your entertainment."

"The farm girl and the rich city boy," Ruby said. "Episode One: the first date."

"Good night, Ruby."

She blew me a kiss, and I went out.

At the bottom of the outside steps, Connor waited. His back was to me, broad beneath a fitted dress shirt, tapering down to a narrow waist in tailored dress pants.

His ass is perfect.

I blinked at my own errant thought, and composed my stare just as he turned around.

"Hey," he said, and the slow smile that spread over his face was better than a thousand compliments. "You look incredible."

"Thank you," I said, my gaze caught on his handsome face. Thick brows, a broad mouth. His eyes were like chips of emeralds fringed by long lashes. A shadow of stubble over his strong jaw.

"Ready?" He offered me his arm.

My fingers slid around his elbow, feeling the smooth skin and muscle beneath his rolled-up shirt sleeve. We walked toward a brand-new-looking sports car, parked at the curb and begging attention. Dark gray with bright red brakes underneath chrome wheels. The front grill made me think of a snarling dog baring its teeth.

"Wow, this is yours?" I said.

"Just got her last month," Connor said, opening the passenger door for me. "She's pretty sweet."

"I love the color."

"The gun metal gray isn't standard. I had her custom-painted."

I sank into luxurious leather and a potent mix of new-car smell and Connor's cologne.

"I don't know much about cars," I said when he got behind the wheel. "What kind is it?"

He grinned and revved the engine. It sounded like a rocket ship readying for takeoff. "Dodge Challenger Hellcat coupe. Seven-hundred-and-seven-horsepower, six-hundred-fifty-foot pounds of torque." He glanced at me slyly. "Does that mean anything to you?"

"Not really."

Connor laughed. "You don't have to know her specs to enjoy how she drives."

He shifted into gear and expertly navigated off the curb and down Pleasant Drive, his car purring beneath us. I sat with my hands folded in my lap, almost afraid to touch anything this expensive. I was a farm girl who rode a bike all over town. Feeling I'd been miscast in a movie, I sought comfort in the beautiful text that brought me here in the first place.

"Did you tell me your major the other night at Yancy's?" I asked. "Was it Creative Writing?"

"Economics."

BRING DOWN the Stars

"Oh. Same as Weston."

"We tend to do things together. A habit since prep school."

"Are you going to join him on Wall Street?"

"I don't know," Connor said. "I haven't figured it out yet. I could go on Wall Street, or work at one of my dad's companies. I'm not really a nine-to-five kind of guy." He laughed. "Hell, I'm not really a ten-to-three kind of guy. I think owning my own sports bar would be pretty perfect. I like hanging out, talking hockey or baseball. Just having a good time, you know?"

"Sure."

No wonder his tone and manner were so easy-going. Connor never had to wake up early unless he wanted to. He needed no crap job to keep money in the bank. No scholarship to pay for school. No lean months when he wondered where rent was going to come from. He slouched in his custom-painted car, a wrist slung over the wheel.

He has no fear, I thought. *No fear it could all be taken away at any second.*

I feared. Working my ass off for what I wanted was ingrained in me. It made me who I was, and fear continued to form me like clay every single day, molding me into the person I had yet to become.

My stomach tightened. I reminded myself that having money didn't guarantee a perfect life, but the feeling of being miscast grew stronger.

"Running your own business is a lot of work," I said.

"I can hire people to do the heavy lifting. I want to hang out and talk to customers, make them feel good. Make 'em laugh, take their minds off their worries."

"That sounds…nice," I said.

"Tell that to my parents." He pulled into the Maison Rostand driveway and found a parking spot.

"They don't like the sports bar idea?"

"Not even a little."

His expression darkened as he killed the engine and abruptly exited the car, unsmiling for the first time since I'd met him. But his smile was back as he opened my door for me, and offered me his arm. A perfect gentleman.

The French restaurant was a tall, elegant building—a bit of 18th century Versailles set smack in the middle of the Massachusetts countryside.

"Have you been here before?" I asked, as we crossed the parking lot.

"Once," Connor said. "My parents came to watch one of my games. They brought me and a couple of teammates here after."

"One of your baseball games, right? What position do you play?"

"Center field," he said. "You ever come to a game?"

"No, I'm usually too busy with classes and Mark wasn't..." I swallowed the rest of the sentence.

Dammit. Now I'm the girl who brings up an ex on a first date.

One of Connor's eyebrows raised. "Mark?"

"My ex-boyfriend," I said. "We broke up at the start of summer. He wasn't a big sports fan and I was too busy. Weston's track meet was the first event I've been to at Amherst."

As he opened the restaurant door, Connor's stunning eyes caught and held mine. "I'm glad you made an exception."

The tightness in my stomach relaxed. "Me too."

The foyer of Rostand's was elegant marble and plaster, with muted lighting and rich décor. The scent of grilled steak and chocolate laced the air.

"It's like a little piece of Paris," I said, glancing around. "I'm trying to imagine a bunch of baseball players in here."

"We were on our best behavior." He shot me a wink. "At Roxy's later...not so much. Ever been?"

"Never heard of it," I said, as we waited to be seated.

"Really? It's a roadhouse about an hour out of town, on this little dirt road. Kind of a rough crowd, but I dig it." He whipped his head to me. "You want to check it out instead of eating here?"

"I don't know if it's my scene," I said, smoothing down my skirt.

"Probably true." Connor's smile thinned out. "Another time."

A silence fell and stretched until the maître d' arrived. He took us up a winding marble staircase to the uppermost floor, where a rooftop terrace overlooked all of Amherst. The sun was just starting to sink in the west, casting a golden hue over the rolling greenery.

"Kind of an old person's place, yeah?" Connor said in a low voice.

I tore my eyes away from the view and saw most of the terrace tables were occupied by couples, all older than us by a good thirty

BRING DOWN the Stars

years.

"Now I remember why we ran out to Roxy's after dinner with my parents."

"I thought you liked it here," I said. "You told me the sunset wasn't to be missed."

"Oh, right. That's just what I heard, but never seen it myself." He turned his beaming smile up a notch. "It'll be a first for me, too."

The moment smoothed out and settled warmly between us, and we took up our menus.

The waiter appeared to take our drink orders.

"Do you have pear cider?" Connor asked the waiter with a wink for me.

I rolled my eyes and laughed as the waiter apologized for the lack of cider on the premises.

"A bottle of red wine then?" Connor asked.

"White, please. And only a glass."

He ordered a glass of sauvignon blanc for me and a craft beer for him.

"Just the one," he said. "Since I'm driving."

The waiter checked our IDs, then retreated.

Connor leaned back in his chair. "I have a confession."

"Oh?"

"Between Yancy's and the track meet, I can't remember what you said about your major, except that it sounded complicated as hell."

"Double major in poli-sci and social anthropology."

"Right. What are you planning to do with that? You mentioned going to Harvard for grad school?"

"I hope to. I'm going to petition to create my own specialized major with an emphasis on a specific area of humanitarian work."

Connor blew out his cheeks. "Wow. Ambitious."

I ran the tip of my finger over the rim of my water glass. "Well, I haven't picked my emphasis yet, but Harvard says they're open to it. I have to send the project in when I apply, so I have only this year to figure it out."

"Sounds like a crap-ton of work, whatever you choose."

"It is, but it'll be worth it. I want to take on a major issue in a meaningful way."

"That's cool."

The waiter came back with our drinks, and Connor ordered for

85

us, filet for me and prime rib for him.

He held up his beer to my wine glass. "Cheers."

"Cheers," I said, disappointed he didn't offer a toast as romantic as the text that brought us here.

Connor took a pull from his beer, set it down, then leaned back in his chair.

"So what else do you do, Autumn, when you're not figuring out how to save the world?"

"That takes up a lot of time," I said, then laughed. "Studying, I mean. And I work at the Panache Blanc bakery. You know it? On Pleasant?"

"Sure," he said. "Wes goes there some nights to study."

"I work the morning shifts."

His shoulders twitched a little. "What time does that start?"

"Six a.m."

Connor mimed being stabbed in the heart. "Six a.m. *every* morning?"

I laughed. "You sound like my roommate. I have Saturdays off but I still wake up early. It's a habit from growing up on a farm."

"What do you do for fun?"

"I like to read. And I listen to music. I love alternative music. Growing up, we didn't hear much of it. The first time I heard New Order, I was ten years behind everyone else." I smiled. "Now I'm all caught up."

"Cool, cool," Connor said. His fingers drummed the table. The fidgety rhythm and the murmur of other patrons' conversations filled the silence between us.

"So, do you have any brothers or sisters?" I asked.

"One brother," Connor said. "Older."

"I have a brother too," I said. "Younger. A senior in high school."

"Jefferson's at Harvard Business School," Connor said. "He's about to graduate with honors. He'll probably work with my mother in the Senate, then run for office himself some day."

His darkened expression told me I'd blundered onto the wrong topic. Being unhappy, I realized, was unnatural to Connor. Like a too-tight suit he itched to take off as soon as possible.

"Is that a bad thing?"

He glanced up and seemed to realize he'd been frowning. "No,

BRING DOWN the Stars

sorry. It's great. He's on track to make a difference in the world. Meanwhile, I want to open a sports bar. My parents remind me of this. Frequently."

"They put a lot of pressure on you?"

"They're high-profile, so they want their kids to be high-profile too." He shook his head, took another pull of beer and shot me a wink. "I'm not trying to save the world like some people I know."

"I think we all have our own paths to follow," I said. "Mine is to go out in the world and bring some relief to some people. I hope, anyway. Yours is to give them a place to come to. A haven."

Connor's smile widened slowly, like a brilliant dawn rising.

"Yeah, exactly," he said. "A haven. I love that."

I basked in that smile. "I'm glad."

His gaze lingered on mine, and I grinned nervously at the tiny *zing* of electricity in the moment. I tucked a lock of hair behind my ear and glanced over his shoulder.

"You were right," I said. "The sunset is really beautiful."

"Yeah," he said softly. "Crazy beautiful."

But he wasn't looking at the sunset, he was looking at me.

Zing.

The rest of the dinner conversation was like a faucet with a faulty spigot. Sometimes the conversation flowed easily; sometimes it dripped. Other times it was shut off completely in awkward stretches of silence.

And no more *zing*.

The sun sank and our waiter came to light the candle in the little glass cup between us. I found my thoughts wandering to the pile of work on my desk at home.

After dessert, we headed back through the parking lot. Two valet attendants were walking around Connor's car, unabashedly admiring it from all angles.

"Hey, fellas," Connor said, hitting the key fob to unarm the car.

"Hey, man," one valet said. "Sweet ride."

"Thanks."

"Do you mind if we hang out while you start her up?" asked

the other.

Connor's grinned turned cocky. "You want to hear the growl?"

"Hell, yeah."

Connor slid in the driver's seat and started up the car while I waited off to the side. He revved the engine twice and the valets were ecstatic. He got out again and the three of them stood there, arms crossed, watching the sports car idle, and talking in low voices I couldn't hear over the car's 'growl.'

Finally, they thanked him and got back to work. Connor hurried over to where I stood, my arms crossed in the cooling night.

"Sorry about the car stuff. I sort of left you hanging," he said. "It's a guy thing."

"No, it's fine."

"You sure?"

"Yeah, I'm just…a little out of my element."

"What do you mean?"

"Maybe this place was setting the bar a little high for me. Don't get me wrong, dinner was lovely. I just mean… I haven't been on a first date in two years…"

Connor nudged me. "Don't be so hard on yourself. You did just fine."

"Oh. Thanks," I muttered.

He helped me into the car, and I picked at the hem of my dress for the duration of our quiet ride home. At the front of the apartment complex, Connor swiveled to me.

"It's early yet. Time for a game of pool at Yancy's, maybe?"

"No, I have to be up at five tomorrow morning."

Connor grimaced. "The agony."

"Right. So… I'll say goodnight."

"If you insist." He got out and came around to open my door. He walked me to the front stoop and slipped his hands around my waist.

"I want to see you again," he said.

"You do?"

"Yeah, I do," he said, and leaned in.

I leaned back. "Connor, wait. Before we go any further… Well, I was trying to tell you something before, and I guess didn't do a great job of it."

His smile tilted. "Okay."

BRING DOWN the Stars

"About this being my first date in two years? I need to be perfectly honest with you. The long-term relationship I just got out of? It didn't end well."

"No?"

"No, and I—"

"How come?"

I flinched a little, my cheeks burning. "Oh. Well."

God, do I have to say it?

Connor waited. Apparently I did.

"He wasn't...faithful."

His grin faltered. "Oh, gotcha."

The air tightened around me and I wanted to turn and run upstairs.

I cleared my throat. "Yes, it was a 'gotcha' moment, all right. And it's made me a little reticent to jump into something new."

"I totally get that," Connor said. "I'm down with keeping it casual. Or whatever you want."

I bit my lip. "Maybe we could grab a coffee sometime and talk—?"

His face lit up. "Hey, you know what? A bunch of us are going to Lake Onota next weekend. Ever been?"

"No."

"It's a blast. Swimming, boating, and a huge bonfire on the beach. One last hurrah before it gets too cold."

"I don't know."

"Just think about it," he murmured, his voice deepening and turning husky. "Okay?"

"I will."

He gently kissed my cheek, his warm breath lingering, and sending a *zing-y* shiver over my skin.

"Talk to you soon."

"Okay," I said. "Bye."

Inside the apartment, I shut the door and rested my back against it, trying to make sense of the night. I pulled out my phone and reread the text he'd sent me a week ago. The beautiful words that set tonight in motion.

You're the Halley's Comet of girls...

It was perfect. And he'd been a perfect gentleman. But our conversation was a seesaw of warm moments and awkward. *Zing* and silence.

I touched my fingers to my cheek where Connor's kiss still lingered.

"God," I sighed, slumping against the door. I needed Ruby, but she was out—a note on the counter said she'd gone to Debra and Julie's place down the hall. *Just in case.*

I thought about joining them but they'd ask a million questions about the date. Including if I was going to see Connor again.

A question I didn't know how to answer.

CHAPTER Ten

Weston

In the space between us
A thousand unspoken words
Hang
A noose tightening
Around my throat
choking me silent
Heart bleeding
For autumn colors
Red and gold
And red again
Drowning in my
every thought
that is
for

you

I put down my pen and blinked at what I'd written.
I'd been working on the Object of Devotion poem a week now. Long stretches of absent-minded doodling, followed by bouts of

writing, letting my mind spill onto the page however it wanted. Pretending the subject of these hopeless words wasn't on a first date with my best friend. Or that I'd had a hand in orchestrating said date.

I read over the lines again, remembering what Professor Ondiwuje said about form—that how a poem looked on a page could have as much as impact as the words themselves.

My poem was arranged in a column. A scaffold of words with a lone *you* at the end, separated from the rest. The object separated from the devotion.

"Not too subtle there, Turner," I muttered.

I flipped to a blank page to start over. I had a shit-ton of Econ reading on exchange rate regimes, but I couldn't concentrate.

Are they hitting it off? Is she falling for him? Is he kissing her right now?

The front door opened, jarring me out of my thoughts.

"Hey," Connor said. He shut the door without taking off his jacket and headed to the kitchen.

I glanced at the clock that read a little before eight o'clock—a solid three hours earlier than his usual date schedule.

"You're early," I said, keeping my eyes on my paper. "How did it go?"

"Different," Connor said. He rummaged in the fridge for a beer, popped the top and leaned against the counter, a strange smile on his lips.

"Different, how?"

"I'm back before dawn, for one thing," Connor said. "It was strictly dinner and goodnight."

"Isn't that what she told you when she agreed to go out in the first place?"

After she read my text.

"Yeah, it was."

I shrugged. "She means what she says."

"Yeah, she does," Connor said. "She's pretty hard-core with her double major and getting up at the ass-crack of dawn for a job that can't pay all that well. And none of the stuff that usually impresses girls impressed her. She couldn't give two shits about the Hellcat. We didn't even kiss."

My head whipped up. "You didn't?"

Connor shook his head. "A peck on the cheek and I'm home by

eight o'clock." He laughed. "The sky must be falling."

It was on the tip of my tongue to tell him I was sorry it didn't work out between them, better luck next time, other fish in the sea…but then a slow smile spread over Connor's lips.

"But you know what? I really dig that about her."

My jaw stiffened. "Oh yeah?"

"Yeah." Connor whipped a chair out to sit across from me. "She *is* different. She's not falling into my lap and I'm pretty sure she doesn't give a shit about my money."

"Yeah," I said, slowly. "You'd never have to wonder if that's all she cared about."

"Right? She's the kind of girl you have to work to keep. My parents would eat her up with a spoon."

"But Con—"

"I know, I know, it's not about them. Yet. I like her. I want to see her again." His smile dimmed. "But it's probably too late."

"Why?"

"She was telling me about her ex. Some guy she'd been with for two years. Mark."

"And?"

"He cheated on her."

Which made Mark not only a dumbass, but king of the dumbasses. But Autumn had pride. She didn't strike me as someone who'd volunteer such a painful piece of information on the first date.

"I'm sort of surprised she brought that up," I said slowly.

Connor's gaze slid away from me. "She didn't. She said her relationship ended badly and I asked how."

"Point blank?"

He nodded.

"Jesus, man."

"I didn't know what to say. I started babbling about keeping things casual and going to Lake Onota or some shit. She wasn't happy."

"Of course she wasn't," I said. "She told you something incredibly personal and embarrassing and you steamrolled over it."

"What the hell should I have said?"

"That the guy was an idiot. You should have reassured her that she's not going to get screwed over again. Or that at the very least, you respect her pain and you don't want to add to it."

Connor sagged and studied his beer bottle. "Yeah, that would've been exactly what she wanted to hear."

Silence fell between us. My heart felt like it was being pulled in two directions—to helping Connor try again with Autumn, or to convince him to move on.

So you can take your shot?

"I wouldn't mind something real with a girl, you know?" Connor said after a moment. "The hookups are fun, but I have a lot more to offer than money. And that stupid car. Jesus, I could've been driving a Pinto for all Autumn cared." He looked at me. "No offense to your beautiful automotive trash heap."

"None taken," I said. *Because Autumn wouldn't care.*

"When I told her about my sports bar idea, she said something amazing."

"Yeah?" I asked, my voice low.

"She said she was going to go out into the world to help people, while I was creating a haven for them to come to. A *haven*." He gave his head a short shake and put his beer bottle to his mouth. "My parents wouldn't think like that. Ever."

My pen scrawled along the blank page.

Haven.

Safety.

I give you my dreams for safekeeping.

"But it's too late now," Connor said. He drained his beer. "I fucked it up."

I studied my best friend, whose inherent happiness was constantly beat down by the Drakes who wanted him to be something he wasn't. Connor never wanted for anything in his life, but didn't ask for much either.

He's asking for her.

"What's she doing now?" I asked.

"Autumn?" He shrugged. "I dropped her off at her place. Why?"

"Give me your phone."

Connor fished it out of his jacket pocket and slid it across the table. "You have a plan?"

"Shh. Let me think."

I opened the thread of messages with Autumn. My thumb hesitated over the key, then I typed a textbook Connor Drake opener:

BRING DOWN the Stars

Hey. I wanted to tell you I had a great time tonight.

Connor brought his chair around to sit beside me. "You just broke my three-day rule," he said. "Again."

Autumn's text came back. **Me too.**

Nothing else.

"Not exactly a ringing endorsement," I said.

"Ha ha."

My thumbs started flying.

And I completely fucked up.

"*Dude,*" Connor said.

"Shut up and watch," I said.

What do you mean? she wrote.

What you told me about your ex caught me off guard. I couldn't believe any guy would be so blind to what he had in you. But I didn't treat you with the respect you deserved either. You put something personal and painful in my hands and I dropped it.

It's okay, she wrote back and I could imagine her soft smile as she leaned her chin on her hand, the phone in the other, reading my words.

No, it's not. He had two years with you and he threw them away. I had only one dinner, but it was enough to make me want to do better. To talk to you.

I hit send and bit my lip, brows furrowed. I felt Connor's anticipation hanging over me, but he kept silent.

Thank you for saying so, Autumn wrote. **I think I'd like that too.**

How about we grab a coffee?

I have to be up early, remember?

I shot Connor a look. He shrugged and tried to grab for his phone. I smacked his hand away.

Decaf coffee.

:) but now?

Right now. Before you sleep and wake up and put me behind you. I don't want to be there. I want to be in front of you, at least one more time.

"Too much," Connor murmured. "She's going to say no."

"Shhh," I hissed.

My heart was pounding like it did before a race. It wasn't my race, but I was already halfway to the finish line and losing was not an

95

option. I ran to *win,* even if it meant this time I'd lose. Hard.

Finally, the rolling dots of Autumn's reply appeared. I held my breath.

I think Claire's Cafe is still open. I could meet you there?

Warmth flooded my chest and my hand clenched in victory under the table.

Perfect, I typed. **See you in a few.**

See you then, Connor.

Connor.

His hand clapped my shoulder and the cold bucket of reality splashed over my 'victory.'

"Holy *shit*." He took his phone back and read over the texts. "You have a gift, my friend."

"Yeah, well, study and learn," I said stiffly, rising from my chair. I wasn't dressed for running but my sweats and T-shirt would suffice. I went to the door to put on my shoes. "Read what I wrote to her and use it. And the comment she made about the sports bar being a haven? Tell her you're still thinking about it. Tell her what it meant to you."

Connor nodded. "I will. Because I am."

"Good, because I'm not doing that again."

"Why not? It worked perfectly."

"It's *dishonest*," I said. "Autumn's already been burned hard by dishonesty. If she finds out, she'll never talk to either of us again."

"It's not all that dishonest." Connor got up and grabbed his wallet and keys from the front table. "You just wrote what I was thinking but couldn't say."

No, I wrote what I was thinking and can never say.

"You're on your own now, Drake." I gave my shoelace a jerk and grabbed my phone and earbuds. "I'm going for a run."

"Okay," Connor said, sounding bewildered. "Hey, man. Thanks."

I found a faint smile. "Don't make her wait."

I ran all the way down Pleasant Drive, past the shops and cafes of the small town. It was quiet for a Saturday night, and my thoughts were loud. I put on a radio app that tuned into the Amherst station. Over the eclectic mix of songs, I played my mantra:

Forget her.
Get over it.
Move on.

I ran to the end of town, where the lights gave way to dark swaths of uninhabited land. I stared out at the black nothing, turned around and headed back. The DJ in my ear announced the next song.

"Here's 'Ocean Eyes', from the sixteen-year-old prodigy, Billie Eilish."

I froze, hands on hips, listening and breathing hard as a young woman sang about a man she'd been watching from afar. How she fell into the depths of his eyes and his diamond mind.

I tore the earbuds out and paced a small circle, anger burning a hole in my chest.

"It's me," I said to the night. "It's fucking me, Autumn. Not him."

I sucked in a deep breath. I had to tell Connor I had a connection with Autumn I couldn't explain and if I didn't admit it out loud, it'd burn me up from the inside.

I started to jog back to town, then ran. Hard. Another race, and only this one meant more than anything I'd done on the track last weekend. I raced to Connor, to tell him the truth, and maybe he'd understand.

Or maybe he'd tell me I was too late…

I was too late.

From across the street, I saw them sitting at a tiny table at Claire's Café, leaning into each other. Connor reached out and cupped Autumn's cheek, drawing her closer so he could kiss her.

He kissed her.

They kissed.

Their first kiss, and I had a front row seat. Because I'd helped make it happen.

A cold lump settled into my gut and my skin shivered under the sweat of my run.

You made your bed, Turner. Now they're going to lie in it.

Chapter Eleven

Autumn

"Do we call this our second date?" Connor Drake's grin was charmingly sheepish. "Or is it my second chance at our first date?"

I smiled. "How about, First Date, part two?"

He turned his grin all the way up to eleven. "That works."

God, he really is beautiful. And more sensitive than he lets on.

I waited for him to prove that in person and talk to me like he said he wanted to in his texts. Instead, a short silence fell. I glanced around the café, with wood furnishings and caramel lighting. Under the table, my foot tapped the backpack of anthro texts I'd brought just in case.

"I like this coffee shop," I said, finally. "Just don't tell my boss at the Panache."

Connor made an X over his chest. "Cross my heart."

The silence threatened again, and we broke it at the same time.

"Connor, I—"

"I wanted to—"

The tension cracked a little, but there was a tightness in my stomach instead of butterflies.

"Go ahead," I said.

"No, ladies first."

BRING DOWN the Stars

I wrapped both hands around my mug. "Okay, well... I read our text exchange on the way over here a dozen times. What you wrote...about Mark being blind?" I tucked a lock of hair behind my ear. "After what happened...my sense of self really took a hit, you know? I thought I was the blind one for missing the signs, so what you said...it was really nice to hear."

"I'm glad," Connor said. He shifted in his chair, leaning a little over our table. "I'll be honest too; I don't always know what to say in the moment. You know how you can think of the perfect clap-back at someone ten minutes after you needed it?"

"I totally do."

"I'm like that when it comes to finding the right things to say when someone—a girl like you, for instance—needs to hear them."

"A girl like me?"

He nodded. "You're different than anyone I've ever gone out with, Autumn. But in a good way."

In a good way. Not exactly poetry, but then his voice softened as did his gaze as his eyes held mine, unwavering.

"And I want you to know that what your ex did...he was an idiot. I don't want you to feel like you're going to get screwed over again. Not with me. Whatever pain he left you with, I don't want to add to it."

That tenseness in my stomach loosened, and I let out a sigh.

"Thank you for saying that," I said softly. "I'd begun to think it was too soon to be dating again. Maybe it still is?"

Connor shook his head. "I hope not. What you said about my sports bar idea...that meant a lot to me. More than you can know."

"I'm so glad, Connor. And I know this is only our first date, but I think it'll be better for both of us if we take things slowly."

"Whatever you want," he said. "I'm just glad to be sitting here right now."

My cheeks warmed. "Me too."

The soft moments piled and that *zingy* feeling filled the space between us. It intensified, building a thickness in the air until Connor laughed and raked a hand through his hair.

"Okay, I can't take it anymore." He reached across the small table to cup my cheek. "We can go as slow as you want, Autumn, but if I don't kiss you right now, I'm going to hate myself in the morning."

I was already leaning in, as if the emerald prisms of his eyes were tractor beams, drawing me to him—to his kiss and everything that came after.

A pleasant shiver slid over my skin at the first touch of his lips, and then he did it again. A brush of his mouth over mine. I was infused with his scent, the nearness of him, his warmth. He pressed in softly and then more deeply. His tongue swept into my mouth and the shiver slipped down my spine at the pure expertise of his kiss.

He broke away before it became too much, and slowly released my cheek, letting a lock of my hair slide through his fingers at the same time.

"That's better," he said, looking at me intently. "Isn't it?"

I nodded. No more tightness in my stomach. Only butterflies.

PART III
October

CHAPTER Twelve

Weston

I sat at the dining room table, paging through my notes and scribbles, stanza after unfinished stanza of the poem for Professor Ondiwuje's assignment. Autumn. There could be no other subject. I was dragging the poem out, because once it was done, I had no other relief but running, and I couldn't run all day, every day.

Connor shuffled into the living room, still in his flannel pants and undershirt, though it was three in the afternoon on a Sunday. "I'm screwed."

"What's up?" I asked.

"I told Mom and Dad all about Autumn, and now they want to invite her to Thanksgiving dinner."

"Oh, yeah?" I asked as my stomach dropped. Thanksgiving was Drake inner-circle only. That they were already inviting Autumn meant either Connor had told them he was getting serious about her...

Or he's actually *getting serious about her.*

Connor went to the fridge and grabbed the black and neon-green can of a Monster energy drink.

"Yeah." He shut the door with a bitter smile. "We were on speakerphone just now, and they were fucking falling all over themselves. My dad actually said the words, *'There's hope for you, yet.*'"

My lip curled. I respected Alan Drake and was grateful for all the help he'd given my mother over the years, but he took the same cut-throat, win-at-any-cost mentality that had earned him billions, and applied it to parenting as well.

"Why do they put so much stake in her?"

"The same reason they love you so much. Because she's on scholarship and working hard at making a difference in the world. They think she'd be a good influence on me."

"Isn't that the precise reason you started dating her in the first place?"

"It's not the *only* reason," Connor said. "And that's why I'm screwed."

"What do you mean?"

He shrugged, sipped his drink. "I don't know if we'll make it to Thanksgiving. I think she's drifting away from me."

I swallowed hard. "You do?"

Connor sighed, contemplated the M on the side of the can. "Feels like she's on the verge of calling it quits."

I sat up straighter, hating and loving the hope that expanded in my chest. "I told you a month ago, she needs romance and you keep taking her to Yancy's for booze and pool."

"She's good at pool. She likes the booze," Connor said. "Dude, she keeps telling me she wants to keep things casual, so that's what I'm doing. I only see her on weekends because of her work, but Christ, for how long? It's been a month and she won't even sleep with me."

"Which is why I haven't transferred out of state," I muttered under my breath.

"What'd you say?"

"Nothing."

It was easy to hang back and stay out of Connor and Autumn's way on group outings to Yancy's. I kept to myself as much as I could, attempted to talk to other girls, and generally ignored Autumn. But the overnight trip a bunch of us took to Lake Onota was an exercise in torture. Through the flames of the campfire, I watched Connor and Autumn slip under his blanket. They may not have screwed then, but my imagination had zero problems conjuring what they were doing or where his hands were.

"Hello? Wes?"

I glanced up. "What, sorry?"

Connor frowned. "I said, I feel like I can't win with her."

"Win?" I asked, swiveling in my chair. "It's bottom of the ninth and you're about to strike out?"

"No, but…"

"Forget what she said about keeping things casual for a sec. What do you *want*? Do you want to get serious with her? Do you want to convince her to take the plunge? Because if so, you're going to have to put some effort into it."

"I'm taking her to that Dickinson museum, like you suggested. That's something, right?"

"It's a start. But man, just *talk* to her."

"I do but then I feel all this pressure to say something smart or meaningful, instead of just…going with the flow." Connor shot me a look. "She loved those texts—"

"Forget it."

He sighed. "You've completely abandoned me."

For my sanity, yes.

"Figure it out," I said. "You have a lot to offer, man. Can't you dig a little and find something deeper to talk about?"

"I do. All the time. I tell her she's pretty, she's smart. When she starts talking about her goals, I tell her how ambitious she is—"

"She knows that already," I said. "She doesn't need compliments, she needs authenticity."

He shrugged and sipped his Monster drink. "I don't know. I guess I'm used to things being easier with girls."

"Do you want to date girls that are easier for you or do you want to date Autumn? What do you *want*?"

Connor's fingers tapped the side of his drink can. "I've never had a real relationship, you know? She's my first shot at something serious and I think that's what I want." He shot me a grin. "*And* I want to sleep with her."

I clenched my teeth, then quickly schooled my face to neutral, but not quick enough.

"Whoa, what was that? You looked like you were about to murder me." Connor laughed and nudged my shoulder. "What's with you, anyway? You've been even more…*you* lately, with your trademark Turner charm. And none of your usual parade of girls has passed through this way. What gives?"

BRING DOWN the Stars

"Nothing," I said. "I'm busy. Doing *your* homework, by the way."

I held up a printed page of the Macro-Econ essay I wrote for him. My words. His name at the top. Just like old times.

"Point taken," Connor said with a laugh. He pushed off the counter and headed for the couch. "Anyway. We're going to that Emily Dickinson museum like you suggested. That should count for something."

I rolled my eyes. Counting, winning, keeping score... Connor belonged on the baseball field, not in a poet's ancestral home. But I was done holding his hand with Autumn.

Or so I kept telling myself.

I refused to write any more texts for him, but I couldn't keep my mouth shut with advice. The bitch of it all was I wanted both of them to be happy. I wasn't counseling Connor just for his sake, but for Autumn's too.

"Don't be hard on yourself," I said. "She needs someone like you to make her laugh and feel good."

Connor sniffed from the couch. "She also needs the poetry and deep conversations, and saying the right thing at the right time. All that shit I'm not good at. I'm telling you, Wes, if you and I merged into one person, we'd be Autumn's perfect guy."

I stared as the truth of it slammed me in the chest. How often had I wished I had Connor's easy-going humor? His open, friendly demeanor that drew people in, instead of my repellant brand of derision and snark.

But repelling was better than losing. That was my sad truth, constructed around me like an exoskeleton of armor I couldn't take off.

"I'm going for a run," I said.

"Cool." Connor yawned, stretched, and reached for his Xbox controller. "I'll order pizza later."

I went out without another word, to run my stupid infatuation with Autumn out of me. But like the words the page, there was always more.

Chapter Thirteen

Autumn

"Hayes, oh my God… *Yes…YES…*"

My roommate's voice carried through the house, her drumming headboard keeping time. I smashed my pillow over my face and rolled onto my stomach. A peek at the clock said it was three a.m. Every weekend for the past month, Ruby and the runner from Wesleyan had played this song, whether I wanted to hear it or not.

Finally, after a screaming crescendo that showed Ruby had inherited some of her mother's vocal prowess, quiet descended on the apartment. But the damage was done—I had to be up in two hours for my double-shift at Panache Blanc.

I rolled onto my back and stared at the ceiling. I couldn't even be mad. What Ruby and Hayes had were #relationshipgoals as far as I was concerned. I envied her sleepy, tumbled-in-a-dryer, rumpled look the morning after. I envied even more her ability to keep things light and fun.

I'd tried my best to do the same with Connor, but the last month had been an expanded version of our first date. Our conversations never seemed to last long or delve as deep as I wanted them to. Most of the time, we waded through the shallow waters of small talk.

BRING DOWN the Stars

And yet...

I closed my eyes, remembering soft moments when Connor swept me off my feet with a look. Said something to make me laugh. Or made me feel beautiful and wanted.

And God, could the man kiss...

In the last week of September, we went with his gang to Lake Onota, to swim in the river and have a bonfire afterward. Connor and I kissed under a blanket in the sand, his hands roaming over me until I had to fight to keep my moans quiet.

He succeeded in easing the pain of my break-up, but we'd come to a standstill. I'd told him I wanted to keep it casual and maybe he was honoring that, both by not pushing me into something physical, and by keeping his more sentimental side to himself. But I wished he wouldn't. Then I could stop fighting and let myself fall.

Or maybe it's better to keep to solid ground and be single.

I hated single. I hated empty beds and silent mornings. I loved long talks, longer kisses and the feeling of having a partner as I navigated the world; one who would fill many chapters in the story of my life. But I couldn't escape a nagging feeling I was trying to see something in Connor that wasn't there; that he would only occupy a few paragraphs in my life's story, and it made me sad.

I'd miss that smile.

At five, I got up, showered, dressed in black pants and a white blouse and pulled my hair up in a ponytail. I came out of my room just in time to catch Ruby and Hayes saying goodbye at the front door.

"Hiya, Auts," Hayes called.

I smiled and gave a little wave. "Hiya, Hayes."

Ruby smacked Hayes playfully on the chest. "Hope this beast didn't keep you up last night with his X-rated shenanigans."

"Me?" Hayes' eyes widened with his smile. "You can't keep your volume down at my X-rated shenanigans."

"It's okay," I said. "I was feeling homesick but you two brought me right back to the farm during mating season."

"Ha ha," Ruby said, while Hayes snickered.

He kissed Ruby a final time. "Bye, baby."

"Ciao, bello. Until next time."

She shut the door and leaned against it, a sleepy smile on her face. Then she joined me in the kitchen.

"Coffee?" I asked through a jaw-cracking yawn.

"Hell, no. I'm going back to bed." She leaned elbows on the counter. "Did we keep you awake?"

"Oh gosh no, I stayed up to listen on purpose."

"Perv," Ruby said. "But I'm sorry we keep doing this to you."

"I'm not even mad. A little jealous, maybe."

"Girl, *why*?" she said. "You have a perfectly good man, ready and willing."

"If I sleep with him, I know what will happen. I'll want more."

"More what, exactly?"

"Everything."

"And?"

"And I don't know that I'm ready to jump in like that again. Or if Connor's the one I should jump with." I toyed with the stack of coffee filters on the counter. "I talked to my counselor on Friday. She spoke to the Dean of Admissions at Harvard."

"What's the dealio?"

"The absolute deadline for me to apply is next October."

Ruby snorted. "That's an entire year away."

"Right," I said. "One year to plan and execute an application project and write the paper to go with it. It sounds like a lot of time but it's not."

"It would probably help if you picked a focus."

"Ya don't say?" I sighed and hit the button to start the coffee brewing. "When I think about picking an emphasis, I feel like I'm abandoning so many other causes that need attention."

Ruby rubbed her eyes. "Honey, there's no shortage of problems that need fixing. You have to pull one of them close to your heart. That's how you'll make a difference." She cocked her head. "How's the farm doing?"

"Struggling," I said. "We always are, to greater or lesser degrees."

"Maybe there's something there."

"Maybe," I said, with a pang of guilt. "I *should* pick something in agriculture or food systems, but…"

"But it doesn't thrill you," Ruby said. "Guilt is a terrible way to choose a career."

"But it feels irresponsible to my family if I don't."

"Speaking of counselors and careers," Ruby said, her finger tracing a line on our counter. "Mine told me I'm one step closer to

BRING DOWN the Stars

getting my year in La Spezia. The study-abroad commission liked my work and it's down to me and a few other applicants." She grinned sleepily. "But I have a good feeling. One year from now I'm going to be on the Italian Riviera, in a cute little village on a beach, rolling in the surf with a hot Italian."

I wrinkled my nose. "What about Hayes?"

"I like to keep my options open," she said and yawned over a smile. "I'm hitting the sack." She gave my arm a squeeze. "You'll figure out your focus for your project. Make lists. Meditate. Hell, throw a dart and see where it lands."

"That's exactly what I've been doing at Yancy's every weekend instead of working."

"Orgasms, too," she tossed over her shoulder, pretending not to have heard me. "Great for decision making. Helps to relax."

I laughed as she retreated back to her room. If Ruby were any more relaxed, she'd melt. I tried to remember the last time I felt truly relaxed and not stressed over work or my family's farm, and couldn't.

During my morning shift at the Panache Blanc, Edmond caught me worrying my lip and staring off into space between customers. He tugged at his mustache, looking at me thoughtfully.

"Ma chère, I would say you wear the face of a girl with two roads ahead of her and she does not know which one to take."

I started to protest, then nodded instead. "You're right. I have some decisions to make about my grad school application and…"

"And?"

"The boy I'm dating."

I braced myself for Edmond's reaction and had to laugh as he gasped and clutched his heart.

"I knew it. It is a matter of love." He burst into pieces of a Puccini aria I'd heard before, and spun me around. "The grad school…" He made a sour face. "I am no help. But when it comes to love, I tell you what I know, ma chère. There are no decisions you make here." He tapped his forehead. "There is only to listen to what your heart tells you."

"I really like this guy," I admitted. "I'd like to think there was something there, but…"

"But?"

"But what if I'm wrong?"

Edmond grinned behind his thick black mustache. "Unfortunately, that is something you can never know until you give your heart. Trust. Trust and love are flour and water. They need each other to stick, non?"

"I guess."

I'd let my heart trust Mark and he'd tossed it away. Maybe it was better to be practical with Connor. Smart. Safe.

It was Connor's idea to visit the Emily Dickinson Museum next Saturday. Half of me struggled to envision the tall baseball player interested in Dickinson's painful history or reading her poetry. The other half felt it might be exactly what he enjoyed doing, if only he'd share that side of himself more.

Maybe we both were holding back, but the only thing I knew was that I desperately needed a little time and perspective.

I picked up my phone and texted Connor.

Hi. I don't think I can make the museum on Saturday.

His reply came in a few minutes later, as I was walking my bike down Pleasant Street under the falling twilight.

Bummer. Yancy's later?

No. I don't think so.

A pause. Then, **Is everything okay?**

I bit my lip. How to answer? That was exactly the source of my unease. Everything wasn't okay but there was nothing wrong either. It was as if my heart was split right down the middle, just like Edmond had said.

I'm really behind on my Harvard project. I need to devote a solid chunk of time to it.

OK. Any thoughts on Thanksgiving?

I stopped walking and leaned against a tall oak tree, my bike against my thigh. Connor hadn't been able to stop talking about the holiday. The thought of meeting his parents felt incredibly flattering and a little bit too soon at the same time.

Not sure. I have to see what I can get done this week and let you know.

OK.

I'm sorry.

BRING DOWN the Stars

It's fine, he wrote.
Talk to you later?
Sure.
And nothing else.

"Shit." I started to walk again but the tight feeling in my stomach strengthened. I had to tackle this head on, not over the phone.

Connor?

A tense ten seconds later, then, **Autumn?** ☺

His sweetness eased my breath a little. **Are you at your place? Can I come over? To talk?**

I'm here, he wrote. **Come over.**
Okay see you in a few.
CU

"Hi," Connor said, opening the door for me. He was handsomely rumpled in his pajama pants and V-neck shirt though it was Sunday evening. He bent to kiss my cheek.

"It's kind of a mess. Ramona comes on Tuesday."

I'd been over to his place a handful of times in the past month, never staying for long. Weston had ceased speaking to me beyond curt hellos and goodbyes, and I never felt welcome when he was there.

Despite Connor's warning, the large apartment was nearly spotless, thanks to the cleaning lady the Drakes paid to come once a week. The only messes were a scatter of papers on the dining area table, and a pizza box beside a few empty beer bottles on the coffee table. *Madden* was paused on their gigantic flat screen TV.

"Is Weston here?" I asked. "I wanted to talk alone."

"He's taking a run," Connor said, and then grinned. "Should I be scared? Call him for back up?"

God, he really is adorable.

I mentally fortified myself against Connor's inherent sexiness and charm. "Nothing to be scared of. In fact…" I sighed. "Now that I'm here, I don't know what to say. But I know it will all come back to me the second I walk out that door."

Connor laced his hands around my waist. "Maybe don't walk out the door." He bent and kissed my mouth softly but with intention behind it. Promises of more if I wanted it. "Stay," he murmured.

"I want to," I said. "But, Connor…"

He kissed me again, deeper, and I felt the floor tip out from under me. I clung to his strong arms, while his hands slipped up my back to tangle in my hair. His phone rang—a classical music ringtone—breaking the moment.

"Shit. My parents." He released me and went to grab his phone from the couch. "Let me just see what they want."

I nodded, still slightly breathless, and watched him answer. His usual smile replaced by a grimace, as if he were bracing himself.

"Hey, Dad. What's up?"

He held up a finger to me and mouthed *sorry, hold on*, then took the call into his room. I wandered to the kitchen for a glass of water. The kitchen was sleek—chrome and gray and masculine. It reminded me of Connor's car. New and expensive. I supposed part of the cost of this luxury was Connor could never let his parents' calls go to voicemail.

I poured a glass of water from the state-of-the-art filtration system on the marble counter and sat at the dining room table to drink it. My fastidious nature fixated on the sprawl of papers. They begged to be gathered up.

Stop. Don't touch other people's stuff.

Minutes passed and Connor didn't come back. I sipped my water, then sat on my hands. The mess on the table was making me itchy. I pulled a few papers together, glancing at an essay on Macroeconomics, Connor's name and date at the top. This was all his work. He wouldn't mind if I straightened it. We were dating, after all…

Class handouts. Articles. Loose pages with handwritten lines of text, arrows to notes in the margin, a few doodles.

I sighed. What was Connor talking about with his parents?

I went on gathering papers into piles and my eye pulled a few lines off one scribbled page, half-hidden beneath another:

Without you,
The hours stretch

I glanced around the empty apartment. Connor's muffled voice came from the other room, still sounding in the middle of a

BRING DOWN the Stars

conversation, not wrapping one up.

Be patient and mind your business, I thought.

I made it all of six seconds before I slid the paper free and read what was there. A poem. The handwriting was a scratchy scrape of the pen, with sharp lines and angles. The words burned hot off the page.

> *Without you,*
> *The hours stretch*
> *into suffocating days;*
> *gasping through nights*
> *in sweated sheets*
> *eyes squeezed shut*
> *your name locked behind*
> *my clenched teeth*
> *grasping at relief*
> *until you're here*
> *and I*
> *can breathe again*
> *and I*
> *can bask again*
> *in the shifting colors*
> *of your gaze;*
> *gold, green, and brown—*
> *your namesake captured*
> *in your eyes.*

My face tingled hot, then cold, then hot again. The poem infused me, each line bending and flowing and breathing into the next, creating one fluid sensation. I didn't see individual words. I felt the whole, like staring at a painting. But the last three lines stood out, demanded I read them again and again.

> *gold, green, and brown—*
> *your namesake captured*
> *in your eyes.*

"*My* namesake?" I murmured.

"Hey, sorry about that."

I jerked my head up, staring, the paper slack in my hand.

Connor stopped midstride into the living area, his brows furrowed in concern for me.

"Are you okay?"

I rose to my feet. "Is this yours?" I offered him the poem.

Connor took the paper, and his eyes scanned it. "Oh this. This is…" He glanced up at me quickly and handed the poem back. "I mean, it's nothing."

"Did you write it? For me?"

He stared at me, a thousand thoughts behind his eyes. His chin lifted the tiniest bit, then lowered.

"You wrote this about me?"

His smile was weak and his gaze slid away, to the floor, the table, then back to me. "I never know what to say when you're standing right in front of me. Still don't."

"God, Connor," I laughed and sighed with relief at the same time. "This is exactly why I'm here. What I wanted to tell you…is that you can talk to me. Whatever you're thinking, I want to hear it. I *need* to hear it. All your thoughts and ideas and dreams. They're as important to me as being with you. I mean…" I held up the sheet of paper again. "Do you want…*this?*"

"I want…" He swallowed hard, his voice firming. "I want to be with you. That…" He jerked his chin at the paper in my hand. "That's what I want. With you."

A warmth spread through my chest, down to my stomach, washing away the tight knot there. I went to him and ringed my arms around his neck.

"I can't be casual," I said. "I wish I could, but I'm not built that way. And that poem…" I shook my head, the warmth heating toward something more. "It's not casual. It's beautiful."

"*You're* beautiful," he said, and kissed me, holding my body to the strong wall of his. His lips trailed down my throat. "And I don't want casual. I want you to stay."

"I do too," I breathed, clinging to him, my fingers sinking into his hair. "I think I just needed a little something more from you. Does that sound totally crazy?"

"No." He kissed the hollow of my throat, and then raised his head to look at me. "I have a lot to give, Autumn. I promise."

I stroked his cheek. "I know you do. And I wish your parents could see that too."

BRING DOWN the Stars

Connor's expression shifted, hardening into something fierce and full of want. His arms around me tightened and he kissed me hard, wide-mouthed and demanding. I took it in, dizzy with him and the words now burned into my brain. I kissed back just as hard, as if I could siphon off the poetry in him.

He lifted me off the ground, never breaking our kiss and carried me to his bedroom, to his king-sized bed where he laid me down. My clothes melted away under his deft hands, and I surrendered myself to his expert machinations in every way.

In sweated sheets...

We tore his bed apart, voracious, as Connor's body on mine—so heavy and thick above me and inside me—worked me into a delirium.

Grasping at relief...

My fingernails raked down his broad back and then clutched at him hard, as that ecstatic release found me.

Again and again, through all the hours of night, and one final time when I was nearly asleep, yet starving for more. I collapsed in the strong ring of his embrace, my body warm and heavy and breathing—

can breathe again

—in perfect cadence to his.

CHAPTER Fourteen

Autumn

The alarm on my phone went off at five a.m. Disoriented, I fumbled my hand on a nightstand that wasn't mine, trying to shut it off.

"The agony," Connor mumbled.

The beeping silenced, I rolled to face him. He lay on his stomach, face half-buried in his pillow, and everything we'd done that night came flooding back to me, bringing a flush of heat to my face.

"Sorry," I whispered. "Go back to sleep."

"I plan to." One green eye peeked open and he gave me a lazy smile.

I bit my own smile with my front teeth. "Last night was really good."

"Really good?" His arm snaked out and pulled me in tighter. "I can't let you leave here with 'really good.'"

I laughed and gave his chest a playful shove. "I have to work. And maybe I was understating it a little."

He kissed me softly. "I'm glad you stayed."

Oh God, the butterflies.

"Me too." I ran my fingers through his hair. "I can't stop smiling."

He kissed me again. "I don't want you to."

BRING DOWN the Stars

"But I'll be late for work."

His eyes went to the window behind me, the blinds drawn. "It's still dark out. You do this every morning?"

"Bakery life starts early." I sat up, holding the sheet around me. "Do you mind if I make some coffee?"

Connor had already settled back into his pillow. "Nope. Make yourself at home."

"Can I borrow one of your T-shirts to wear while I do?"

I wasn't quite ready to put my dress back on; I wanted Connor's arms around me. Wearing his shirt—something he wears close to his skin and catching the smell of his cologne, his laundry soap and the indescribable scent of *him*—was the next best thing.

"Dresser," he said. "Second drawer."

I slipped out of Connor's bed naked and went to his dresser. I found a dark gray V-neck shirt in the drawer. It looked a tad too small for Connor, but still plenty large to cover me. I pulled it over my head and inhaled.

Wow.

A tingle of electricity danced over my skin. The residue of cologne under the laundry soap was different than Connor's usual scent—sharper and more potent—and it went straight to my head. It woke up my blood cells better than coffee and I had to press my thighs together.

What in the world?

Padding toward the kitchen to get my muddled brain some coffee, I put the soft cotton of his shirt to my nose and inhaled again.

Wow again.

It was like taking a hit off of pure masculine pheromones, but somehow different from what I'd felt and sensed lying in Connor's bed.

"Oh, stop."

I vowed to quit with the weird thoughts and to bask in the newness of it all. If there was one truth I had after reading that poem, it was that Connor had many facets, and clearly I hadn't discovered them all yet.

That prospect of discovery—one of my favorite parts of a new relationship—brought a slow smile over my lips as I came around the corner of the hall. The light was on, and I stopped short with a little yelp. "Oh."

Weston stood at the dining room table, furiously cramming books and papers into his bag, as if he were stealing them. His head shot up at my little gasp and his gaze raked me up and down. Over my bare legs, my thighs and my small breasts. I immediately crossed my arms over them as if I were naked.

"Hi," I stammered. "I didn't know you were here. I mean, awake."

Weston stared. His mouth parted and the tip of his tongue touched his upper lip. Then, like a man waking from a dream, his head gave a twitch and his entire expression went hard and sharp.

"What the hell are you wearing?"

I flinched and looked down. "One of Connor's shirts?"

"That's *my* shirt." He stared a moment more, then tore his gaze from me to jerk at the zipper on his bag.

"Oh," I said, my cheeks inexplicably burning, the heat racing through my veins to every part of my body. "It was in his drawer."

"It's *mine*," he said.

"Sorry. I'll take it off," I said.

His head flicked back to me, eyes wide.

"Not *now*," I said. "I mean, I was—"

"Forget it," Weston said, standing straight and shouldering his bag. "The Drakes send a cleaning lady once a week. She does the laundry…mixes up our clothes sometimes."

His gaze flicked up and down along my body, and I could have sworn I saw a flash of pain in the blue-green depths, before they turned icy again.

"I'm going. See you."

A soft pain swelled in my chest at his refusal to be in the same room with me for longer than a minute. I tugged the hem of the shirt—Weston's shirt—lower over my thighs.

"Weston?"

"Yeah?" he said at the door without turning.

"I miss our talks."

His shoulders flinched almost imperceptibly. A silence fell between us in which the air grew thick. Then he sliced through it with his cold tone.

"What talks?"

I slumped against the kitchen counter. "Nothing. Have a good day."

BRING DOWN the Stars

Weston hesitated a moment more, than grunted from his throat and headed out, shutting the door hard behind him.

The silence felt thick and heavy and the apartment seemed cold and dim now. I went back to Connor's room. I changed out of Weston's shirt and put it in the hamper, then reached for my dress that was a crumpled ball on the floor.

"Got your coffee?" Connor mumbled.

"No, I need to get back to my place anyway," I said, buttoning my dress up the front. "Shower and change."

"'Kay."

I grabbed my shoes and purse, then bent to kiss Connor.

"Have a good day," I said. I hesitated for a second, then bent to kiss him again, trying to recapture the warmth of the morning that Weston's cold snap had ruined.

Connor's lazy smile widened. "You sure you can't stay?"

"No, I'll be late."

"I'll call you later."

"Okay," I said. "Bye."

I hurried out of the apartment, one of my father's sayings in my thoughts.

If you hear the snake's rattle, best to listen to it.

Weston was an asshole. That was his rep, and I had no concrete reason to think otherwise. He'd hardly spoken a handful of words to me over the last month. He left a room minutes after I walked into it, often with a cutting remark. And yet…

I always felt there was more to Weston than he let on, and that he did nothing to alter his asshole reputation because it *guarded* him. I couldn't prove it, but I knew it. Instinctively. And it made me immune to his crankiness.

But it hurts a little, I thought as I walked home, shivering in the gray, misty morning. *Just a little.*

CHAPTER Fifteen

Weston

Shit shit shit…

I fled the apartment as if it were on fire, my blood running just as hot. I thought those two fucking in Connor's room all night was the worst thing that could happen.

How wrong I was.

Last night, I ran at the track, pushing myself faster and faster, trying to marathon Autumn out of my system. I ran until I puked, then walked home hollowed out with exhaustion. I'd opened the door to the unmistakable rhythm of a headboard banging against the wall, and Autumn's cries filling the rooms of the apartment.

It slammed me in the chest. Rock bottom. The absolute worst. Nothing could bring me lower.

I'd immediately turned around and headed for Matt Decker's place, and a sleepless night on his couch, but had forgotten nearly all of my books for class. Naturally, I timed my return to get them perfectly with Autumn emerging from Connor's room. There she stood, straight from Connor's bed, looking freshly fucked and so damn beautiful I could hardly breathe.

"Why the hell was she wearing my shirt?" I muttered under my breath as I stalked down the quiet street toward the university, trying

BRING DOWN the Stars

to outpace the memory of Autumn, her copper hair tousled, her legs bare and showing porcelain skin. My shirt barely covering her nakedness.

A raging hard-on began to strain at the front of my jeans.

"For fuck's sake."

I walked faster, nearly a jog, but I couldn't get away from how badly I wanted her.

Feeling like the world's biggest jackass, I found a bathroom on campus—mercifully empty—on the first floor of the Business and Economics Building. I locked myself in the handicap stall, grabbed a wad of toilet paper off the roll, yanked my fly open and took myself in hand.

I was rock-hard. Autumn in my shirt and nothing else would haunt me until I died if I didn't do something. I closed my eyes, letting my fertile imagination reset the scene as my hand worked to give me some relief.

"I thought you left," she says, biting her lower lip that's still swollen from my kisses. She rests one bare foot on the other and her eyes rake me up and down. The way we fucked all night with relentless abandon is reflected in the hazel depths of her eyes, darkening them with renewed want.

"I did," I say, my voice thick with need. "I came back."

"For me?" she asks coyly.

I nod. My bag drops to the ground.

"What are you waiting for?" Then her sweet smile fades and she lowers her hands to the tops of her thighs, lifting my shirt an inch. "Come here, Weston, and put your mouth on me."

In three long strides, I'm in front of her, kneeling, pressing my tongue into her…

I bit back a sound and barely managed to contain it to a grunt. Tasting Autumn in my fevered imagination, I came hard. My body shuddered with release, delirium suffusing me and leaving me drained.

I leaned against the stall with one hand, sucking in deep breaths. Someone came in the bathroom to take a piss. I tossed the wad of paper in the toilet, tucked myself back in my jeans and flushed.

Fucking pathetic, I thought, grabbing my bag.

I washed my hands and got the hell out of there, hoping the cold air would bring me around. Hoping that jerking off to my best friend's new girlfriend would relieve some of the deep ache in my gut—and heart, if I were being honest. The physical lust was satiated for the time being, but that pang of longing ate away at me from the inside out.

I miss our talks.

"Me too," I'd nearly replied, but of course that wouldn't fly. The more Autumn and I spoke, the more I knew her and spent time with her, the harder it would be on me.

They're sleeping together.

I stopped midstride and sagged against the wall of the Econ building and took a minute to gather up what I felt and push it down.

"You're surprised, Sock Boy?" I muttered. "Keep going."

After Econ—a new economics class, since I'd dropped the one Autumn took too—I grabbed a coffee at the student union, then headed to Professor Ondiwuje's poetry class. I sat slouched in my seat, my pen twirling around and around as the echo of Autumn's voice on the other side of Connor's bedroom door resounded in my head. I gripped the pen so tightly my knuckles turned white and then nearly dropped it in shock as a hand clapped my shoulder.

I whipped around to see Connor in the row behind me.

"Jesus, you scared the shit out of me," I hissed. "What the hell are you doing here?"

"I'm auditing the class," he whispered back, looking calm, relaxed, confident, and radiating his own brand of *I got epically laid last night.*

I could've hated him if he didn't look so happy. Then a sense of territorial defensiveness washed over me.

This is my fucking class. My refuge. My outlet.

"You're auditing *this* class?"

"I sort of have to."

"Why?"

He shifted in his seat. "I figure I should learn a thing or two about poetry, now that Autumn and I are a thing."

I narrowed my eyes. "What's that mean?"

His smile widened, blinding me with white teeth and triumph. "We did the deed last night. All night."

BRING DOWN the Stars

"Congratulations," I said through clenched teeth. The words coming out of his mouth hit me like fists to the gut all over again. "That's not what I was asking. Why are you here?"

Connor was lost in his memories of last night. "Sorry if we kept you awake but damn... She's nothing like I expected. A firecracker."

Nausea boiled in my guts. I glanced at the nearest classmates who didn't need to hear these private details about Autumn.

"She's also really fucking intelligent," I muttered, as if I hadn't been jerking off to her in a goddamn public bathroom hours earlier.

"She is," Connor said. "That's sort of why I'm here. If I hope to keep her, I need to brush up on my romance." He gave me a knowing, hopeful look. "I was hoping to enlist your help—"

"*No,*" I said loudly.

Professor O turned his gaze my way. "Not a fan of assonance, Mr. Turner?"

The class tittered.

"Sorry," I muttered.

The professor resumed his lesson, and after a moment, Connor leaned over my shoulder again.

"So, here's the thing..." he whispered hesitantly.

"No, there is no thing," I hissed back. "You need to shut up. I'm trying to actually learn something."

Connor was stunned into silence, and sat back in his seat, his confusion wafting over my shoulder.

After class, I gathered my shit and headed up the auditorium stairs instead of down, to the back stairwell without a word to Connor. He followed, his voice echoing down the two flights in the back stairwell.

Outside, he grabbed my shoulder on the back pathway of the Creative Arts Building and turned me around.

"Wes, Jesus, will you wait a second?"

"I don't have a second."

"Dude, talk to me."

"I'm late for—"

"Autumn read your poem."

I froze. My stomach tightened. "What poem?"

He rummaged in his bag and then he handed me a paper. One of *my* papers with my words on it.

Without you,
The hours stretch
into suffocating days;
gasping through nights

My hand made a fist, crumpling the paper before I could read the rest, as the world suddenly felt airless.

Fuck, she knows...

I divided straight down the center: anxiety at being exposed coupled with a strange sense of relief.

She knows.

But she slept with Connor.

Now a swirl of confusion battered me, a terrible suspicion making its way up through the storm.

"She read it," I said slowly. "And?"

"And, well, it's kind of funny, actually." He coughed. "She thought I wrote it."

"But you told her you didn't," I said, already knowing the answer.

"I kind of just…went with it."

"Is that why she slept with you?" I asked. A pit of dread settled into my stomach. "Because she read that poem?"

It was one thing to write a couple of texts to help a friend out. Another if my words affected Autumn enough to convince her to get naked with that friend, to lie in his bed and share her body with him.

Connor shook his head. "Not entirely."

"Partially? Fractionally?" My lip curled. "Give me a ballpark percentage."

"I don't know, it was like the…catalyst?" He held up his hands. "Let's put it this way, it sure as hell didn't hurt."

I thought I was going to be sick. My jaw and fists clenched.

"So that's why I'm here." Connor gestured at the Creative Arts Building. "If I take this class and you help me out a little—"

"No."

"Why not?"

"Forget it."

I turned to go and his hand gripped my shoulder again.

"What the hell is your problem?" Connor demanded, spinning

me around. "Why are you being such a dick about this? Because she slept with me? I told you, your stupid poem wasn't the only reason—"

"Isn't it? Let's examine the chain of events, shall we? You thought she was going to break up with you. She read the poem. She let you fuck her. Have I got that right?"

I started walking again and Connor followed.

"Hey. Asshole. I'm not completely helpless, you know. She likes *me*."

"Good for you," I said. "But don't steal my shit again."

"Why are you so pissed? I didn't steal your damn poem. Autumn found it under an econ paper and thought it was mine."

"And you let her keep thinking that."

"Yeah? So? What's the big deal? Damn poem told the truth, anyway. You think I haven't jerked off a hundred times this month, waiting for her?" He stopped, his brows coming together. "Hold on…Why are *you* writing about jerking off to her?"

"I'm not. It's not her," I said quickly, shifting my backpack to my other shoulder, my heart pounding now with guilt instead of anger. "It's…thoughts. Words. Shit I dream up."

"Really?" Connor crossed his arms. "It's not about Autumn?"

"No," I said, and the flat lie tasted like acid in my mouth. "Ever hear of write-what-you-know? She's around a lot. I haven't been with a girl in months so it came out in the poem, but it's not about *her*."

"Well, Autumn sure as shit thought it was about her."

"Yeah, and look how well that turned out for you."

My hands were still balled into fists. Against Connor. We'd never been this at odds with each other. It felt like the solid foundation between us had sprouted its first cracks and I hated it.

Connor must've felt the same. He backed off and held up his hands.

"I'm sorry I stole your poem. It just sort of happened. The way she was looking at me…no girl has *ever* looked at me that way. Not over a feeling. Or thoughts. It felt fucking good so I went with it, okay?"

I shook my head. "If she finds out…"

"So let's not tell her," Connor said. "If it comes up again, help me out a little, like you did with the texts."

I ran my hand through my hair then jabbed a finger at the Creative Arts Building. "If you're serious about auditing that class, then do it and pay attention. But I'm not writing a damn thing for you. Not one word."

He held up his hands. "What the hell is the big deal? It's like an econ paper—"

"It's nothing like an econ paper. It's about her. Her feelings. She's serious about you now, right?"

Connor shrugged. "Yeah, she is. We are."

I closed my eyes for a second. "You have to be careful. Don't…"

Don't break her heart.

"…fuck around with her."

"I won't," Connor said. "It may shock you, but I actually care about her."

"Good." I shouldered my bag. "I gotta go."

I took a few steps and then Connor called my name. His voice sounded like it did when he spoke on the phone with his dad. Unsettled and full of worry.

It made me turn around.

"Yeah, man."

His uncertain smile nearly cracked my damn heart. "See you at home?"

He needs me.

"See you at home."

CHAPTER Sixteen

Autumn

"Someone didn't come home last night," Ruby called in a sing-song voice.

I sank down on the grass at our usual lunchtime spot in front of the Admin building. "Will you hush? Half the campus heard you."

"Oh, who cares?" Ruby said. "You did the deed with Connor Drake. You should be singing it from the rooftops." She made a face. "Unless it was bad." Her eyes widened. "Was it bad? Oh my God, it was bad."

"Not at all," I said. "He's very…skilled."

She sighed in relief. "And here you were, ready to dump his cute ass. Must've been a pretty good reason to get you to jump in the sack instead."

I frowned. "What do you mean?"

"You told me you needed a better reason to fuck him other than he's hot."

"Oh, right."

"So?"

The cool October breeze swept over us. I wrapped my cardigan around me more tightly and tucked my legs underneath me. I wore black pants and flats, but soon enough it would be time for jackets and scarves. The leaves from the trees were already carpeting the ground in sprays of color.

gold, green, and brown—
your namesake captured
in your eyes.

I bit my lip over a smile. "You're going to think I'm the biggest sap in the world."

"Too late."

I plucked at a blade of grass. "He wrote a poem."

Ruby did a double-take. "Come again? Connor Drake wrote a poem?"

"*Yes*," I said. "About me."

Her expression brightened. "That kind of thing's right up your alley. You should be over the moon, right?"

"I am," I said, and sighed. "Or I should be. Instead I feel…I don't know. Fragile. I can't do one-night stands and this is exactly why. Sex is so intimate." I shook my head. "It's like part of me is still naked. I have to trust he feels it was just as special."

"How was the morning after?" Ruby asked. "That can be a deal breaker, right there."

"It was perfect."

Until I ran into Weston.

Like lightning, it hit me I hadn't felt fragile or naked about sleeping with Connor until I'd mistakenly put on Weston's shirt. Or rather, until Weston *saw* me wearing his shirt. His reaction unsettled me to the core and I couldn't figure out why.

"Connor did everything right." I slumped over, covering my hands. "God, I am the queen of overthinking, aren't I? Why I can't just enjoy something for what it is?"

"Because you're a big softy," Ruby said. "So tell me about this poem."

"It was simple," I said. "A little window into a different, deeper layer of him. Feelings and thoughts he doesn't share with me when we're together."

Ruby nodded. "I'm still trying to imagine him writing a poem."

"Why? Because he's a jock who drives a sportscar?"

"Whoa, put your sword away, Khaleesi," she said. "And yes,

call me a judgmental bitch, but I can't picture it."

"I can. I've seen it. And now it makes sense why he wants to take me to the Dickinson Museum this Saturday after Weston's track meet."

Ruby shrugged, and got to her feet, brushing grass off her jeans. "Well, I'm happy for you. Sounds like you landed the perfect guy—hot, rich, and deep."

I nodded, rising too.

"Hey," she said, taking me by the shoulders. "Don't apologize for who you are. You're a slut for poetry. Own it."

I burst out laughing. "Is that what I am?"

"But seriously. Hai una bella anima."

"Bella anima?"

"You're a beautiful soul," Ruby said and shrugged. "It sounds better in Italian. Fact: most things sound better in Italian. And if Connor doesn't treat you right, prendilo a calci in culo. I'll kick his ass."

I smiled and hugged my friend, even as my unease deepened. Connor treated me perfectly. He'd done and said everything right. But Weston…

I didn't know how or why it was important, but if I was going to feel good about my relationship with Connor, I needed to fix things with Weston. I gave myself a solid list of reasons: they were best friends. I wouldn't feel comfortable spending the night at their place if Weston kept giving me the cold shoulder. I didn't want my boyfriend's best friend to hate me…

Not to mention putting on Weston's shirt turned you on.

I stopped short and glanced around, mortified.

"Jesus, that is *not* what happened." I walked faster toward the library, head down and muttering into my books, "I thought it was Connor's."

I hurried up the steps of the library, hoping Wes would be there. Determined to meet this head on and kill these ridiculous thoughts. But he wasn't. Since Connor and I began dating, I never saw Weston here anymore.

My phone buzzed a text from Connor.

Hey you.

I smiled, butterflies taking off in my stomach.

Hi, I texted back. **What's up?**

I just got wind of a party at Delta Psi this Friday. Want to go?

I sank down into a chair at one of the library's long tables. **Sounds fun, but I have to study.**

Bummer. You care if I go?

No, of course not, I replied. **Are we still on for the museum after W's races on Sat?**

Definitely. :)

Okay, I wrote. **Great.**

Call you later.

But he didn't call me later, and aside from a few checking in texts, I didn't hear from him for the rest of the week.

Friday, working my morning shift at the Panache Blanc, it dawned on me that Weston usually ate here the night before a track meet. After classes, I killed time in the library, then headed back to the bakery, hoping he hadn't changed that routine.

He sat at a corner table. Dark and sharp in a black shirt and jeans, his long legs stretched out and his nose buried in an econ book. A half-eaten sprout and cucumber sandwich sat on a plate in front of him. Edmond de Guiche was singing in the back room.

Heart stuttering, I went to stand by his table. "Hi."

He lowered his book, and his eyes widened for a second, before his expression reverted to hard neutral. "Hey."

"Can we talk?"

"Sure." He moved his legs and indicated for me to take the chair opposite him.

I sat with my purse in my lap, needing some kind of barrier between me and Weston's barbed stare. "I wanted to apologize for Sunday night—"

"Don't," Wes said. "Nothing to apologize for."

"There is," I said. "It's a little tacky to have disturbed your sleep. If we did. And then coming out wearing your shirt."

"Forget it." Weston shifted in his seat, his blue-green eyes turbulent like a stormy sea. "No big deal."

"It's a big deal to me," I said. "Connor and I are getting more serious and I don't want there to be any weirdness between you and me."

He stared for a second, then nodded. "Right. Weirdness."

I puffed my cheeks full of air. "I was hoping you and I could be friends. I don't want to come over and feel like an intruder."

"You're not. It's me." His long fingers toyed with his pen. "I can be a dick. Ask anyone."

"I don't think you're a dick," I said and grinned. "Maybe not the softest or fuzziest of guys, but you have potential."

"Potential?"

"Sure. Maybe if you rolled around with a basket full of puppies or held a baby chick or two like we have on the farm… Fix you right up."

The faintest of smiles touched his lips then vanished again. "Are you hungry? Do you want something to eat?" He cleared his throat. "You're probably sick of eating here."

"I like the food here," I said, touched at the offer. "But no thanks. I have a late night of studying. Actually, a coffee might be a good idea."

I started to rise, but Weston was quicker.

"I'll get it."

"Don't, I have an employee discount."

But Weston ignored me. He took his lean, muscled body to the counter and interrupted Phil's usual phone scrolling to order me a coffee. Edmond burst from the back, a blue windbreaker jacket on over his white uniform, just as Weston was paying.

"What is this?" Edmond said, spying me. "Autumn, ma chère."

I smiled and waved. "Hi, Edmond."

The baker's gaze moved between Weston and me. "Monsieur Turner never drinks coffee before racing day. It is for Autumn?" He shot Phil a dirty look. "Philippe, return to him his money."

I suppressed a laugh as Phil rolled his eyes and hunted for the refund button, but Weston waved him off. "It's okay, Edmond. I got it."

"Thank you," I said, as Weston returned to the table and set down the steaming mug in front of me. "You and Edmond know each other?"

"Of course we do," Edmond answered, swooping over to us. "Weston is un homme tranquille. Our quiet man, always reading.

Always writing. Very still. But tomorrow? He runs very fast, non?"

I glanced at Weston, expecting him to chafe under Edmond's bluster, but he was almost smiling.

"Yeah, that pretty much sums me up."

"And you two, together?" Edmond beamed under his mustache. "My thoughtful girl and the quiet man. This, I like."

"We're friends," I said. Then glanced at Weston. "Aren't we?"

He nodded, his eyes soft on mine. "Yeah. Friends."

"Ah," Edmond said, his gaze going between us, his dark eyes narrowing. "Parfois, le cœur se cache derrière l'esprit." He clapped his hands together. "But what do I know? I am but a silly old baker. I leave you to your coffee. Philippe! Don't forget to mop the back room. We will get rats and then what will the customers think of us?"

"I won't," Phil muttered, eyes rolling again.

Edmond shot Weston and me a wink and swept out of the bakery, a bellowed aria in his wake.

Chapter Seventeen

Weston

"Edmond," Autumn said with a stunning smile, "is why I love working here." Her delicate brows furrowed. "But I wonder what he said. Something about the heart? You don't happen to speak French, do you?"

"Afraid not," I said, lying. Between Sinclair Prep and the Academy, I slogged through six years of French. Tonight, was the first time I was glad for it.

Parfois, le cœur se cache derrière l'esprit.
Sometimes the heart hides itself behind the mind.
Story of my life, Edmond, I thought

"Too bad," Autumn said. "It sounded pretty. Poetic." She smiled behind a sip of coffee.

Not touching that with a ten-foot pole.

Connor and I had hardly spoken in a week. I pretended I was too busy with classwork. I didn't have a choice. The more I showed I was angry at him for using my poem to get Autumn into his bed, the more he'd wonder why I was angry at all.

"Connor's going to the Delta party tonight," I said. "You're not going with him?"

She shook her head. "I have too much studying to do. Ruby's

going to go, but I'm too busy."

"Did he at least ask you to go with him?"

"Of course."

"Good." I met her raised eyebrows with a shrug. "He can get careless about important things."

She smiled but it faded quickly. "We haven't spoken much since Sunday, actually."

I clenched my teeth.

Connor, you asshole.

"Oh, yeah?"

"No, but we're both busy." Her expression brightened. "Did you know Connor wrote poetry?"

"You don't say."

"I've only read one. About me." Her cheeks turned pink. "Did you read it?"

"Suffocating days?" I said. "Sweaty sheets?"

"Oh my God." She covered her face with her hands, then peeked at me between her fingers. "Yes, that's the one."

I laughed a little. Her embarrassment was fucking cute as hell. "It wasn't a very good poem."

Her face bloomed into surprised amusement. She tossed a napkin at me, laughing. "Yes, it was! I suppose you're giving him a ton of shit about it."

"Only because he can do better," I said.

"You think?" Her laughter melted into something warm and private. "I wish he would. Write more, I mean."

"You do?"

She pursed her lips and gave me a look. "Oh no, one love poem is all a gal needs, thanks. It'll tide me over until Valentine's Day. At least."

I laughed. "I just meant, poetry isn't for everybody."

"No, but it is for me."

I knew that. I just wish it wasn't so true. I would write to you every day...

"You once told me pretty words weren't enough without something real behind them," I said slowly.

"They're not," Autumn said. "But his poem felt very real to me. More than pretty words. It felt…"

"Honest," I said.

BRING DOWN the Stars

"Yes!" Her face lit up. "It felt honest and yet beautiful. And coming from him, it was unexpected."

"He wants to express himself," I said. "How he feels about you. For a guy like him, it's not always easy." My pen tapped. "That's what he told me, anyway."

She nodded. "I'm so glad he did. I'm the first to admit I have ridiculous expectations in relationships. And I was trying my best to keep things between us causal, but…" She shrugged. "I don't do casual."

Translation: going for a week without hearing from the guy she slept with is too long.

"Connor's been busy all week too," I said, biting out the words. "But he talks about you. A lot."

Her face brightened. "He does?"

"Yep." My pen madly tapped my notebook. "He's auditing a poetry class," I said. "To get better at the poetry thing. For you."

"Really?" Her eyes were molten gemstones in the dim light.

I nodded.

"That's so sweet." She shook her head. "More than sweet. After the way things ended with my last boyfriend, I was sure starting something new was a bad idea. Especially since I tend to become *invested* rather quickly."

"Nothing wrong with that," I said. "Some people live their entire fucking lives without showing their hand." My pen doodled on a blank page of my notebook. "It's brave to put yourself out there, especially after someone screwed you over."

"Thank you. I hated how what Mark did made me feel shitty about myself. Like I was to blame, you know?"

"Trust me, he's the asshole in the picture. But it still hurts like hell, right?"

"That's the great thing about dating Connor," she said. "It's almost impossible to be around him and not smile and laugh. And to discover he has this deeper, poetic side?" She shook her head, lost in a dreamy thought. Her wrist rolled, turning her palm up. Empty.

I could fill her soft hand
with all of my words,
Curl her fingers around them
Protected now

My soul in her safekeeping

"If only he'd show that to me more," Autumn said. "He'd be…"

"Perfect?"

"Nobody's perfect, but the combination of his good humor and sensitivity makes me feel we have a chance at being happy."

If the two of us were one person, we'd make her happy. I can help Connor make her happy.

"Happy is the most important thing," I said quietly.

She curled her fingers and drew her hand back into her lap. "But not at your expense. It's important to me that you're okay with us. With me being over at your place. In your life."

At my expense, I thought. *Yes, at my expense. I'm going to pay. Every day they're together, I'm going to pay. Because their happiness is worth the price.*

"I'm okay with it," I said.

Her smile was radiant. "I'm so glad. I—" Her ringing phone—Chris Isaac's "Wicked Game"—cut her off and she rummaged in her bag. "Sorry. That's my brother." She put the phone to her ear. "Hey, Trav. What's up?"

Within three seconds, her smile vanished and her mouth slowly dropped open. Her eyes widened, fear and worry blooming in them like a dark shadow.

"Oh my God," she said.

I half-rose out of my seat. "What is it?"

Her eyes darted to me helplessly as she listened. "My dad…he had a heart attack. They're rushing him to surgery." She listened a moment. "Okay." Nodded vigorously. "Right. Okay, I will. I'll call you back when I get a flight. It'll be okay, Trav. I'm coming. Okay. Bye."

Her hand shook as she ended the call and stared at the display, thumb hovering over the buttons. "Holy *shit*," she murmured. "This is so bad. So bad…"

"What can I do?"

"I need…a flight. I have to go. Tonight. Oh God…" The phone slipped from her hand. I caught it before it fell in her coffee cup.

"Easy, easy," I said, opening the Google App. "We'll get you home. What airport do you fly into? Lincoln?"

BRING DOWN the Stars

"Omaha," she said, her hands digging in her hair.

"Got it." I punched in the info on her phone.

"Travis said he'd had chest pains for days. but he wouldn't go to the doctor. Didn't want to miss a day's work for the money it might lose him."

I stopped scrolling through flights to meet her eyes. I gave her a quick, tight nod to tell her I got it. I understood how fear of missed work and less money could take over your life. "It's gonna be okay," I said.

"I have to get to him, Weston. I have to see him."

"I know. We'll get you there, I promise," I said. "Here. Direct to Omaha Eppley. Leaves Logan at eight p.m."

She reached for the phone. "How much?" Tears spilled from her eyes. "God, it's over five hundred dollars. I can't..."

"I know, I know. Last minute flight."

She looked up at me. "I don't have it. Even if I cleaned out my savings, I don't have it."

I didn't have it either. I'd opted for my scholarship stipend to pay out in monthly installments, and I was already tapped out.

Fuck everything, everywhere.

"Where's Edmond?" Autumn glanced around. "Maybe he can give me an advance on my paycheck."

"He wandered outside." I tore out of my seat and onto the street. I looked up and down, but the singing baker was nowhere in sight.

You idiot, Edmond's not the answer. Connor. Connor can take care of this.

"He's not there," I said, rushing back inside. I fished my phone out of my pocket and jabbed a number with my thumb.

"What are you doing?" Autumn asked.

"Calling Connor."

She was already shaking her head. "Why...? No. I can't ask him for five hundred dollars."

"You're not. I am."

"No, it's too much."

I ignored her. The phone was ringing. "Come with me now," I told Autumn. "Get your bag. Let's go."

"But I can't—"

"This is plan B," I said, putting my arm around her, helping her

137

to her feet. She smelled like cinnamon and apples. She was soft and small under my hand.

I led her to my parked car and opened the passenger door for her.

"Hey," Connor answered, as I helped Autumn in.

"Are you home?"

"Yeah, what's up?"

"I'm with Autumn. Her dad is sick. She needs a flight to Nebraska and a ride to Logan."

"Her dad is sick?"

"Heart attack. He's in surgery now."

"Goddamn. Hold on, let me get my laptop."

I climbed behind the wheel, fumbling my seatbelt with one hand as I juggled my phone

Autumn's voice was breathy and high. "Weston…"

"It's going to be okay," I said, starting my car, which, by some miracle, turned over on the first try.

Autumn turned away, elbow on the window ledge and forehead in her palm, fighting back tears. Caught in the no man's land between pride and hope. The same war I fought every time the Drakes bailed my mother out of one catastrophe or another.

I pulled from the curb and Autumn's phone rang.

"Oh God, it's my mother. Hello? Mom? How is he, what's happening?"

Don't let it be too late, I prayed to any god that would listen. *Please, she has to see him.*

"He is? Okay. Yes, I'm coming tonight. Right now." She glanced at me. "My friend is helping me. I'm on my way. Okay, love you. See you soon."

I blew out a breath of relief as Connor came back on my phone. I told him about the flight I'd found. By the time I screeched to a stop in front of our place, he'd booked the ticket and was waiting outside, jacket and keys in hand, the Hellcat idling at the curb. Autumn burst out of my car and flew up the walk. Connor was already striding to meet her. He wrapped his arms around her and they held each other tight.

I exhaled the story of my life, killed the engine and got out.

"Hey, it's okay." Connor stroked Autumn's hair as she buried her face against his chest, her shoulders shaking. "It's going to be all right. You'll be home in a few hours. You'll be right there with him. It's okay."

He met my eye over her head and said again, "It's okay." And a week's worth of awkwardness between us blew away.

"I'll pay you back," Autumn was saying.

"Hell no," Connor said. "Don't worry about it. It's done."

"Thank you." Autumn stepped back, wiped her eyes and checked her watch. "God, it's five-thirty. Are we going to make it to Logan in time?"

"We can make it," Connor said, leading her by the hand toward the Hellcat. "I'll get you there, I swear."

"I can't thank you enough."

Connor opened the passenger door and Autumn had a foot in the well when she abruptly reversed directions and rushed back down the sidewalk.

To me.

She jumped at me, wrapped her arms around my neck, her feet off the ground for a second. Not giving me a hug of gratitude, but taking something from me instead.

"I'm going to be strong, like you," she said against my neck. "I have to get to my dad."

"That's right," I said. I held her tight and inhaled everything I loved about her. "And you will."

"Thank you," she whispered. Then she released me and hurried to Connor's waiting car.

Connor texted around eight o'clock that Autumn made her flight. I was already in bed, reading and resting my body for the next day's track meet. I should've gone to sleep then. Instead I lay awake, waiting for the sound of Connor's key in the door.

He came home around quarter after ten and I met him in the living room.

"Well?" I demanded, as if he were late for curfew.

He gave me a strange look. "Well, what? I told you she made the flight."

"Right, right," I said, dialing it down. "I was just worried about her. Is she okay?"

"She's scared for her dad and relieved to be on the way to him." He shrugged out of his jacket and tossed it toward a chair. "Good thing you were with her when she got the news."

"I know. I was doing my pre-race carb load and she came in for...something. Her work schedule, I guess."

"Yeah."

"Hey," I said. "You did a good thing for her."

A shade of Connor's usual smile came back. "We both did."

"You bought her a flight home to see her dad. I bought her a coffee."

And that, friends and neighbors, sums it all up, doesn't it?

Connor's smile widened. "Between the two of us, she got there. What time is it?" He glanced at his watch. "Early yet. I'm all jacked up from that crazy drive to Boston. I could actually still make the Delta party. Try to chill."

"Isn't Autumn going to text you or something, when she knows how her dad is?"

He nodded. "She lands around one a.m. her time. I probably won't hear from her until tomorrow."

His expression was growing curious, which I cut off at the pass.

"Cool. Well, whenever you talk to her, tell her I hope all is well."

Connor's brow smoothed out. "Sure thing." He pointed toward the hallway. "Now get your ass in bed. You're running tomorrow."

He went out to party and I lay flat on my bed again. Sleep eluded me. Every passing minute I was awake was one step closer to a shitty track meet, but my thoughts were full of Autumn. And her dad. They were close. Hell, he was still around. Married to her mom. A solid human being of flesh and blood, instead of a ghost. I needed him to be okay for her. I needed to imagine them in their house, having breakfast together, a family.

I dozed and dreamt of a large house in a sea of green cornstalks, and baby chicks hopping around a yard.

At three a.m., my best friend's drunken stumble woke me as he navigated his way to the kitchen for some water. I listened for voices—especially that of the female persuasion. Connor rarely came home from a party alone.

BRING DOWN the Stars

He was alone.

And hungover or not, he'd still come to my meet. Or so I hoped.

He's a good guy at heart.

I listened to him shuffle to bed, then crept out of my room. As usual, Connor had left his keys, phone and wallet on the table by the front door.

I opened his phone and searched for a message from Autumn. Nothing. I did some math: if she arrived at Omaha at 1 a.m., she still had an hour drive to Lincoln, putting her at the hospital around two. Which meant she could be texting Connor any minute now.

I stretched out on the couch with Connor's phone on my chest. Sleep pulled at me but my brain wouldn't quit.

If it's his time, at least let her say goodbye. Let her have that with him, instead of nothing. Instead of desertion.

I dozed again and dreamt of the start of the race. I took my mark and the track vibrated beneath my fingers. I jerked awake. Connor's phone vibrated a text. Heart pounding, I read the message.

Hey. It's late, I hope this doesn't wake you. I'm at the hospital. He's made it through surgery. Quad bypass. He's in ICU now, stable, and we're waiting to get the okay to see him.

Relief gusted out of me. The rolling dots told me she was writing another text, but my thumbs flew to reply first: **So fucking glad.**

The rolling dots of her reply stopped. A pause. Then: **OMG, you're awake.**

If you don't sleep, I don't sleep.

I'm crying (again.) You got me here. I don't know how to thank you.

You don't have to, I typed. **I'm just happy you made it.**

Me too. It's a gift, beyond money, to be here right now.

My lack of sleep must've been catching up with me since my eyes stung.

Tell Weston good luck on his track meet, she wrote. **And thank him for me too, okay?**

I will. Good night, Autumn.

Good night, Connor. <3

I stared at the words, the name and the heart a long time. Then I got up and put Connor's phone back on the table.

Her dad made it, I thought as I flopped face first onto my pillow in my bed.

I was asleep instantly.

Chapter Eighteen

Weston

My alarm went off at six, and I felt as hungover as Connor probably was. I showered and dressed, then grabbed an energy bar and some water. I was tired as hell and couldn't give two shits about the meet.

"Suck it up, Turner," I muttered. "Your fans are waiting. All one of them."

But Connor was still sleeping. He wouldn't show up at the meet until one minute before the first race.

I paused at the door, wondering if Connor *would* show today, or if he were pissed enough that I refused to help him with Autumn.

I glanced at his phone on the front table.

I sure as shit helped you out this morning.

An ironic sense of calm came over me. Autumn's happiness was worth sacrificing my own. Even if it meant my words in Connor's mouth. My thoughts on the page with his signature at the bottom. Answering Autumn's texts made him look good, but it made me feel better as well. To be there for her.

Even if she never knew it.

It took three tries to get my car's engine to turn over. The sound wheezing from under the hood made my teeth clench.

"It would be inconvenient as fuck if you were to die on me," I told the car.

I let her warm up a little before putting her in drive, and breathed a sigh of relief that quickly turned into a yawn. The car complained the whole way, but she got me to the stadium's backlot for staff and athletes.

I joined my teammates and Coach Braun in the locker room. The other guys were talking and joking around, heels planted on benches to stretch hamstrings. A couple of them gave me a nod as I entered. I nodded back.

After giving the team his standard pre-race pep talk, Coach Braun pulled me aside.

"We got some NCAA people here today, Wes," he said, his hand heavy on my shoulder. "It's early in the season, but scholarship-wise, this could be good for you."

I shifted out from under his hand, while a steady stream of cursing crossed my thoughts. "Really?" I asked. "Today?"

"I only just got wind of it. I don't want to freak you out, but one of them is a liaison to the regional Olympic Committee."

"But you don't want to freak me out."

"Accurate."

His friendly smile faltered when I said nothing else, and he moved off.

Well, fuck me sideways.

My scholarship was done and I had no idea how I was going to pay for my final year at Amherst. Now, on the one fucking day I had a bowling ball of sleeplessness on my back, the NCAA people were here.

I gave my shoelaces a yank. "This should be fun."

The sky was overcast and cold. I hopped up and down and did high, rapid goose-steps to get my blood flowing. Our opponents today were MIT, Wesleyan, and Boston College. Hayes, the Wesleyan runner who was dating Autumn's roommate, spied me from his group and jerked his chin in greeting. I stared back until he rolled his eyes and turned away.

"Hey, baby boy! Yoo hoo!"

I whipped my head toward the stands. They were sparsely

BRING DOWN the Stars

populated with diehard track fans willing to brave the cold for these last prelims.

And, apparently, my mother.

"You have got to be fucking kidding me," I muttered.

There she was, Miranda Turner, in a purple and white Amherst jersey, customized with *W. Turner* on the back. Her bleached blonde hair was tied up in a ponytail, showing her plated-gold hoop earrings.

She waved jazz hands at me, then pointed with both fingers at the man sitting beside her. I couldn't see much from the field, but my initial impression was of a fifth-grade science teacher. Balding head, oversized glasses, mustache and a windbreaker.

Ma cupped her hands over her mouth. "This is Paul I was telling you about, remember?"

Her thick accent carried over the cool air. *This is Pawl I was tellin' yoo 'bout, remembah?*

I gave a quick wave and pretended that stretching my leaden muscles required all my concentration. No sign of Connor in the stands yet. Maybe he was too hungover to show. He didn't owe it to me to come to the meets. But it would be the first one he had ever missed.

"That would be the perfect topper to this shit sandwich of a day."

My first race was the 200-meter dash. Hayes lined up in the lane next to me.

"Got your mama here to see you, Turner? That's so cute, I could puke. But I'll leave the puking to you, after."

I opened my mouth to shoot back a cutting insult but nothing came out. My brain was too sluggish and tired.

"Nothing to say?" Hayes clucked his tongue. "I'm disappointed. Has the Amherst Asshole changed his ways?"

I ignored him, took my starting position and concentrated on driving oxygen deep into my lungs, hoping the cold air would snap some energy into me.

The gun fired.

Normally, I could anticipate the shot, my muscles coiled like a spring, ready to take off the instant the sound cut the air. Not today.

Three strides in and I knew it was over.

For the first time in a long time, I had four guys ahead of me, including Hayes. I dug deep to give it everything I had, driving my legs faster and faster. I caught up and passed a few of the runners, but

Hayes was uncatchable.

I crossed the finish line after him, and came to a slow jog. Hands planted on my hips, chest wheezing worse than my car had this morning. I didn't have to look at the scoreboard to know my time was a good second and a half behind my best.

"Second place," Hayes said, hardly winded. "This is new. Or were you trying to get a look at my ass? My girlfriend's in the stands, don't make her jealous."

I sucked in air and glanced up at the bleachers. Ruby was there, in bright yellow. And sitting next to her, with my mother and Paul to his right, was Connor.

He cupped his hands over his mouth. *"You're still my boy, blue."*

"You'll get 'em next time, baby!" my mother shouted.

I hid a smile in my shoulder and blinked stinging sweat out of my eyes.

Coach Braun approached. "Talk to me," he said in his no-nonsense coach voice.

"Shitty sleep," I said. "I'm okay. I'll push through."

Coach pursed his lips, nodding. "Settle in. Focus. We're still in prelims and today isn't the last day you'll see the NCAA."

"I know. I'm good."

Forty minutes later, I was lining up again for the hurdles.

I'm so fucked.

My legs felt like dead weight after the first race. I felt the pressure of my mother's presence and Paul sitting next to her. Sitting where my father should've been. Autumn wasn't there to trick my male ego into a better performance. The NCAA people *were* there, and I felt the catastrophe coming even before the starting gun went off.

I cleared the first three hurdles, but getting my body over each one grew harder and harder. On the fourth hurdle, I didn't tuck my right foot enough and my toe hit the board. Not hard enough to knock it over, but enough to throw me off my rhythm. My three-step cadence faltered, and my muscle memory short-circuited.

I shouldn't have even tried for the next hurdle, but I was moving too fast. My left foot hit the board and my right foot hooked under it as it tipped. I crashed down hard and flung my hands out to save me from smashing face first into the turf. I tumbled with the hurdle tangling in my legs, then lay flat on my back, the wind knocked

BRING DOWN the Stars

out of me.

Sucking in deep breaths, I took inventory. Nothing broken. Nothing sprained. But I ached all over and my palms were scraped all to hell. My right knee stung like a bitch. I sat up slowly to visually assess the damage. I'd scraped the skin off my knee cap and a steady stream of blood was oozing down my shin and calf.

The medical team and Coach Braun rushed over. Before they could surround me, I saw my mother, Paul, Connor and Ruby on their feet in concern. My mother clutched Paul's shoulder and he had his arm around her.

"Wes." Coach Braun crouched down. "Hey. Look at me. How bad?"

I couldn't meet his eye. "I'm fine. Road rash and some bruises."

I kept looking at the ground as I hobbled off the track to a smattering of applause. A medic sat me down on a cooler, cleaned up my leg and bandaged my scraped knee.

"Not your day," Coach said, his hands on his hips, a sympathetic softness over his face.

"Of all the days," I said.

"They got all your times from the last two years, Wes. This season is only starting. We all have shitty days. This is yours."

I nodded. I was supposed to anchor the 4x400 relay but that was out of the question. "Sorry, Coach."

"It happens," Coach said aloud, while his expression spoke, *Me too.*

I looked away from him to see Hayes casually walking over.

"Hey, man," he said. "You okay?"

"All in a day's work."

"You tangled with the hurdle pretty fucking hard. I don't know how you managed not to face-plant or snap a leg."

"Sorry to disappoint."

Hayes looked at the sky with a disbelieving little laugh. "Okay, whatever, bro. I'm sorry you got hurt. I enjoyed kicking your ass in the two hundred and was looking forward to doing it again in the four-by-four."

I swallowed the sharp comeback. What was the fucking point? I was only the Amherst Asshole when I was winning. Without my speed, I was…

I believe 'Sock Boy' is the word you're looking for.

After the meet, Connor, Ma and Paul came onto the field.

"My poor baby boy," Ma said, holding out her arms to me. I bent to give her a hug and was enveloped in a cloud of cheap perfume. "Honey, what happened? I never seen you fall so hard."

"It happens."

"Hey, man," Connor said, clapping my shoulder. "That looked fucking rough. Haven't seen you take a digger like that since freshman year."

"Thanks for noticing."

"Let me see your hands," Ma said. "Oh God, you're a mess." She looked up at Paul. "Every other day, he wins all his races. But of course, bring someone special to see my boy and he wipes out. But I'm glad you're okay. That's the most important thing, right? This is Paul. Paul Winfield. Paul, this is my son, Weston."

"Good to meet you," Paul said.

"Likewise," I said.

"I'd shake your hand, but I don't want to add insult to injury."

I sized him up, trying to discern any signs he was a bum like all the rest of the guys Ma hung around with. Freeloaders who moved in to live rent free, eat her food and drink her beer while she worked at the hair salon.

Paul weathered my scrutiny with calm, smiling placidly under his mustache as he put his hands in the pockets of his khakis, rocking on his heels.

"Now, don't you give him that look, Weston Jacob Turner," Ma said, wagging her finger with its gold and pink acrylic curve. "Paul's a good man and he's good to me, so you just take that attitude and stuff it." She gestured to Connor. "Why can't you be more like this one? Mr. Handsome, always smiling." She reached over and patted Connor's cheek. He had his shades on, despite the cloud cover, and looked a little pale and a lot tired.

"You feel like eating, Wes?" Paul asked quietly. "Or maybe just sit and ice the knee?"

"Yes," Ma answered. "Where are we going to lunch? Hannigan's? I just love that little country bumpkin breakfast joint."

Connor grinned. "Lunch at Hannigan's then. On me."

"Well, aren't you the sweetest," Ma said. "Sounds perfect."

I studied my best friend. He called to where Ruby stood with

BRING DOWN the Stars

Hayes. "Ruby. Lunch?"

"Love to," she called back, but Hayes's smile vanished as he and I exchanged glances. She conferred with him and then sighed. "Rain check, okay?"

"Definitely." Connor turned to us and gestured across the field. "Shall we?"

We headed to the parking lot, my mother walking ahead with her arm linked in Paul's, gabbling away, while Connor matched my slow limp.

"How's the knee?" he asked.

"Hurts like a sonofabitch, but I'll live. How's your hangover?"

"Hurts like a sonofabitch, but I'll live."

My glance slid to him then away. "How late did you get in?"

"Around three. I didn't think I was so wasted, but apparently I had a whole conversation with Autumn on text that I don't even remember."

"Oh yeah?" I said, securing my Academy Award nomination for Casual as Fuck. "How's she doing?"

"Good. Really grateful that she made it to be with her dad."

"Thanks to you."

"So what happened out there today?" he asked, shooting me a glance. "Did you not get enough sleep?"

No, as a matter of fact. I was up until three in the morning texting your girlfriend for you.

"I don't know what happened. Bad day. Couldn't be worse timing either."

"Why not?"

"NCAA people were here."

"Shut up."

"One of them was a liaison to the regional Olympic Committee."

"Oh fuck," Connor said. "Man, that sucks."

I shrugged. "I guess."

"You guess? *The Olympics.*"

"I don't know about the Olympics," I said. "The Olympics won't pay for next year's tuition. If the NCAA people were feeling generous today, I blew it."

Connor looked about to say more, but we'd arrived at his Hellcat and Paul's silver sedan.

"There's four of us," Ma said. "Let's all ride together. Weston, go up front with Paul. Connor, you come sit by this old lady."

Paul and I exchanged glances over the hood of his car as we climbed in. He offered a smile I didn't take or return.

Hannigan's was hopping and we crowded into a small booth.

"Connor, that Ruby seems like a nice young girl," Ma said, after the waitress took our order. "You say she's your girlfriend's roommate?"

"I did," Conner said. "Ruby's all kinds of fun."

"She's a hoot," Ma said. "But where is your girlfriend again? Nebraska?"

"Family emergency," Connor said. "Her dad had a heart attack."

"Oh no, that's awful," Paul said quietly. "Any word on his prognosis?"

"Not yet," Connor said. "But I'm supposed to hear from her again tonight."

"Well, give her our best," Ma said. "Too bad, I'd like to meet her. And too bad about your race," she said to me. "I've been telling Paul about how fast you are. It was his idea to come watch the meet, since you won't take the hour drive to come visit your mother."

"I've been busy, Ma," I said.

"Busy," she said. "Where's *your* girlfriend? How come you don't got a girlfriend? With your face and your brain, they should be falling all over themselves for you. I'll tell you what it is—you don't smile enough."

"Jesus, Ma."

She nudged Paul with her elbow. "For years, I've been telling Wes he's a sweet, handsome guy, but he don't smile. How you can attract pretty girls looking like you've got a stick up your ass all the time?"

"Miranda, leave him be," Paul said mildly.

Beside me, Connor was laughing into his napkin, shoulders shuddering silently.

"Look at Connor," Ma said. "Always smiling, showing those beautiful teeth. And let me tell you, Wes." She started counting off on her fingers. "You're a beautiful boy. You're the fastest runner out there when you're not falling on your face. And you're a brilliant writer. Paul, did I tell you he's a brilliant writer?"

BRING DOWN the Stars

"Once or twice." Paul smiled at me. "I heard you wrote a winning essay for a scholarship to a very prestigious prep school in Boston."

"It's all true," Ma said. "That's how he met this one." She patted Connor on the shoulder. "This one…" She shook her head, her lips pursed to hold back a sudden rush of emotion as she took Connor's face in both of her hands. "I don't know what we would've done without him. And his family. They took care of me. Took care of us…"

I clenched my teeth. *That was my dad's job. And since he's fucking gone, it's my job…*

"Come on, Miranda," Connor said, hugging Ma's shoulders.

"Times are tough and I just feel so grateful to have these beautiful boys." She turned to Paul. "And now you. I'm surrounded by good men. How did I get so lucky?"

The waitress appeared with a tray, laden with plates of pancakes, eggs, and bacon. After she sorted out who got what—with Ma's loud assistance—we dug in.

I glanced at Paul beside me as we ate, still searching for the scumbag that lurked within his mild-mannered, nice guy act.

"What do you do for living, Paul?" I asked.

Are you 'between opportunities'? Taking some time off? Crashing with Ma until you get back on your feet?

Paul opened his mouth to answer but Ma swooped in with a proud smile.

"He's a regional sales manager for a lumber distribution company, how about that? The buildings you see going up all over? That lumber gets there because of him."

That lumbah gets they-ah cuzza him. Ma's accent seemed stronger every time I saw her, and listening to her drew mine out of me against my will, when I worked so hard to kill it.

Paul chuckled. "Miranda makes my job sound loftier than it is."

"Don't minimize yourself," she scolded. "And I'm so happy you took time off to drive out here to see my son. Wish it was a better performance."

"Thanks, Ma," I said over my coffee cup, just as Connor dropped his gaze toward his plate and Paul mumbled, "Miranda…"

"Well? Am I wrong?" she said. "You're always the best one

151

out there. What happened today?"

"I tripped on a hurdle, Ma," I said. "It happens."

She shook her head, clucking her tongue. "Such a shame."

"I thought you were terrific in your first race," Paul said.

"He came in second," Ma said. "He never comes in second. That's how he got the NCAA scholarship, for being so fast." She ripped open a packet of Sweet & Low and dumped it into her coffee. "Speaking of which, baby, what are you going to do about next year?"

"What happens next year?" Paul asked.

"No more scholarship, that's what happens."

I exchanged glances with Connor and shook my head slightly. If I told her the NCAA people had been there on the same afternoon I DQ'd a race, her head would explode.

"You know my friend Gilly?" Ma said. "Her son's about your age. He was on the verge of jailbird city. Well, this recruiter comes from the Army Reserves and signs him up. Now he's got a few grand coming in per month, health bennies *and* they'll pay for his college."

"You want me to join the Army, Ma?"

She shrugged and stirred her coffee with a spoon. "I'm just saying the Army Reserves is only one weekend a month."

"Things are heating up in Syria," Paul said to his oatmeal.

Ma waved her hand. "Things blow over. They always do."

"What if that weekend per month interferes with track?" I asked.

"Track's not paying for your college anymore." She pointed her spoon at me. "*You* still got to pay for college." She tilted her head and half-shrugged and said in a lower voice, "And the monthly pay wouldn't be so terrible, would it?"

"You don't need it," Paul said to her. He put his hand on my arm. "Keep running, Wes."

I glanced down at his hand, smattered with dark hair and pudgy at the knuckles. A dad's hand. It patted me, then retreated back toward oatmeal and coffee. And it wasn't so bad.

"So tell me, Connor," Paul said brightly. "What's your sport? You look like a baseball man to me."

BRING DOWN the Stars

We said our goodbyes in the parking lot. Ma took my face in her hands and smacked a kiss on my cheek.

"You did good. Not your best show, but I'm still proud of you."

"Thanks, Ma," I said.

She turned to hug Connor, leaving Paul and me face to face.

"Good to meet you, Weston." He put out his hand for a shake, then grimaced. "Keep forgetting you're bearing war wounds."

I wouldn't have minded shaking his hand. "Good to meet you, too," I said, with the most honest smile I could find.

"We'll see you soon I hope," Ma said. "Thanksgiving? Can you manage to haul your butt out east for Thanksgiving?"

"He'll be there," Connor said. "My mother is looking forward to seeing you. Felicia and Kimberly, too." He turned to Paul, and they shook hands. "You as well, Mr. Winfield. Please come. We'd love to have you."

"My God, is he not a treasure?" Ma took Connor's face too, kissed his cheek. "Good bye, my angels."

"Drive safe," Connor called as she and Paul climbed into his sedan.

A huge sigh gusted out of me as the car drove away.

"I heard that." Connor's hand dropped. "I love your mother, but I'm exhausted."

"Try living with her," I said. "Paul must be a glutton for punishment."

"Or he really likes her," Connor said. "Your mom's really likable, you know that? *You're* really likable when you're not so busy being a dickhead." Connor reached to pinch my cheek and said in a high falsetto, "Weston, you sweet, handsome boy. You'd get all the girls if you just smiled more."

I laughed and knocked his hand away. "You and your beautiful teeth can fuck off."

He gave me a lift to backlot where my car was parked at the stadium. Before I could get out he killed the engine and turned to look at me.

"Listen, I know you don't want to hear this, but if you need help paying next year's tuition—"

"Forget it."

"My parents can help you. They would want to help you."

"I'll figure it out, Connor," I said.

"It's not a big deal—"

"It's a big deal to me, okay? I take enough from you. I need to figure my own shit out, and take care of Ma."

"How? The Army?"

"If I have to."

Connor shook his head and blew out his cheeks. "You're really fucking smart, Wes. But sometimes you're really fucking stupid."

"How's that?"

"You think this is all one-sided? You think you don't help me out? You write my damn papers. You got me through the SATs. Hell, the only reason I'm here is because of you."

"That's not true."

"It is true, and that's why you're fucking stupid. Because you can't see what kind of talent you have. A brain and…fucking *soul* like yours is majoring in Economics? Why aren't you writing a book? Why aren't you taking your running seriously? Maybe I don't have the balls to open my own sports bar yet, but at least I know what I *want*."

"Where the hell is this coming from?"

Connor shrugged, his trademark smile all but vanished. "I don't know. Thanksgiving. I feel like I have to brace myself for battle against my parents while they slobber all over you and you don't even know why."

"They don't slobber on me."

"You and Autumn are my secret weapons. But she hasn't even said yes to the invite yet." He sighed. "I'm just going to fuck it up with her anyway. If we make it to Thanksgiving, it'll be a miracle."

I shifted in my seat, glanced down at my raw, scraped palms. "You're not going to fuck up with Autumn. She cares about you. What you did for her last night was a lot."

Connor smirked and wore an expression I'd never seen him wear before. "That's just money."

I started to protest but he cut me off.

"I know you wrote those texts to her last night, Wes."

I froze. "I…"

"You said you wouldn't help me and then you did. Why?"

"I don't know," I said. "I couldn't sleep. I heard your phone. It made you look good and made her happy. Win-win."

Connor nodded, absorbing this. "You know… It never

BRING DOWN the Stars

occurred to me to check in with her. I care about her but it never occurred to me. But it did to you." He looked at me. "Does this mean you're helping me again?"

"I guess so. If you need me."

If she *needs me. She deserves to be happy.*

"I mean…you don't need my help," I said. "It's all there, man. You just need to—"

"Put in the effort?" Connor asked with the rueful smile. "Go on, get out of here before they tow your piece of shit to the junkyard."

I nodded. "Yeah, okay. I'll see you at home."

"See ya."

I climbed out of Connor's $80,000 sports car and into my junker. The contrast between our lives had never been more obvious. Connor was wrong—sometimes money counted for a lot. Sometimes it was the difference between watching the girl you cared about worry over her dad, and getting her on a plane to be with him.

I turned the key in the ignition, but the car was dead.

I rested my forehead on the steering wheel, feeling as if I spilled out on the track again in front of hundreds of people, and I didn't want to get up again.

Connor was still parked across from me. Connor might not have thought to call Autumn in her hour of need, but he'd never miss one of my meets. He'd never let me be alone on Thanksgiving. And he'd never drive out of the parking lot until he heard my engine turn over.

He deserves to be happy too.

Connor smiled, waved me over, and gave me a lift home.

Chapter Nineteen

Autumn

I sat in the ICU waiting room, slumped against my brother's shoulder. My mother sat on my other side, our hands clasped tight. Mom's red hair was graying at the temples. Her face, always weathered, now showed signs of worry that seemed to have aged her another ten years.

My father said if he were the grease that kept the engine of our family going, Lynette Caldwell was the nuts and bolts that held it all together. I hadn't seen her shed any tears since I'd arrived. Her blue eyes stayed sharp, vigilant, and dry as she watched the nurses come and go. I inherited my red hair and pragmatism from Mom, but I had my father's hard work ethic and his soft heart.

The heart that almost gave out.

The doctor said Dad's arterial blockage was 97% and it was a miracle he was still alive. But he *was* alive and any second now—thanks to Connor—I would see him.

My eyes fell shut and my head lolled against my brother's shoulder. Travis, at eighteen, was a carbon copy of my father in both looks and soul. Kind and hard-working. But Mom said Travis had so many clouds in his head, she was surprised he didn't float away. He was content to be a farmer. The love of the land ran simple and true in his blood. Growing up, he spent summer nights in our front-yard

BRING DOWN the Stars

hammock, drinking lemonade and watching the fireflies, while I sat at the porch table with my schoolwork.

My dream was to go to college and get out into the world. Travis felt the world was already there in his backyard.

We all sat up together as a nurse emerged from the hallway and headed straight for us. "You can see him now."

We followed her down the hallway toward the ICU. At Room 2014, the nurse opened the door. Tears sprang immediately to my eyes. If Mom looked ten years older, Dad had time-traveled twenty years into the future. His tanned, weathered face was now gaunt and pale. His hair had been salt-and-pepper when I saw him over the summer. Now it lay thin and white against his head, so small on the pillow. All of him looking so diminished, lying within a nest of tubes and wires and machines that breathed for him.

But he was alive.

"He may go in and out of consciousness," the nurse said from the door. "I'll leave you to visit for a little while, but then he must rest."

"Hello, Henry," Mom said, and sank into a chair beside the bed, as if her vigil against death was over and she had won. For now.

I went to the other side and slipped my hand in my father's. Once a hearty and strong grip, now weak and limp.

"Hi, Daddy," I whispered. "I'm here."

"Hey, Dad," Travis said from the foot of the bed.

For a handful of seconds, there was only the steady push of oxygen from the machine, and then my father opened his eyes and looked right at me. A small, weak smile stretched his lips.

He was too weak to do more than twitch his fingers against my hand. But he was there with me, and I was there with him. And I wouldn't have traded that moment for anything in the world.

After the nurses shooed us out to let Dad rest, we went down to the cafeteria to grab an early breakfast.

"Tell me about this boy you're seeing, Autumn," Mom said, as we sat down with our trays of oatmeal, fruit, and coffee. She folded her napkin in her lap and nudged my brother's elbows off the table as if we were back at home. "Connor, was it?"

"He's not like anyone I've dated before," I said. "Certainly not like Mark."

My mother pursed her lips. "Good to hear."

"He's really the son of a senator?" Travis asked. "And a billionaire?"

"Yes, but that's the least important thing about him," I said, earning an approving nod from my mother. "Until last night, his money had no bearing on how I felt about him. It still doesn't, except that I'm grateful to him."

"As are we." Mom took a bite of her sandwich, chewed, and swallowed. "So are things serious with him?"

I had no idea how to answer that. "Yes and no," I said. "Mostly yes, but…it's complicated."

"Mm. How's your Harvard application coming along?"

"It's not. I've been a little distracted. Honestly, I still don't know where to put my focus." I toyed with my spoon. "How are things with the farm?"

Travis glanced at me, then Mom.

"First things first," Mom said, shooting him a look. "Your father's health is the most important thing right now. Let's concentrate our energies there."

"Yes, ma'am," Travis said.

"Okay, Mom," I said.

My brother and I exchanged smiles. Lynette Caldwell, rain, shine, or tragedy, never changed.

We spent the afternoon in Dad's room, mostly holding his hand while he slept. He couldn't speak with the breathing tube in place. So many tubes: in his chest, his neck, his stomach, plus an IV in his arm and an oxygen monitor on his finger. A thin white bandage poked up from his hospital gown, covering the seam where his chest had been cracked open.

While he slept, Mom worked on her cross-stitch and Travis sat on the window ledge, scrolling his phone. I sat in one of the chairs beside Dad's bed, eyes drooping. I hadn't slept in more than twenty-

BRING DOWN the Stars

four hours, and my thoughts became nonsensical. Breaking apart and reforming. Visions shifting and scattering until finally, I was in Connor's arms, his beautiful green eyes gazing into mine.

There's so much I want to tell you, he said.
Tell me, I whispered.

He bent to kiss me instead. I got lost in the sensation of pure want that bloomed in my belly and the heat that swept through my veins. I clung to him as the kiss became urgent, deeper, my mouth opening wide to take everything he could give me. We kissed like breathing until finally, I broke away.

Now it was ocean eyes holding my gaze. Blue-green and a million miles deep.

It was Weston's arms around me. Weston's hard body pressed to mine. He held my face in his hands, his thumbs stroking my cheeks, and the way he looked at me…

I'd never in my life felt so cherished.

There's so much I want to tell you, he said.
Tell me, I whispered.

He opened his mouth to speak, then raised his head to look at something over my shoulder.

It's time to go.
What? No…

"Auts? It's time to go."

I came awake with a start to my brother shaking my shoulder.

"What…"

"They're kicking us out."

I blinked and glanced around, the dream still clinging to me. I could feel Connor's mouth lingering on mine. Or was it Weston's? It had felt so real, both kisses. Connor's, I could still feel on my mouth and body, while Weston's, I felt somewhere deep, in the center of me…

I shook off the dream and leaned to kiss my father's cheek. "Bye, Daddy," I whispered. "Sleep tight. We'll be back first thing in the morning."

I had flown to Nebraska literally with nothing but the clothes on my back, so Travis drove me to Wal-Mart so I could get a toothbrush, toothpaste, hairbrush, and underwear. Then we grabbed barbecue chicken from Sully's BBQ and took it home.

Home.

The big rickety farmhouse with its old wallpaper and creaking boards. The kitchen's smell of wood and time and my mother's cooking. The sound of the chickens a little ways down the path to the barn, and the cows lowing in the field. As we drove up, the sun sank behind the crops, casting a gold and lavender hue over the horizon that seem to stretch on forever.

I understood why my brother was content to live here all his life. I loved it here but I'd always known, since I was little, that I wasn't meant to stay. I would leave, but one day, I'd come back with the man I was going to marry and show him the sunset over our farm. I wanted to share my beginning with him, and see the place where he began. His home. Then we'd venture out to find the place that was ours.

After dinner, I settled myself in my room that still had posters of *Moulin Rouge* and Keira Knightley's *Pride and Prejudice* hung over the bluebell wallpaper. I still had some clothes stashed in the old dresser. I took a shower and changed out of the dress I'd been wearing, into an old set of men's style pajamas. I bundled myself up in one of Mom's afghans, and sat on the porch swing to watch the stars come out.

Around nine o'clock, I opened my phone and reread the last text exchange with Connor. Smiling, I pushed the call button. He answered in three rings.

"Hey you," he said in his deep voice.

"Hi," I said. "Are you busy?"

"No, I'm just hanging around here at home. How's your dad?"

"He's okay. He made it through the surgery and he opened his eyes." The tears were already coming. "Thank you so much."

"It was nothing."

"It's everything," I said, my voice breaking.

"Don't cry. It's not a big deal."

"It is to me," I said, wiping my eyes with the cuff of my PJs. "It's a very big deal."

A short silence fell.

"Okay, well…" I pressed my lips together. "I guess that's all I wanted to tell you."

I heard a shuffling and muffled voices, then Connor said, "Autumn, can you hold on for a second? Just give me a second."

"Uh, sure."

BRING DOWN the Stars

More shuffling and I thought I heard someone swear, then Connor came back on the line, his voice whispery and rough.

"Hi. Sorry about that. I was just…getting my thoughts together. Long day."

"Are you getting a cold?" I asked.

"Hmm?"

"Your voice sounds a little hoarse."

"Yeah, I got this little tickle going on." He cleared his throat. "Driving me crazy. And I have to keep it down. Wes is trying to sleep."

"Oh, I forgot he had a meet this morning," I said. "How'd it go?"

"Not good. He crashed bad on the hurdles."

I sat up on the porch swing. "He did? Is he okay?"

"Some bruises and road rash, but he'll be all right. I think his pride took the brunt of it."

I laughed a little and sank back down.

"So your father is okay?" he asked.

"They're taking the breathing tube out tomorrow, which is good. It means he's on track. God, he looks so weak, though. Frail."

"You're there," he said. "I'm sure that means everything to him. He'll be up in no time."

"You think so?"

"You're worth getting out of bed for, Autumn."

"That's sweet of you to say." I sniffed a laugh and wiped my eyes. "And you do say the sweetest things. Sometimes."

"But not enough?"

I smiled, cradling the phone closer. "Well…"

"I have a lot to say. I just wish it didn't take me so long to find my voice."

"It's worth waiting for. And worth getting *into* bed for," I heard myself add.

The gruff whisper of his voice deepened. "If only."

"Hmm?"

"Nothing. I just miss you."

"Me too, but…" I swallowed hard. "I mean, I don't know if it's the time to tell you this…"

"Tell me everything."

"It hurt when I didn't hear from you after we spent the night

161

together."

"I know it did." He heaved a sigh. "I'm sorry, Autumn."

"It's funny, but when we're talking on the phone right now? Or texting? I feel so close to you. I feel closer to you than when I'm actually *with* you."

"I know."

"You told me you don't always know what to say, but—"

"I always know what to say," he said. "Always. But I can't *say* it. Like I'm drunk when I'm with you. I'm drunk *off* of you and then I…I don't know. I have to step back. And it takes a cold shower of reality to slap some sense into me."

"I love everything you're saying now," I said softly. "But I'm scared."

"I know. I am too."

"You are?"

"Sure. Of fucking this up. Of hurting you. I don't want to hurt you, Autumn. I just want you to be happy. That's it. End of story."

My breath became a little shallower. My heart beat a little faster.

"I don't want to hurt you either," I said. "Or ask more than you can give, but a part of me wishes you'd share this side of yourself with the world. I know your parents put so much pressure on you."

"Yeah," he said. "They do."

A yawn I couldn't stop came over me.

"You should sleep," he said.

"I've lost all sense of time. Feels like ages since Mom called me," I said. "Thank you again. And tell Weston thank you."

"For what?"

"For being there for me at the bakery. He took care of me when I was freaking out."

"He has his moments."

I closed my eyes to the sense memories of the dream. Closing my eyes and falling into Connor's kiss. Opening my eyes and falling out of Weston's kiss.

They both helped me that night. They're both special to me in different ways.

"Connor?"

He coughed a little, his voice growing more gruff. "Yeah?"

"If my dad gets better like they think he will, then I'll head back to Boston. And if I can do that, then I'd like to go to Thanksgiving at your parents' house."

"You would?"

"If you still want me to."

"It would mean everything to…me. But are you sure?"

"I never spend Thanksgiving at the farm. I can only ever afford one holiday flight and Christmas wins."

"I can help with any flight, Autumn."

"I know. But this is the one that counted." I leaned back against the swing. "I can't wait to see you."

"Me too. And I'm here if you need me."

"That's all I need." Tears filled my eyes again.

"Don't cry," he said, his whispering voice softer. "It's going to be okay."

"How did you know I was crying?"

I heard him take a long, slow breath. Full of hesitation. "I'm starting to memorize you," he said. "Not just your words but how you talk. The silences between words. The sound you make when you're thinking. The quiet where you try to hold back, and the little floods where you don't."

I pressed my fingertips to my mouth, listening, absorbing every word straight into my heart.

"I know you're crying because I can hear you," he said. "And I can't hold you but I want to hold you. So much."

"Me too. I need to feel you." I curled hard around the phone, holding it tightly.

"I can't hold you and be there for you, but I hear you. And I changed my mind; if you need to cry, go ahead. I'm listening. I'll take anything you need to give. Anything and everything. I'm right here. You can give it to me. I can take it. I want to."

His words unlocked something deep inside me. What I thought would be a tired little cry turned into a flood of tears, pouring into the phone. Fear for my father. For the farm that was already struggling. For gratitude that I was home, and for the longing to be with this man who was hundreds of miles away.

"Thank you," I said, voice reduced to a croak.

"Try to get some sleep," he said, his whispered voice thick now. "But call me if you can't. I'll stay up with you. As long as it takes."

"Okay."
A pause.
"Autumn?"
"I'm going now."
"All right."
Another silence, and then we laughed.
"For real this time. Good night, Connor."
Another short pause, then, "Goodnight, Autumn."

CHAPTER Twenty

Weston

I hung up the phone and stared at it, shocked at what I'd just done. What I'd said to her. The truth that poured out of my heart and the emotion flooding back from Autumn to me.

You mean, to him.

Connor was staring at me, eyes wide. "Dude…"

Disgust flooded me, slugged through my veins—thick and cold—dousing the warmth I'd had with Autumn on the phone.

You didn't have anything with Autumn, you selfish asshole. You tricked her…

"Wes?"

I blinked and gave my head a shake.

"That was awesome, man," Connor said. "You said everything right. Perfect."

"Yeah," I muttered. "Perfect."

Connor frowned. "Don't do that."

"Do what?"

"Overthink it. It's not a big deal," he said. "When she started to cry, my mind went blank. It's so much easier to shut up and hug a girl when she's upset, you know? I'm better with that. Over the phone, it's rough. But you knew just what to say. To make her feel better."

To make her happy. That's all that matters.

I clung to that thought, fighting the rising tide of wrongness for deceiving Autumn. Again.

"She'll come to Boston for Thanksgiving," I said, my Southie accent coming back after being carefully locked up for the phone call. My jaw ached.

"Thanks, man," Connor said. "That's awesome. You're a miracle worker."

"Yeah."

He cocked his head. "You're good, right?"

"What? Yeah. Fine. Just tired. And sore from the track spill."

He nodded. "So. Can I have my phone back?"

I realized I was still holding it. "Oh, right." Reluctantly, I handed it back.

Handed Autumn back to Connor.

"Thanks, man."

"Yeah, no problem."

No problem at all. Except that I've dug us in deeper. Dug Autumn in deeper to Connor. Dug myself deeper into lies, and she'll never forgive me...

A little more than a week later, Autumn surprised him by flying home and coming directly over to our place.

"Hi," she said softly, dropping her bag.

"Hi," he said.

They kissed deeply at the door, then he took her to his room.

She can never know. Never.

I took a run. Faster and faster, until exhaustion hollowed me out. Hopelessly trying to burn out what I felt for Autumn, and pretending I was filling myself back up with their happiness. Both of them, the two people I cared for most in the world.

The two people I loved.

PART IV
November

Chapter Twenty-One

Autumn

Friday before Thanksgiving, I went to Panache Blanc to pick up my paycheck. It was the first time I ever dreaded a payday. It wasn't going to be enough to get me out of the hole from spending ten days in Nebraska.

Dad was released from the hospital and Mom had set him up in the downstairs den. It had an adjoining bathroom so he wouldn't have to deal with stairs. He insisted I go back to Massachusetts before I fell further behind in my classes and work. I hated to leave. He still looked so pale and thin. Things were bad at the farm and getting worse with every day he had to stay in bed.

"There's nothing you can do here," he told me. "If you want to do something to help, get back to school. Pursue your dream."

"I don't know what my dream is, Daddy," I'd said.

"You will. It'll come to you, and when it does, you'll wonder how you never saw it there, waiting for you all this time."

At the bakery, Weston was at his usual table in the corner, head bent over his work. His pen moved quickly over a page, his jaw hard, his eyes nowhere else. I said hi to Phil, slipped into the back room to get my paycheck, and slipped out again. I tore into the envelope, wanting to face the disaster head-on.

BRING DOWN the Stars

I stopped short, mouth falling open and tears flooding my eyes as I read the amount on the check—an extra five hundred dollars that had no business being there.

God, Edmond...

"Are you okay?"

From his table, Weston stared at me, the angular lines of his face drawn down with concern. I wiped my face and slumped into the chair opposite him. I set my paycheck on the table.

"Edmond's kindness is making me emotional. He's giving me a 'Thanksgiving bonus.'" I made air quotes around the word. "Only there's no such thing. He's making up for the pay I lost while I was in Nebraska."

"Sounds like Edmond. But you don't like taking charity," Weston said, not quite a question.

I shook my head. "Pride is a weird thing. If the situation were reversed and someone I cared about needed money, I'd give it without a second thought. Why is taking it so much harder?"

Weston nodded. "Yeah, I know how that is. But are you going to be okay?" He gestured to the envelope. "Money-wise, I mean."

"I don't know." Dread lay heavy in my stomach. "I really don't know if I'm going to be able to stay in school. Or if I even should. It feels selfish when my family is suffering so much. I feel like there's nothing I can do to help, and I'm so far away."

"How bad is it?" he asked.

"Not great. Dad was already shorthanded before the heart attack. He was probably working himself harder to make up for it, but it's the planting season. The most important part of the year, and my brother says that we owe the bank money from an old loan. Dad's going to have to sell off some acreage to make up for it."

Weston's expression was thoughtful as he nodded. This guy observed everything and missed nothing.

His diamond mind...

I huffed a breath and waved my hand. "Anyway, I hate talking about money. I thought the prelim track season was over until spring. What's a runner like you doing in a place like this?"

"Best carbs in town."

I laughed and pointed to the crust of sandwich left on his plate. "You going to eat that?"

"Help yourself."

I took a bit of wheat bread crust. "Carbs I can accept. Money, not so much."

"Bread is easier to accept than bread," Weston said.

I laughed again and gestured to his work. "Am I keeping you?"

"I'm okay," he said. His eyes were soft. "You?"

"Not really. On top of everything else, I'm panicking about my grades. As opposed to panicking about my Harvard application." I ran my hands over my hair, yanking it back from my face and letting it fall again. "I'm really sinking. If I don't maintain my GPA I'm going to be in trouble with *this* school, never mind Harvard."

Weston nodded. "I had a partial NCAA and it ran out last year. I've been able to stretch the living stipend through this year because Connor's parents are paying our rent. But next year?" He raised his lean-muscled shoulders in a shrug.

"Student loans?" I asked.

"I don't want to be saddled with that kind of debt. My mother's been in debt her entire life. It scares the shit out of me. I'm thinking about Army Reserves."

I sat back in my chair. "The Army. Really? Things are really a mess in Syria right now. And the war in Afghanistan seems like it will go on forever."

"It's only the Reserves," he said. "One weekend a month."

"What if the service falls on a track meet weekend?"

He shrugged again. "Bottom line, I have to take care of my mom and sisters and I need a degree and a decent job to do it."

Mother and sisters. No father. Weston never mentions his father.

"I'm looking forward to meeting your family next weekend," I said.

"Brace yourself," Weston said. "You're basically going to walk into a Mark Wahlberg movie."

I laughed. "Connor seems really nervous about the day. Are his parents really that hard on him?"

"The Drakes are good people at heart," Weston said. "They want Connor to be his best self. But they don't get that his best self doesn't involve being in his dad's business, or politics, or even being in college."

I nodded. "I think he'd be happy with his own sports bar."

"He'd be good at it." Weston's pen tapped his page. "At least

BRING DOWN the Stars

an economics degree could come in handy for it, even if it's not what he wants."

"Can I ask you a question?"

"Sure."

"Is economics what *you* really want to do too? Wall Street?"

"Why wouldn't I?" he asked slowly.

"I don't know," I said, and narrowed my eyes at him with a small smile. "Part of me thinks you working with numbers and money makes no sense. The other half thinks you'd make an excellent, cutthroat Wall Street vulture."

His eyes widened first, then his smile unfolded—a genuine smile free of irony or dryness. It kept growing, unleashing a full-throated laugh in his deep—*sexy*—voice.

"Oh, you *can* laugh," I said, my own smile growing. "I have to say, I'm feeling pretty proud of myself right now."

His laughter tapered to a chuckle. "I don't know which title I like better—Amherst Asshole, or Wall Street Vulture."

I made a face. "I don't like that name, Amherst Asshole. Where did it come from?"

"Track guys, mostly."

"That's because you don't let them know you. You have facets just like everybody else. Even for a guy who thinks feelings are like tonsils."

His brow furrowed. "When did I say that?"

"The day we met in the library. You said feelings were like tonsils and if only you could rip them out just as easily."

"I did say that."

"Do you still think it's true?"

His ocean eyes poured into mine. "More than ever."

The air between us suddenly grew thin. The distance between us felt like inches instead of feet. The dream I had in Nebraska filled my memory. Kissing Connor, then opening my eyes to find Weston holding my face in his hands...

I cleared my throat and looked away, even as some deep part of me wanted to be closer. To know more.

"What?" he said softly.

"I can't get a read on you, Weston Turner."

"Why do you always call me Weston, instead of Wes?"

I shrugged. "Wes is usually short for Wesley. Weston is

171

unique."

"You're the only one that calls me that."

"Then I guess I'm unique, too."

The smallest of smiles touched his lips. "You are."

"Can I exploit my unique status to ask you another, more personal question?"

"Ask away. But I may exploit my Amherst Asshole status to refrain from answering."

I softened my voice. "Where's your dad?"

A flicker along his jaw as his teeth clenched. A flare of anger burned hot in the blue-green waters of his eyes, then extinguished just as quickly.

"*That*," he said, "is the million-dollar question."

"You don't know?"

"He took off when I was seven."

"He just…left?"

"Tried to sneak out like the fucking coward he is without having the balls to tell my mom. Or to look my sisters and me in the eye and say he was leaving without us. But we caught him."

My eyes widened. "You caught him?"

"Ma and I," he said, "I came down with a fever at school. Ma took me home, and we arrived just as my dad was packing up the car."

"Oh my God." My hand itched to grab his. "Weston… What did you do?"

He shrugged, a hard jerk of his shoulders. "He drove off without a word and I chased him."

"You chased him."

He nodded. "I chased him. But he didn't stop."

I slumped back in my chair. "God. I'm so sorry."

"Yeah, well…"

My heart ached as pieces of Weston Turner clicked into place for me. Not an asshole, but an abandoned, bewildered kid, grown into a man, chasing that car, always.

"It must've been so hard for you, not knowing why he left," I said.

"*Why* doesn't bother me," Weston said. "The *why* is he's weak, cowardly, a pathetic excuse for a man. Plus, a million other insults I've called him over the years. *Why* is easy." He flicked the edge of his empty plate. "*What now* is the bitch to accept."

BRING DOWN the Stars

"What do you mean?"

Weston watched me for a long moment.

"He left my mom with the mortgage and only a haircutting job to pay it. He left her with three kids to support. *What now?* It was screaming at us from inside our empty house. And that question stretches over the years: *What now?*"

I leaned forward, silent, listening as Weston spoke more words at one time than I'd ever heard him speak. His voice was low, gravelly, and his accent grew thicker, as he drifted away from me and the bakery, and deeper into the thoughts and memories of his childhood.

"Who do I talk to if I have a crush on a girl?" he said. "Who teaches me how to shave? Or to drive? Ma is crying her eyes out every night, and the crying becomes drinking too many beers, so what can I do? My sisters drop out of school to get jobs and have shitty relationships with shitty guys because they've never seen it any other way. A cycle for them, but for me, it was like a pendulum. My childhood swung between *What now?* and *What did I do wrong?*"

His long fingers toyed with his pen, doodling hashmarks, tallies on a wall.

"You didn't do anything wrong," I said, my throat thick. "You were a little boy. It wasn't your fault."

Weston glanced up, his eyes soft. "Sometimes that's harder to accept than money." He dropped the pen and pressed the knuckles of one hand into the palm of the other, cracking them. "Anyway, that's my sob story. We all have one."

Mine was a fairytale in comparison. I tried to imagine my dad leaving Mom, Travis and me. Without a word or warning. I'd blame myself, too. I'd seek protection. Build thick walls and insulate them against feeling that kind of pain ever again. A parent's promise is unconditional love, and Weston's father broke it.

No wonder he's angry, I thought. *No wonder he's walled off, holding himself back.* The old saying filtered into my thoughts, *We accept the love we think we deserve.* Sadness clenched my heart because for Weston, it seemed that meant none at all.

"Whatever," he said, watching me. "I didn't mean to dump all that on you."

"I asked you to."

Weston watched me again, the blue-green of his eyes like sea glass under the café lights.

"We all have our shit. Connor's life isn't any easier because he's got money or both his parents. He's got double the pressure bearing down on him. I have the responsibility to my mother and sisters."

"Taking on that responsibility makes you the opposite of an asshole."

"I know," he said. "But…"

"But what?"

"Nothing. It is what it is. I'm pissed at my dad and I don't know how not to be."

I reached across the table to touch his hand, because I had nothing to say or offer but my presence.

His gaze held mine, the blue-green warm and deep, then it dropped to our hands on the table. His closed around mine, his long fingers folding under my palm, his thumb sliding against my skin. Just as it had done against my cheek in my dream…

My heart began to pound, and I swallowed hard.

"Weston…"

The wind whistled hard against the bakery windows just then. A newspaper slapped hard against the glass, then swirled away in the cold eddies of encroaching winter. Weston stiffened and withdrew his hand.

"It's cold out," he said. "How are you getting home?"

"Connor was supposed to meet me." I checked my wristwatch. "Five minutes ago. We're going to grab something to eat. You want to come with us?"

"No."

I bit my lip, not wanting to leave him alone. I wanted to hold his hand again, or put my arms around him and give him a hug. He was a grown man, but my mind kept picturing a little blond boy, standing on an empty street and watching his father drive away.

I want to keep touching him.

The thought was both completely wrong and felt completely right. I fought for something neutral to say.

"You sure? I heard your car broke down."

"It did," he said. "But Connor and a buddy of his took it to the garage and had it fixed while I was in class last Monday."

Warmth spread through my chest, feeling like relief. "That's a classic Connor thing to do," I said. "He has a generous heart."

BRING DOWN the Stars

Weston nodded and abruptly began packing up his things. "Next week, when you meet his parents, it couldn't hurt to tell them that."

"I will."

"Speak of the devil." Weston tilted his head toward the door.

With a blast of chilly wind, Connor came into the bakery, eyes scanning the tables. His smile widened when he found me, then faltered to see Weston.

"Hey," Connor said. "How's it going?"

I got up and put my arms around his neck. "We were just talking about you."

"Oh yeah?" He kissed me briefly, his gaze over my head.

Weston got to his feet. "I was just leaving."

"We're heading out to get something at Boko 6," Connor said. "You hungry?"

"Nah, I'm good." Weston shouldered his bag. "See you at home."

"Bye, Weston," I said.

"Yep."

He pushed out the door. Connor watched him go, brows furrowed. I buried my hand that had been holding Weston's in Connor's hair.

"Everything okay?" I asked, feeling like a liar. A fraud. A *cheater.*

I was only comforting Weston. That's all.

Connor blinked and then looked down at me. "I guess. I'm nervous about Thanksgiving, actually. Distracted."

"Don't be," I said. "I'm really looking forward to it."

"Then I changed my mind." His smile returned and his arms around me tightened as he kissed me deeply. "Everything's great."

It is, I thought as we headed out into the cold November wind, Connor's strong arm around me, keeping me warm. I watched Weston walk to his car a block ahead and climb in alone.

Isn't it?

175

CHAPTER Twenty-Two

Weston

Wednesday evening, we drove to Boston in Connor's Hellcat, four days' worth of luggage for three people crammed in the trunk. Autumn rode shotgun. I sat in the back with earbuds in, my music cranked up so I wouldn't have to listen to their small talk. The sight of their twined hands on the console was unavoidable.

Connor was a wreck. Autumn did her best to comfort him, but I had to wonder if she regretted coming, instead of spending Thanksgiving with her own father.

We arrived at the Drake residence off of Dartmouth Street. Connor parked at the curb and peered up at the huge row house.

"I feel like I'm about to stand trial," he said. "Exhibit A," he added, with a nod at the silver Jaguar parked in front of us. "Jefferson is here."

Autumn slipped her hand across his shoulders and into his hair. "I hate that this is so hard for you."

Connor forced a smile. "Nah, I need to chill. My parents will love you."

Autumn didn't say anything, but I could almost read her thoughts in the downward curve of her lips.

It's not me they need to love.

BRING DOWN the Stars

Connor punched in the security code on a panel at the front door and opened it.

"Abandon all hope, ye who enter here," he said.

The house hummed with talk and laughter. The scent of cooking hung in the air—baking bread, roasting meat, vegetables simmering in thick sauces.

"Wow, this is beautiful," Autumn said. Her neck craned from the ruffled collar of her simple blue dress. As she turned this way and that to gaze up at the high-vaulted ceiling with its crystal chandelier, the tendrils falling from her loose bun danced around her porcelain face. She started fidgeting with her bag on her shoulder. "Now I just got nervous."

Connor's mother emerged from the sitting room then. "Hello, my darlings."

Senator Victoria Drake wore an elegant, pale beige pantsuit with a string of pearls at her throat. Her hair was down instead of the severe coil she wore in D.C. She radiated refined elegance with an underlying mom warmth, but her eyes were sharp. A woman who wrote laws for a living, for Massachusetts and the Drake household.

"Hi, Mom," Connor said.

Victoria embraced him and held his face in her palms a moment, then turned to me.

"Wonderful to see you, Wes," she said. "You look handsome as ever."

"Thanks, Mrs. Drake." I gave her light peck on the cheek and was suffused with perfume, and the chalky smell of her makeup.

"And you must be Autumn." Victoria offered her hand for a brisk shake. "So lovely to meet you."

"Wonderful to meet you too, Mrs. Drake," Autumn said, then bit her lip. "Or…Senator…?"

"Please. Call me Victoria."

I smirked. Mrs. Drake had been asking me to call her by her first name for years, and it was impossible. Connor's mother exuded the aura of a famous person—one step removed from mere flesh and blood like the rest of us. She was far warmer than Mr. Drake, but still intimidating. If Autumn ever felt comfortable enough to call her Victoria, I'd eat my shorts.

"Connor tells me you've petitioned Harvard to create your own major?" Mrs. Drake asked.

177

"I will be," Autumn said. "I'm still putting the project together."

"Connor's older brother, Jefferson, is set to graduate Harvard Business School with Honors this spring."

"I heard," Autumn said, her gaze flickering to Connor for a moment, her smile stiffening. "What an amazing accomplishment."

"We're very proud." Mrs. Drake beckoned us deeper into the house. "Come. Everyone's here except for your mother and sisters, Wes. Miranda called and said they're all driving up tomorrow."

"The Wahlberg show will have to wait," I muttered to Autumn.

She grinned. "Whatta pissah."

I barely contained the laugh that threatened to bust out of me.

God, this girl.

We adjourned to the lavish sitting room of polished mahogany and glass tables. A fire burned in the fireplace. Mr. Drake and Connor's older brother sat with a tall blonde woman dressed impeccably in slacks, and a cashmere sweater. Jefferson's fiancée, I presumed. Perfectly put together, not a hair out of place. A dystopian film director's wet dream of the perfect woman.

I glanced down at Autumn—small and delicate, but holding her own in this intimidating space, a genuine smile on her full lips.

She's fucking perfect.

The Drake men exchanged handshakes and greetings. "Dad, this is my girlfriend, Autumn Caldwell," Connor said.

Alan Drake nodded curtly at Autumn. "A pleasure."

"Thank you for having me, Mr. Drake," Autumn said.

"Hey, Wes," Jefferson called, walking over and shaking my hand with a grip a tad stronger than necessary. "Good to see you again. This is my fiancée, Cassandra Malloy."

Through the introductions, Mrs. Drake motioned over a caterer in a white blouse and apron, holding a tray of small dessert tarts. "We've had dinner, but you're just in time for these and please, help yourself to any drink."

"Autumn, can I get you anything?" Connor asked.

"I'm fine," she said.

"Wes?"

"I'm good," I said. Something told me not to leave Autumn's side as Jefferson indicated she should sit with him and Cassandra.

I clapped Connor's shoulder as he headed to a glass table

BRING DOWN the Stars

covered in bottles of expensive liquor. Autumn sank into one of the high-backed chairs by the fireplace and I leaned on its arm. Casual on the outside, but holding a machine gun on the inside.

The senator left the room to take a call. Mr. Drake stood at the fireplace, his arm resting on the mantle, grim-faced and quiet, as usual.

"Tell me, Autumn," Cassandra said. "Victoria said you're applying to Harvard for grad school?"

"That's right."

"What's your area of study?"

"Social anthropology," she replied.

"I wasn't aware that Harvard had a *social* anthropology department," Jefferson said, putting one ankle on the other knee.

"It doesn't," Autumn said. "I'm petitioning the Anthropology department with an application that includes a project focused on an area of socially-conscious reform in order to create a special degree for me."

Jefferson pursed his lips as if reluctantly—and condescendingly—impressed. "And what area do you feel is in dire need of reform?"

Autumn folded her hands in her lap as Connor returned with a glass of, at least three fingers of Scotch. I reluctantly relinquished my post to him.

"I'm still working that out," Autumn said. "Several areas I'm leaning toward. Population impact on the environment, the effects of racism at different economic levels, or the rights of the disabled and urban planning."

"So, we have a social justice warrior in our midst." Jefferson surveyed his audience to see if we shared his amusement.

My teeth clenched at the patronizing tone, but loosened as Autumn replied, "Yes, you do." Her voice was cool and steady, her gaze unblinking. "Social change on a large scale usually begins with micro-protests or rebellions. Warriors who take a stand. Rosa Parks sitting at the front of the bus is the most famous example. The Me Too movement, being a modern day parallel."

Cassandra sipped her wine. "Broad stroke, isn't it?"

Jefferson sniffed. "Indeed. One can't compare the Civil Rights Movement to a hashtag on Twitter."

"I think the argument can be made that they have important similarities," Autumn said, her voice stiffening. "In the same way that

Ms. Parks' action was a catalyst for the Civil Rights Movement, Me Too opened the floodgates of women—and men—coming forward to tell their stories of abuse, often in environments where sexual harassment was considered an unchangeable reality. For the first time, we're seeing real consequences for abuse of power and voices are demanding to be heard. My aim is to be one of those voices, and if that makes me a social justice warrior, then so be it."

I rocked back on my heels.

So there, you sanctimonious pricks.

Connor's gaze flickered nervously to his father, who was studying his cocktail. The room quieted, as if waiting for Mr. Drake to weigh in, like a judge with a final verdict.

Mr. Drake pursed his lips, thinking, then said, "Jefferson, whatever happened to your friend Reginald? He was a good man. How come we haven't seen much of him lately?"

Jefferson answered as if the abrupt conversation shift was perfectly natural. Which of course, in the Drake household, it was; if the Lord and Master didn't like a subject, he simply changed it.

I went over to the liquor cabinet and cracked a craft beer from the mini fridge. Autumn slipped away from the group to join me.

"Had a nice chat, did you?" I asked.

"Who doesn't enjoy a good dose of condescension?" She nodded her head at the brandy. "Pour me one of those, will you?"

"Are you sure that's a good idea?" I asked. "Two pear ciders seem to be your limit."

"I need alcohol or I'll never make it through the night."

I popped a craft bottle for her and we clinked glasses.

"I like Mrs. Drake," she said. "Can't get a read on Mr. Drake yet."

I nodded at Jefferson and Cassandra sitting primly at Mr. Drake's feet. "What do you think of the Commander and Serena Joy?"

Autumn sputtered over the rim of her bottle as she was taking a sip. "Oh my God, Weston. You're terrible." After a moment, she leaned into me to whisper, "Their Handmaid must be waiting in the car."

I grinned behind my beer. "Poor Ofjefferson. I hope they cracked a window."

She let out a loud laugh, then pressed her lips together. "We're going to hell."

BRING DOWN the Stars

"I know," I said. "But they're so creepily perfect for each other. I wonder if they met on Tinder? 'Hi, I'm Cassandra, and my hobbies include sitting on the porch at sunset with a glass of Chablis and making jewelry from the bones of small animals.'"

Autumn nudged my arm, her face straining to hold back her laughter. "Weston, shh."

"He enjoys fishing, boating, and keeping a journal of the size and frequency of his dumps."

She shook her head, unable to speak.

"Just think of the beautiful children their nanny is going to raise."

Autumn buried her forehead against my shoulder, her shoulders shaking. I fought the impulse to put my arm around her.

"Time out," she said when she caught her breath. She handed me her beer bottle and wiped her eyes on a cocktail napkin. "Thank you, I needed that."

"Any time."

Autumn's hazel eyes were still shining and liquid from laugh-crying when Connor extricated himself from his family and joined us. Autumn slipped her arms around his waist.

"How are you holding up?" she asked softly. "You look tired."

"I'm great," Connor, holding her close. "*You* were great. Wasn't she great? I love how you stood up for yourself like that. I think my dad was impressed. Jefferson and Cassandra can be a little stiff."

"A little," I muttered.

"Your dad didn't seem impressed," Autumn said, her voice low. "He hardly looked my way."

"How can they not love you?" Connor said, the volume rising in his voice. The scotch had loosened him up.

Victoria Drake joined us. "I've had Autumn's things taken up to your room, Connor. Wes, the guestroom is made up for you."

"Thanks, Mrs. Drake."

She frowned at me. "You were more than welcome to bring a guest, Wes. I didn't even think to ask if you were seeing someone…?"

"No worries." I stuck my hands in my pockets, feeling Autumn's eyes on me. "Nobody worthy of your company."

Mrs. Drake made a face and swatted my arm. "Aren't you a charmer? Good night, then. Breakfast at nine tomorrow, dinner at

181

one."

I watched Connor and Autumn go upstairs together, then I slipped into my own room on the first floor.

Lying in bed, I stared at the ceiling. Above me, Connor was probably wrapped in Autumn's arms, falling asleep to the soft cadence of her breath against his chest. Or having sex with her quietly…

Or fucking her brains out.

"You've no one to blame but yourself," I muttered to the dark, and wrapped myself in cold sheets and silence.

Around one o'clock the next afternoon, the subdued Drake household was bombarded by my mother.

"This must be Connor's girl," Miranda said in the foyer, pulling Autumn into a hug, then holding her at arm's length. "My gosh, she's an angel. Look at this face."

"Okay, Ma," I said, my cheeks burning.

"Is it not true? She's an angel."

"Thank you, Mrs. Turner," Autumn said. Her smile was a hundred times more relaxed than it was with the Drakes. "It's a pleasure to meet you."

Ma shook her head. "An angel." She turned to me. "Why can't you find yourself a girl like this?" She patted Autumn's cheek. "Beautiful. I hope Connor is treating you right."

"I do my best," Connor said, his gaze flicking to me and back.

It's a group effort.

"This is Paul Winfield," Ma said. "He treats me like gold, in case you were curious."

"I do my best," Paul said with a wink. "A pleasure, Autumn."

"Where are Kim and Felicia?" I asked.

Ma crossed herself. "Don't get me started on those two. *Suddenly*, we had other engagements. *Suddenly*, our social calendars are full and we can't be bothered to tell our own mother." She turned to Mrs. Drake who joined us in the foyer. "I'm so sorry, Victoria. Those girls do their own thing. Come and go. I have no say. I don't know where they are from one minute to the next. It's a travesty."

"They're grown women, free to make their own decisions,"

BRING DOWN the Stars

Victoria said placidly. "I'm glad you're here though." She and my mother kissed cheeks. "And you must be Paul."

Paul offered his hand. "Thank—"

"Don't be shy, now," Ma said. "Paul Winfield, this is Victoria Drake. She and Alan are like a second set of parents to my Wes. I don't know what I would've done without them when he was a wild boy on the streets, getting into fights every other minute."

I looked upward, as if patience could rain down on me from the ceiling.

"Wes has been the best friend Connor could hope for," Mrs. Drake said. "We're so happy to have you both as part of this family."

"Here I go," Ma said, wiping her eyes with a hanky Paul had at the ready. "All of five minutes and I'm already crying with gratitude. Paul, didn't I tell you she was a gem?"

"I believe dinner is almost ready," Mrs. Drake said, just as one of the cooks appeared in the hall and motioned to her. "I stand corrected. Dinner *is* ready."

We gathered around the Drakes' immense table in the formal dining room where the two place settings for Felicia and Kimberly were surreptitiously ghosted away. Mr. and Mrs. Drake sat at the heads of the table. Autumn and Connor on one side, with my mother and Paul. Jefferson, Cassandra and me, sat on the other. Mrs. Drake had us all hold hands while Mr. Drake offered up the Thanksgiving blessing.

"That was lovely, dear," Mrs. Drake said when he finished. "Now please, everyone, enjoy."

"Wait, wait, wait," Ma said.

My stomach clenched.

"I think we all should go around the table and say something we're thankful for. Okay, I'll go first. No, no, I changed my mind. I want to go last. Mine's a big one. Wes, baby, why don't you go first?"

I inhaled and let out a slow breath, careful to keep my eyes away from Connor who was going to do his best to make me crack. My gaze landed on Autumn.

I'm thankful for that smile of hers,
Even when it's not meant for me.

I coughed. "I'm grateful that we're all here together, and thanks to Mr. and Mrs. Drake for having us."

Eloquence, thy name is Wes Turner.

Ma sniffed. "You can't do better than that? All those beautiful words you wr—"

"Hey, Connor, how about you go next?" I said. Loudly.

"Yes, yeah, sure," Connor said, shifting in his chair. He turned to Autumn and took her hand.

"I'm grateful for being with family, and that this amazing woman is by my side. Thank you for being here with me."

He leaned and kissed her softly.

"I'm thankful to be here with you too. And all of you." Autumn's gaze swept up the rest of us before finding him again. "I'm thankful you didn't give up when I kept saying I was too busy or too heartbroken. I'm grateful for your sense of humor when I need to laugh, and for your poetry that makes me cry."

"Poetry?" Ma said. "Since when do you write poetry, Connor baby?"

My hands tightened into fists under the table.

"It's just something I do on the side," Connor said.

Mr. and Mrs. Drake shared a look I couldn't read.

"That's what a liberal arts college will do to a man," Jefferson said with a wink. "Do you still play baseball or is it too rough a sport for you now?"

"Connor happens to write beautiful poetry," Autumn said, her voice hard, her back straight. "I think a lot of issues in this country would be solved if men felt free enough to express themselves, instead of being forced to suppress their emotions under the guise of masculine prowess or strength."

"Here, here," Paul said, raising his wine glass.

Autumn touched Connor's cheeks with the backs of her fingers. "Don't ever stop writing me poems."

"I won't," he said, and coughed, his gaze darting everywhere but at me.

Ma blew out her cheeks. "Will wonders never cease?" she said with a shrug. She leaned over the table toward Jefferson. "What are you thankful for, honey, besides your gorgeous fiancée?"

Jefferson's frown vanished. "I'm proud and grateful this wonderful woman has agreed to be my wife. And I'm also truly grateful to Mom and Dad for releasing my trust at the end of this year, so that she and I can start our life together. I look forward to being a part of your business, Dad. Not only to carry on the family name, but ensure it endures for generations to come."

BRING DOWN the Stars

Mr. Drake raised his glass. "Your mother and I share the same proud gratitude for your accomplishments and commitment to this family.

Connor drew in a breath and let it out slowly and shot me a hopeful look that I read instantly. If his parents were releasing Jefferson's trust upon graduation, they'd likely do the same for Connor. I didn't share the same hope.

"Okay, okay, my turn, my turn," Ma said. "I am just so, so thankful we're all here today. For Connor, who is like a son to me. For Victoria and Alan, who took care of my family over the years. But no words can describe how grateful I am for your latest act of generosity."

My head whipped up. I turned questioning eyes at Connor—*what the hell?*—but he only shook his head—*I have no fucking idea.*

"What are you talking about, Ma?" I asked.

"Yes, what do you mean?" Paul asked, frowning in confusion.

"I'm talking about home. Victoria and Alan have rescued me from a lifetime of worry."

"Ma," I said, a cold pit of unease settling in my gut.

"They bought me *a house,*" she cried. "Isn't that something? That cute little number on Union Street?" she said to Paul. "Victoria tells me to take a look, tell me what you think. The next week—this was last Tuesday now—she's handing me the keys. Can you believe it? Can you believe it, Wes?"

"No," I said slowly. "No, I can't."

Ma dabbed her eyes and Paul put his arm around her stiffly. His eyes met mine and his frown deepened.

He doesn't approve. The thought was comforting at first until bitterness drowned it. *Yippee fuckin' do, it's not his business either.*

"It was a good investment," Mr. Drake said. "And if it helps you at the same time, then so be it."

"It was an investment in our gratitude to you," Mrs. Drake said. "Especially to Wes, for being such a good influence on Connor."

"Jesus," Connor muttered.

Autumn's gaze went between him and me, her expression a study in confusion.

Mrs. Drake held up her fork. "Now, please, let's eat before this feast grows cold."

I pushed food around with my fork, humiliation coursing

through my veins instead of blood. I knew Union Street. It wasn't exactly Park Avenue. The cost of a house in that neighborhood was pocket change to the Drakes, but monumental to my mother.

The weight of everything I owed this family tripled. My mother's final burden lifted off her shoulders and placed onto mine. I hated how insignificant I'd become. Hated my father for putting me in this position in the first place.

After the feast, I slipped out to the backyard. I didn't bother with a jacket or coat—I literally needed to cool off. My breath plumed in the November cold as I paced. It was fucking ridiculous to be pissed at the Drakes for helping my mother, yet it felt completely correct.

Finally, I sat on the stone steps, my hands over my knees, my head hung down. Caught between my pride and my mother's happiness.

One of the French doors opened behind me, and then Autumn sat down, her sweater wrapped tight around her.

"You okay?"

"Sure," I said. "Why wouldn't I be? The Drakes just bought my mother a fucking house."

"I know. I get it."

I tossed a pebble from the steps into the grass. "I feel like I've been publicly castrated."

She laughed softly and nudged my shoulder with hers. "Paul didn't seem to like it much either. He's cool. I get a good feeling from him."

"You do?"

She frowned at me. "You don't?"

I shrugged. "Most guys she hangs around are leeches."

"Not him," Autumn said. "He's protective. I like them together."

"I guess. I wish she didn't make such an embarrassment of herself over the whole damn thing."

"She's just being herself. I like her, too. She's genuine. And I like Mrs. Drake for liking your mom almost more than anything else."

Thank you for saying that. Thank you for fucking understanding when it feels like I'm insane. Thank you for being here with me in this moment, in the moonlit cold, with your cheeks pink and your mouth parted. If only I could kiss you, I would...

"Weston?"

BRING DOWN the Stars

I blinked. "Sorry, what?"

"I said, try to think about how less stressed your mom will be. After you graduate, you'll become a Wall Street Vulture and buy her a bigger house." She grinned. "Or a honeymoon in Tahiti for her and Paul."

A silence grew warm and soft between us, even in the cold crisp air of falling night. Autumn stared straight ahead over the vast expanse of the Drakes' backyard. A coppery red tendril danced across the white porcelain of her cheek. Her hazel eyes full of thoughts of the world and the people in it.

She's too sweet for my bitterness. Too kind for my mean streak.

Voices rose in anger from inside. Autumn and I exchanged glances and scrambled off the steps, into the small sitting room off the kitchen where Connor argued with his parents.

"… She's a very sweet girl," Mr. Drake was saying. "But you really see something happening long-term with her?"

Autumn froze, clutching my arm.

"So, she's not good enough for you either?" Connor said.

"You don't want to hear this," I said in a low voice and tried to steer Autumn away. She shrugged out of my grasp and stood rooted to the spot.

"It's not a matter of good enough," Mr. Drake said. "It's a matter of your future."

"I'm twenty-two years old," Connor spat back. "I have to figure out my entire future right now? Well, okay, great. I know what I want. I don't want to work for you, Dad. I don't want a life in politics, Mom. Why are you punishing me for wanting something different?"

"No one is punishing you," Mrs. Drake said. "We're preventing you from making a huge mistake."

"You have not demonstrated responsibility enough to open your own business," Mr. Drake said. "Using your grandparents' money to open a sports bar does not, in our minds, constitute a responsible business decision with an eye toward the future."

"It's not your money."

"It's not yours either and it won't be if you continue on this vein. You don't see Wes throwing his future away by pursuing something trivial."

Autumn's grip tightened on the sleeve of my shirt.

"Wes has been working his ass off for years to make something of himself," Mr. Drake said. "Without his wherewithal, I doubt you'd have been accepted into college in the first place, though a liberal arts college seems to be turning your brain to mush. Poetry? I hope your girlfriend isn't filling your head with hippie-dippy nonsense."

"At least she understands what I'm trying to do. To create a haven—"

"A haven for drunks? What a prestigious use of the Drake name."

"I'm not trying to *use* anything. It's what I want to do. Why can't you get that?"

"It's lazy and irresponsible."

"Oh, so you need a demonstration of my responsibility," Connor said.

"Before we summarily hand you six-million-dollars? I don't think it's an unreasonable request."

"No, God knows you're nothing if not *reasonable*."

"Where are you going?"

"Out. To demonstrate my responsibility."

A few moments of silence and the front door slammed shut so loudly, I felt it in my chest where my heart was already pounding.

CHAPTER Twenty-Three

Weston

Autumn stared at me a moment, thoughts whirling behind her eyes, then she tore through the house, and out the front door. I followed her down the walkway, just as Connor's Hellcat screeched away. Autumn whipped her phone from her pocket and called him, but let her arm drop a minute later.

"Not answering. Should we be worried? I'm worried."

"He has a ton of friends in the city," I said. "He's probably gone to crash with one of them."

"Are you sure?"

I started to tell her yes, but the truth popped out instead. "I've never seen him like this."

"I don't understand what happened," she said, sitting on the front porch swing, already shivering as the night descended. "What money is he talking about?"

"Connor's grandparents left him and Jefferson a twelve-million-dollar trust. Six for each. Their will stated the money was payable upon evidence of their maturity and responsibility. Connor always assumed that meant graduating from college, but apparently his parents have other ideas."

"Why doesn't Connor just break free?" Autumn asked. "Take

out a loan on his own so he doesn't have to be under their thumb?"

"Six-million is a lot of money to walk away from," I said, sitting on the other side of the bench. "But more than that, he wants to be treated with the same respect as his brother. Hell, he just wants to be loved because he's their kid."

"I had no idea it was this bad." Autumn pulled out her phone and texted Connor. We waited a few minutes then she shook her head. "No answer."

Where are you? I sent from my phone.

Nothing.

Where are you, man?

For the first time ever, I didn't know what he was thinking or where his head was at. And it scared me more than I could admit.

The next morning there was still no sign of Connor. The Drakes, Ma, and Paul were gathered around the immense spread of breakfast food that could have served twenty. Jefferson and Cassandra were out for a walk, unconcerned by this family drama.

Autumn's hair was a mess and her eyes ringed by shadows. Mrs. Drake didn't look much better.

"He's a grown man, Victoria," Mr. Drake said over his coffee cup. "He's probably staying with one of his friends. Right, Wes?"

For Mrs. Drake's sake, I nodded. "That's my guess."

"He'll be fine," Ma said, her plate piled high with cinnamon buns, eggs, and bacon. "God knows, if I sent out a search party every time this one" —she pointed her fork at me— "got a wild hair up his ass, I probably woulda wound up married to the police chief."

She laughed. No one else did.

The front door opened and slammed shut. Footsteps stomped through the hall and Connor strode into the kitchen, unshaven and still wearing yesterday's clothes. He slammed a paper palm down onto the table.

"There, Dad," he said. "You want responsible. Here's responsible."

No one moved as Connor went to the fridge for some orange juice. Autumn tried to meet his eye, and failed.

BRING DOWN the Stars

Mr. Drake reached across the table to snatch up the paper, scanned it, and then his hands dropped. "You joined the Army Reserves?"

I sucked in a breath as if I'd been punched in the gut.

Holy fucking shit Connor...

Mrs. Drake's hand flew to her throat. "You're serious? The Army?"

"The Reserves?" Ma crowed. "Terrific. I was just telling Wes-"

Paul put a gentle hand on her arm and she fell silent.

"Is there something wrong with that?" Connor asked.

His mother stared, all of her poise and public persona falling away and leaving a scared mother in its wake. "The war in Afghanistan... And now Syria... Haven't you been paying attention to the news? It's all getting worse."

"Then I'll serve," Connor said, his face hard, mouth set in a grim determination I'd never seen before. He drained his glass and set it down, then surveyed the awestruck faces around him. "What? *Serving my country* isn't good enough?"

The senator started to speak, but Mr. Drake cut her off.

"No, it's extremely responsible. A brave and an honorable thing to serve. It's not what I envisioned for you, but the ROTC is there and you could become an officer—"

"I'm not going to be an officer. If I serve, I'll be infantry. On the ground, front lines if I have to."

Mrs. Drake's face paled. "Front lines..."

Connor nodded. "Yep. I'm going to serve my two years, graduate college in the meanwhile, and if I'm called up to defend this country, I'll go."

"Very well," Mr. Drake said. His fingers toyed with the edge of the paperwork Connor had dropped like a bomb onto the table. "Right. Very well."

He pushed back his chair and left the room. Mrs. Drake stared after him, her mouth hung open. Slowly, her gaze went to Connor.

"Very well," he repeated. He grabbed a slice of bacon and went out the door to the backyard. He kicked it shut behind him with his heel. Autumn stared for a second, then quickly followed.

"Excuse me, Miranda," Mrs. Drake said, getting up. "Paul. I need to talk to Wes a moment. Alone."

I pushed back my chair and followed her into the family room.

"Wes," she said, her voice cracking open to reveal the fear beneath. "It's so dangerous. He's not cut out to be a soldier. He's not cut out to…hold a gun. To fight…" She shook her head, her eyes wide in disbelief. "I don't understand. Where did he get this idea?"

"From me," I said over a hard rock in my throat. "He got it from me. I was working out how to pay for my last year of college. I was thinking about joining the Reserves."

She clutched my arms. "Wes…"

"I'll sign up. I'll go with him. We'll do it together, like we do everything together."

"You will?" Hope was drowning in the tears of her eyes.

How could I not?

"I will. It'll be fine."

"You can watch over him? He doesn't have a head for that kind of life." She pressed her lips together. "God, is it too late? Can we go back to the recruiting office and tell them—?"

"It's going to be okay," I said. "One weekend a month."

"But the war…"

"It's going to be okay," I said again.

I had nothing else to offer her. I couldn't predict the future, nor could I tell her I was just as fucking scared for Connor as she was. The idea of my happy-go-lucky friend taking up arms, never mind taking aim at another human being, made me sick to my stomach.

"It's not going to come to that," I said out loud. "It's going to be okay."

Victoria rested her head against my chest. I held her awkwardly a moment, then she pulled away to compose herself.

"Thank you, Wes. I'm sorry, I had a moment of… It's a mother's greatest fear."

"I know."

She looked up at me. "We take care of each other. My family and yours."

"Yeah," I said. "We do."

"You'll take care of him, Wes. Won't you?"

"I'll do my best."

She dabbed beneath her eyes with the heels of her hand, then straightened her skirt. "I'll just go see about packing some leftovers for your mother."

I joined Autumn and Connor outside. Connor sat on the back

porch steps. Autumn stood a little ways away in the grass, her back to us.

"Is Mom freaking out?" Connor asked. His earlier bravado was gone now. His voice was dull and drained out.

"A little," I said, my eyes on Autumn. "I told her I'd do it with you."

Autumn whipped around. "You'll *what*?"

Connor shook his head. "No. You don't have to—"

"I put the damn idea in your head. And I need to pay for my last year at Amherst. I was probably going to sign up anyway. Seemed like my best bet. So, we'll do it together."

Autumn stared at us both, then turned her back again.

"Jesus, Wes." Connor sighed again, blowing his cheeks out. But I knew him. It was relief in that heavy exhale.

He needs me.

"It'll be good, right? It's a good thing to serve our country."

"Of course it is." A small laugh escaped me. "You are one crazy motherfucker. You realize what this means?"

"We're going to Boot Camp," Connor said, and his grin was back.

"Fucking Boot Camp," I said. "It's going to suck so hard for you."

"Me? I'm going to keep track how many times the drill instructor tells you to drop and give him fifty to get that smirk off your face."

Autumn turned, her arms crossed tightly though I didn't think it was against the cold. She started for the house.

Connor reached for her hand. "Hey," he said. "Hey…"

She kept out of his reach. "I'm sorry I wasn't a better help to you with your parents," she said, her voice thick.

He stood, cut off her path, and pulled her into his arms. He tilted her chin up. "You were. You did a good thing for me. No girl's stood up to them like that. It meant a lot to me."

Tears filled her eyes and I averted my gaze.

"I'm scared," she whispered. "For both of you."

He pulled her in close, held her tight and stroked her hair.

"I'd like to go back to Amherst now," she finally said. "I'll take a bus if you want to stay."

"No, we can go. This visit is over with a capital O."

She nodded. "Good. I'll just go pack."

Autumn went back inside, and Connor turned to me.

"I hate that she's scared, but it's too late for me. Not too late for you." His tone was sober now. "What about track?"

I shrugged. "The offers aren't pouring in."

"But you're so fast."

"I'll be the fastest one at Boot Camp."

Connor laughed and then pulled me in for a sudden hug. "I love you," he said. "No bullshit, no fucking around. I do."

I stiffened automatically. A reflex when someone tried to touch me. But Connor was already sunk into my marrow, blood, and bones.

I need him just as much.

I hugged him back hard.

I'd die for him.

I couldn't say it. Couldn't speak the words out loud.

But give me a pen and paper... Or an Army sign-up sheet... And I'll write it down.

The following Monday, I went to the recruiter's office and signed my name on the dotted line.

Wednesday, the United States Consulate in Adana, Turkey, near the Syrian border, was gassed and the Syrian leader boldly took the credit. Eighty-four dead.

A week later, an orphanage in Ankara was bombed.

Three nights after that, I was working at the dining room table on my Object of Devotion poem. It was due in a week, but it wasn't done. I doubted it would ever be done. Connor was watching a football game, which was pre-empted by the president speaking to the nation. He had, with the full cooperation of Congress, officially declared war on the regime in Syria.

Connor craned around to look at me. I half expected the phone to ring that very minute to tell us to pack up for Boot Camp. We'd intended to wait until summer break to finish the school year, but U.S. forces were stretched to the breaking point. Deployment was inevitable.

We signed our names on the line. If they call us, we have to go.

Connor must've had the same thought as we both jumped when his phone rang.

"Hello? Hey, baby. Yeah, we're watching now. No. Autumn, don't cry. Everything's going to be okay."

BRING DOWN the Stars

My pen doodled across the page. *Everything's going to be okay,* I wrote, and then scratched it out.

PART V
January

Chapter Twenty-Four

Weston

Rain water streamed off the brim of Drill Sergeant Denroy's round-brimmed hat. If he were cold under his rain slicker, he didn't show it.

"Who's smirking now, Turner?" he bellowed at me. "You? You still smirking?"

"Sir, no, sir," I breathed between push-ups. The mud squelched between my fingers. The cold water soaked me through, making my jaw shake.

"Are you going to cry now, maggot?"

"Sir, no, sir."

"I heard you were a fast one, is that right?"

"Sir, yes, sir."

My shoulders were screaming, my biceps were on fire. Halfway through the fourth set of fifty push-ups I'd been forced to do today.

Three weeks into Boot Camp, and I still couldn't keep my disdain for the entire operation off my face. Call it Sock Boy Psychology, but the only grown man who had authority over me had given up the job. In the real world, it built me a rep for being an asshole. Here, it got me push-ups. Hundreds of push-ups.

"A braggart, are you, Turner?"

"Sir, no, sir."

"Sounds to me like you are. Three weeks of you walking around here like your shit don't stink."

Thirty-seven, thirty-eight.

"You got a problem with authority?"

"Sir, no, sir."

My face was a grimace as I pushed through the last ten push-ups that made two hundred on the day. So far.

"Don't you fucking lie to me, Turner. I'll ask you one more time and if you don't tell me the truth, you'll clean the latrine with your toothbrush. Do you have a problem with authority?"

"Sir, yes, sir."

Drill Sergeant Denroy bent lower, red-faced, a vein bulging in his neck as he screamed at me.

"Are you fucking kidding me, Turner? You must be some kind of Einstein to disrespect authority and then sign up for the Army. A shit for brains. Are you a shit for brains?"

"Sir, no, sir," I gritted out.

Forty-eight, forty-nine…

"The hell you aren't. Get your ass up."

I jumped to my feet and stood at attention, the cold rain making my standard issue shirt cling to my body. Gooseflesh broke out over my aching arms.

The rest of the company had to stand at attention and watch me do push-ups, instead of going in for dinner. Sarge walked up and down the company line with his hands behind his back, the rain sliding down his slicker in rivulets.

"I learned a few things about Einstein just now. He's not a fan of authority, he enjoys the ever-loving hell out of push-ups, and he's fast runner. Faster than all of you. We can't have that, can we? No, indeed. We got to get the rest of you slugs up to speed. Bravo Company is going to do fifty fifty-yard sprints."

No one grumbled. No one said a word. No one's shoulders even slumped. But I could feel the wave of animosity and exhaustion coming off the company. It was the end of the day, almost chow time and the pouring rain would not relent.

"Sure, you might be saying to yourself, *But Sarge, it's dinner time.* I could give a rat's puckered little asshole what time it is. You got a problem with it, take it up with Einstein. Now, move!"

BRING DOWN the Stars

Sarge had me stand at attention while the fifty men of Bravo Company ran to the fifty-yard mark and back twenty-five times. By the time the last guy staggered back into formation, most were shooting me looks that promised retribution later.

I made it through dinner and Personal Time at eight p.m. without incident, but as I came back from the shower in Bravo's barracks, Sam Bradbury and Isaiah Erickson were leaning casually against my bunk. Connor and a bunch of other guys were playing poker at the rec table in the corner. The rest were reading, sleeping, or writing home.

"Do you *want* to get your ass kicked?" Erickson demanded. "Are you some kind of fucking masochist?"

"I hate running, Turner," Bradbury said. He was a no-nonsense, quiet kind of guy who looked like he worked for the Genius Bar, took a wrong turn to work one day, and somehow ended up in the Army. "I mean, I really fucking hate running," he said. "We do enough of it as it is."

Erickson crossed his thick arms over his chest. "Maybe Sarge won't be able to see your fucking smirking face if I beat it all to hell."

Other guys, smelling blood in the water, gathered around, glowering. I braced myself for an ass kicking. My Southie street fighting instincts coiled in my muscles, feeding off the murderous anger in the hostile eyes all around me. It was a rush. I'd fed off it on the track and missed it. I hadn't realized how badly. If I fought here, I was going to lose, but at least with physical pain you could point to the source and watch it heal.

I got up in Isaiah's face, chest to chest. "You don't scare me, Erickson, but A for effort."

He shoved me back. "Fuck off, Turner. That was your one fucking warning."

"Do I look like I want a warning?"

Connor pushed through the crowd and wedged himself between Isaiah and me. "*Chill...the...fuck...out,*" he said to me. "This is only Week Three, guys. We're all going to be where Wes was today before Basic is over."

"Sarge makes him drop and give him fifty at least three times a day," Erickson said. "Only it's going to be on us when he fucks up from now on."

"I hate push-ups almost as much as I hate running," Bradbury

199

muttered to no one. "Maybe the Army wasn't such a good idea after all."

"It's cool, guys," Connor said. His smile was relaxed and calm, as if we were on a beach in the Bahamas instead of South Carolina in a hurricane, getting our asses handed to us every day. "Wes gets that, right? He has our back."

I nodded. For Connor. I had his back and no one else's.

"Yeah, guys," I muttered. "It's cool."

For a moment, I thought nothing was cool at all, and my ass kicking would go on as scheduled. But out of deference for Connor, the guys disbursed, many of them shooting me dark, warning looks.

Connor shook his head. "Dude."

"I know."

"You gotta stop with *the face*." He reached out to slap my cheek lightly and laughed as I ducked out of his reach. Connor was having the time of his life. He was physically fit enough that the PT didn't kill him. The DI's grilled him but he was hardly ever singled out. And the guys loved him.

In other words, business as usual.

"You want to join us?" he asked, with a nod toward the poker table.

"No, I was going to write to Ma." I glanced at him sideways. "You going to write to Autumn?"

"Oh yeah, I should," Connor said. "I miss her."

"You do?"

He gave me a look. "Of course I do. But I suck at writing, as we've established. You could write something for me. Since you're already writing letters, and all."

Yes, I could. But for me. Not you.

It was wrong and stupid, but I needed to write to Autumn. I needed *her*, any way I could.

"Drop her a line for me," Connor said. "News and weather. Tell her I'm thinking about her and I miss her." He grinned and chucked my arm. "But make it pretty. No harm in that, right?"

"No harm," I muttered.

Connor beamed, chucked my shoulder again, and headed back to the table.

"All right, boys, what'd I miss? You cheating, Mendez?"

I retrieved a pen and notebook from my footlocker and lay on my back on my bunk. Since email and cell phones weren't allowed, we had to resort to pen and paper. Which was how I did all my writing anyway. A flow of thoughts and words into the ink and onto the page felt natural to me. Like breathing.

But this is wrong...

I should've told Connor to write his own letters. The last time I'd spoken to Autumn on the phone, pretending to be Connor, was months ago when she was in Nebraska, and I'd felt like shit for deceiving her. It was wrong and risky, but I missed her too much. The disgust I'd felt was distant compared to the hunger that gnawed at my insides now. I was starving. No matter how hard I tried to resist, the machine of Boot Camp was hollowing me out. Its job was to strip men down, turn them into war drones who could do the job that needed to be done. To kill if necessary.

Staying connected to Autumn was like holding onto a piece of myself. I needed to indulge in her now; gorge myself on my helpless, hopeless feelings for her, and hate myself for it later.

I'm in love with her.

The truth was bold and stark on the blank page of my heart.

I put my pen to paper and began to write.

CHAPTER Twenty-Five

Autumn

Fort Jackson
South Carolina
Feb 19th

Autumn,

    We are seven weeks in and the physical pain of PT is imbedded in our muscle memory. Sarge's insults are the music by which we march. Softness. Warmth. Beauty. They're mirages in the distance, where you are. There is nothing of you here, but what I create in my mind and memory, and that is harder to endure than any physical pain. Not holding you hurts my hands more that having my palms scraped raw on the ropes. Not hearing your voice cuts deeper than any insult. Boot Camp has stripped me down to the bone, where what I feel for you is stark and naked, and the distance between us is longer than the last mile on the last run of the day.

    And it hurts so bad.

"*Auts,*" Ruby said, loudly.

I blinked and looked up from the letter in my hand. "Sorry,

BRING DOWN the Stars

what?"

"I said, let's go to Yancy's. I need to get out of this apartment. Dress up a little. Drink a lot."

She'd broken up with Hayes over the Christmas break, while I was in Nebraska visiting my family.

I glanced at the mound of work on my table, ignored in favor of Connor's latest letter. I'd read it ten times, just like the others. He held nothing back and my eyes—and heart—couldn't keep from drinking the words in, over and over.

"Give me five minutes," I told Ruby, my gaze sliding back to the page.

I feel invincible when I think about you. Bottomless. The more you take of my heart, the more I have to give.

"Good lord, woman, I can see the stars in your eyes from here," Ruby said. "What, is that another letter from Connor?"

"Yes, his tenth."

"Actual snail mail. I can't remember the last time I got a real letter."

"It feels more intimate and personal," I said. "He was so distracted and stressed about going to Boot Camp but now…"

My gaze was drawn back to the words.

These letters are only placeholders until I see you. A game of words, but I know we'll suffer if we play it too long…

"He was probably nervous about Basic Training," Ruby said. "I saw *Full Metal Jacket*. They're being called pansy-asses a hundred times a day and being worked to the bone." Ruby shook her head. "On the plus side, he's going to come back *ripped.*"

I smiled a little and set the letter down. "It's deployment that scares me."

"Try not to worry. They could be sent anywhere. My friend's cousin was just deployed. War's in Syria. They sent him to Japan. And Connor and Wes are staying together. That's something."

"That's Senator Drake pulling strings."

Ruby patted my hand. "It's something."

I nodded but with every one of Connor's beautiful letters, I felt my heart linking tighter to his, which made the thought of deployment—anywhere—harder and harder to take…

Ruby reached for her coat. "Come on, let's get out. I need a stiff one." She winked. "And a strong drink too."

At Yancy's, Ruby ordered a cranberry vodka for herself and a pear cider for me. We set up at a small table near the pool tables and dart boards. Guys were playing at both. None of them were from Connor's circle of friends. "The Night We Met" by Lord Huron played on the sound system.

"Talk to me, Goose," Ruby said. "Distract me from my post-Hayes haze."

"I have too much distraction," I said. "I haven't taken one damn step toward my project. My grades are slipping. And when I'm not worrying about Connor and Wes, I'm worrying about the farm. At Christmas, I made Travis tell me the truth about our finances."

Ruby made a wincing face. "And?"

"We're in the hole for more than thirty grand, and this year's harvest isn't going to be as profitable as last." I rubbed my eyes. "It feels like everything is falling apart. Even you and Hayes broke up."

"It was fun while it lasted," Ruby said. "I never go into anything with expectations, so I don't feel the burn."

"Meanwhile, I did the exact opposite. Everything with Connor happened exactly as I feared—and hoped—it would. The intimacy made me invested, and now I'm *beyond* invested."

Ruby reached across the table to touch my hand. "Are you falling in love with him?"

I shook my head miserably. "I don't know what to think. Or feel. For so long, we were up and down," I said. "For months, it was like he was afraid to be himself around me without a buffer. But on the phone the night Dad was sick, and now when he writes, I get a purer sense of who Connor is. It sounds cheesy but it's like looking through a window he keeps shuttered up tight. Looking into his soul. And after Thanksgiving, I know why he keeps that side of him so guarded. His parents and brother refuse to let him be himself. They stifle him. So he covers it up with jokes and smiles."

Ruby cocked her head. "Is that a yes?"

"I think it might be," I said, tears filling my eyes. "But I'm scared. A lot. Not only because my heart is on the line, but because there's actual danger here. Real, life-threatening risk. The stakes are so much higher. Life-changing."

BRING DOWN the Stars

Or life ending.

I shivered and pulled my hands from my glass.

"And it's worse, because I could lose Weston too."

"Wes?" Ruby wrinkled her nose. "I didn't realize you were close."

"We have good talks. I like him. I can be myself around him."

My truest self.

The thought slipped in like a cat through a cracked door. The same way the memory of that damn kissing dream came to me, sometimes bringing along little details like our hands locked on the bakery table, or our private jokes, or the song 'Ocean Eyes' that seemed as if it were written about him.

Dreams don't mean anything. We're friends. We have history. I can care about him and still love Connor.

The thought felt...wrong somehow. As if it scratched at the truth but wasn't all of it.

"I can't be with Connor and not have Wes in my life, too," I said, shooing the errant thought away. "And I'm scared I could lose them both."

"It's going to be okay," Ruby said. "They'll come back from Boot Camp and you'll have some time with Connor. Enjoy it. See what happens. Take it one day at a time."

I forced a smile. "I should get back and try to get some sleep. Or some work done. Stay if you want."

"We just got here," Ruby said, pouting.

"I know, I'm sorry. I'm not feeling it."

Ruby pursed her lips again. "I see Lisa Dean over there with some people." She inclined her head to a booth in the corner. "I can hang with her, since you're ditching me so cruelly."

I hid my small sigh of relief in my coat collar. "Are you sure you're okay? About Hayes?"

She sighed. "Yeah. Stings a little, but it's not the end of the world."

"Okay. See you at home."

"Are *you* going to be okay?"

"Once I put some real time into my classwork, I will be."

"You party animal," Ruby said. "See you later tonight."

I slipped off the stool and headed out, speed-walking the entire way to our apartment. Inside, I dumped my coat and purse on the floor

205

and went immediately to my desk where Connor's letters lay on top of population growth graphs and political science texts.

My heart cries out to you, from behind walls that are years' deep and stacked tall with old memories that demand I keep quiet. They say I don't deserve to be heard, and that happiness belongs to those more worthy. I'm scared, Autumn, that they're right.

Tears blurred my eyes and I held the page to my heart.

"They're not, love," I whispered. "I hear you."

Chapter Twenty-Six

Weston

The brilliant South Carolina sun shone in a clear blue sky, while a cool breeze made standing at attention bearable. Bravo Company stood on the field in block formation with the other graduating battalions and companies. Now that we'd made it to Basic Training graduation, I hardly felt the heat. Nor the itch of the thick wool and polyester of my blue dress uniform. My expression was empty. No more smirks. I'd pushed them all out and left them on this field.

We'd been trained within an inch of our lives—screamed at, berated, worked to exhaustion, yet the Army hadn't been able to smother Connor's smile. It lived in his eyes as he nudged my arm with the slightest nod of his head toward the stands. Ma, Paul, my sisters, the Drakes, Ruby and Autumn sat in the front row.

After the drill sergeants were honored, the Lt. Colonel gave a welcome speech. Then the band began its march that would parade us in front of the stands. An officer named off the companies and battalions, and their DIs as we filed past the crowd.

"Bravo Company, led by Drill Sergeant John Denroy."

"That's my boy!" Ma cried out among the applause. "Proud of you, baby!"

We were instructed to keep our eyes forward, heads straight

while marching in time, but I let my periphery—guided by Ma's voice—steal a glance at Autumn.

She was on her feet with the rest of our people. Her hair fell over her shoulders in ribbons of red streaked with gold. It was like looking at a beautiful sunrise after ten weeks of Arctic ice and gray.

Before we were released to the field, Sarge addressed us one last time, with respect in his voice this time. He offered his congratulations before informing us our time as Reservists was over before it began.

"Your country needs you," he said. "And I'm proud to say, you're ready."

We were Active Duty now, likely to be deployed straight out of specialty training. In two weeks, we'd fly to Fort Benning, Georgia for that training, then to the Al-Udeid Airbase in Qatar. All further information was classified until arrival.

Which meant combat zone.

"It's all happening so fast," Connor said, his smile slipping as we walked to meet our friends and family.

"We're soldiers now. Soldiers go to war," I said.

I could've wondered at the speed in which our lives had changed direction, if my stomach weren't so heavy with dread. Connor's face was pale, too. The pride he'd built in himself during Basic looked shaken.

I nudged his arm. "One weekend a month, my ass."

He laughed and the tight fear in his eyes loosened.

That's better, I thought. All my life, Connor's happiness was my constant. It gave me hope I could find something like it one day. I'd take his fear like a second rucksack on my shoulders if I had to.

Our people drew nearer to us on the field.

"Here they come," Connor said. "Look at Autumn."

Like I needed the direction. She wore a cream-colored dress with little blue flowers on it. My heart stuttered at her smile and her sun-burnished hair.

"What do I say?" Connor murmured. "I need something special after being separated for so long. Something to sweep her off her feet."

"You ask how it's possible for her to be that beautiful," I said. "Tell her you have to be dreaming, and if you are dreaming, you hope you never wake up."

Connor's heavy hand on my shoulder jolted me. "Exactly what

BRING DOWN the Stars

I was thinking."

He stepped up his pace and Autumn broke into a run. She threw her arms around Connor's neck. He put his mouth to her ear and said what I'd told him to say. She pulled back to look up at him, then kissed him passionately. Deeply. As if the field weren't filled with hundreds of people.

"Oh my God, I missed you. And here you are, and you're perfect," Autumn was saying as I drew near them. Her small hands held his square jaw, eyes devouring his face. "I can't stop looking at you."

"I second that," Ma said to me. "*Your soldier,* they said. Go meet *your soldier.*" She dabbed her eyes and sniffed. "I've never been more proud. My God, have you ever seen a more handsome pair of boys in your life? Though I'm not a fan of the haircuts, to be honest."

Ma's hand ran over the back of my head and I let her. It was the first soft touch I'd felt in ten weeks.

The second was Autumn's hug.

With a little whoop, she flung her arms around my shoulders. I hugged back loosely when really I wanted to grab her hard, lift her off her feet. I took a quick inhale of the apple-cinnamon scent of her hair, when I only wanted to bury my face and hands in it.

"Congratulations," she whispered against my neck. "I'm glad you're back." Her lips brushed my cheek, then she let go of me. Moved back to slip under Connor's arm and let him claim her.

Mrs. Drake hugged Connor and kissed his cheek and Mr. Drake shook his hand, then pulled him in for a hug. Connor's wide eyes met mine over his dad's shoulder and shone with unshed tears. In all the years I'd known the Drakes, Connor's father had never hugged his son. Until today.

Miracles do happen...

"Hey."

I glanced down to see Ruby in front of me. "Hey."

She laughed and rolled her eyes, then gave me a hug that I needed more than I thought.

"You did good," she said and pretended to sock my chin.

"I survived," I said, with an answering smile.

"All right, Ruby, hands off our brother..."

Felicia and Kimberly took their turns giving me a hug. Both of my sisters had Dad's dark hair and brown eyes. Kimberly wore tight jeans, a short-waisted jacket, and bright blue eye shadow. Felicia wore no makeup and a baggy Sox sweatshirt. She was already starting to have the same rundown, old-before-her-years look Ma had.

"Damn, Wes," Kimberly said, stepping back to give me a once-over. "You know what they say about a man in uniform."

Felicia made a face. "Don't be gross. He's our brother."

"He cleans up good, is all."

"Agreed, but maybe don't look at our own flesh and blood like you wanna hit that."

"Maybe fuck yourself."

Mebbe fuck ya-self.

Felicia rolled her eyes and smacked a smoky kiss on my cheek. "She's a perv. You look great, Wes. But I'm with Ma about the haircut."

"Thanks, Leesh," I said. Carefully. Another minute in my sisters' strongly-accented company would pull my own Southie out of my mouth.

Paul came over, hand outstretched. "Congratulations, Wes," he said. "I hope it's not too forward, but I'm proud of you."

I'm proud of you, son.

I shook his hand but let go quickly. "Thanks."

The two families joined up and for a moment, we stood in silence under the afternoon sun, exchanging glances. No one wanting to voice the inevitable question, *What now?*

"Any word on your deployment?" Mr. Drake asked and his wife closed her eyes slowly, then opened them. "When or where?"

"Fort Benning, in two weeks," Connor said. "Then Qatar. From there, we don't know yet."

"To the front? Where the fighting is?" Kimberly asked.

"We don't know yet," I repeated, slowly.

"But we have you both for now," Autumn said. "For two weeks."

It felt like nothing.

Paul put his arm around Ma. "It's a beautiful day, isn't it? Let's enjoy the picnic and having these young men home."

The feeling of dread lodged itself deeper. Not for the combat we might face—I was trained to deal with that. But for the first time, I couldn't see my future. No track, no writing, no job on Wall Street or even a life in the military. After this two weeks' of leave, there was

BRING DOWN the Stars

nothing but ominous blackness.

"Weston?"

I blinked. The group had begun to walk off the field, but Autumn waited for me. A few steps beyond, Connor waited as well.

"Coming, man?" Connor asked.

"Yep."

I caught up to them and we walked together, Connor and I, with Autumn in the middle.

At the family picnic, Sergeant Denroy morphed into a different guy. He took off his Drill Instructor personality and set it aside, like a tool he was finished using until his next company of new recruits. He smiled wide and easily as he congratulated Connor and me in front of our families, as if he hadn't spent the last ten weeks screaming that we were no better than dog shit on the bottom of his shoe.

Autumn's hand looked welded to Connor's, and every time I snuck a glance at her—which was often—she was gazing up at him.

I managed to peel him from our group, and we watched our people eat and drink and talk.

"Listen, Autumn might mention the letters."

"What letters?"

"The ones I wrote to her. I mean, wrote for you. To her."

He shrugged. "Okay."

"I'm just saying, she's probably going to bring them up."

He frowned. "Okay," he said again, drawing the word out. "How many did you write?"

"A few."

"How many is a few? Like, once a week?"

"More or less." I coughed. "Or more."

Connor's eyes widened. "Every day?"

"Not *every* day."

"Well shit, Wes, what did you say? How did you have *so much* to say?"

"Calm down," I said. "I wrote what you told me to write. News and weather. And... sometimes I got in the groove and kept going. I needed the outlet after all that damn PT."

Connor scratched his chin. "What else? Anything in there I'll need for reference?"

Only that her happiness is the ultimate measure of yours. No big deal.

"You care about her, right?"

"Of course I do," he said. "She stood up for me at Thanksgiving. *I* stood up for me at Thanksgiving. And now here we are, made it through fucking *Army Basic Training,* man. My dad *hugged* me. We're going to serve our country and I have a girl like Autumn, waiting for me at home."

He inclined his head to Autumn, who sat at one end of a picnic table, speaking animatedly to Mr. and Mrs. Drake who listened with warmer interest than at Thanksgiving.

"For the first time, my parents are taking me seriously," Connor said. "And goddammit, I've earned it."

"Yeah, you have," I said. "And I've been right there with you to see it, and that's what I wrote about. It's all there, stretched out over a few letters."

A metric shit-ton of letters.

"You're sort of like my interpreter." Connor slugged my shoulder. "And you're the fucking best, Wes. For real."

He pulled me in tight, and I hugged him back.

"Look at the…what do they call 'em? BFFs," Ma called from the other side of the table. "For life."

For life.

Connor rejoined the group, but I hung back to lean on the fence and stare out at the parade grounds.

Autumn joined me a few minutes later. Every muscle in my body tightened at her nearness, fighting the magnetic pull that wanted to touch her again. Hug her again, and kiss her, and that kiss would be my confession. Every word I'd written to her was hanging in the air between us; a fog only I could see. But if I kissed her, the truth of who authored those letters would come pouring out, and she would know it had been me then… that it had been me all along.

Right. And ruin Connor in front of everyone. No dice, Sock Boy.

"It's strange, isn't it?" she asked, her eyes on the grounds.

"What is?"

"This graduation ceremony. We're celebrating that you're

BRING DOWN the Stars

back, and trained enough to go away again." Her hazel eyes were crushed emeralds and gold over chocolate brown. "Two weeks. It's so short."

I opened my mouth to ask her how she was. Or how her father and the farm were doing. But that black hole in my gut sucked all my words away.

Or maybe I'd given them all to her already.

"Feels like everything is slipping away so fast," she said. She glanced up at me. "You didn't have to do this. You did it for him."

"I did it for me too. To pay for college."

Autumn shook her head. "You could've found another way. But you stuck by him."

"He's my best friend."

I'd die for him.

She craned up on her toes and kissed my cheek. Cinnamon and the softness of her lips suffused me. "Most definitely not an asshole, Weston Turner."

No, just a liar and a fraud who loves you.

Two days later, we were back at Amherst. I dropped my bags in our apartment, traded my uniform for running clothes and took off while Connor made a pit stop at Autumn's place. I didn't want to think about how they were celebrating our homecoming, but my imagination helpfully offered scenario after scenario: her dress being torn off, buttons clattering, kisses that were full of moans, and his hands on her body, touching her everywhere…

I ran up Pleasant Drive, toward the Amherst campus, pushing myself faster and faster until—mercifully—the visions of my imagination burnt up. Thanks to Basic, I was in the best shape of my life. Olympic level-speed and fitness. I didn't need a stopwatch to tell me I'd destroy all of my old times in every race, if I had the chance.

But that door was closed. I'd shut and locked it, and handed the key to the United States Army.

Sir Sly's "&Run" played in my earbuds.

Heavy as the setting sun…

The sun sank in a cold, leaden sky as I ran along paths that wound through the green expanses of grass between buildings. Frost bearded the lawns, turning them silver, and my breath puffed in front of me like a locomotive. I sped past students on their way to class, hunched into their coats. I didn't recognize any faces, since I never bothered to make friends. Except for Matt Decker. And Connor. I never needed more.

I count all the numbers between zero and one…

At the Creative Arts Building, I shut off the music and leaned against the wall to catch my breath. I was hardly winded, but my lungs ached with scratchy regret. I'd chosen this path, and now I was so far down it, I couldn't turn back. My throat and chest burned with the realization that the path I'd been on, the one I questioned and sidestepped and denied for years, was where I belonged all along.

I didn't expect Professor Ondiwuje to be around. Maybe he was teaching a class, or maybe he'd taken the semester off for sabbatical. I knocked on his office door anyway.

"Come in."

I took off my knit cap and opened the door.

"Weston Turner," he said, leaning back in his chair, a smile breaking over his face. "Or is it Private Turner, now?"

"Wes is fine," I said. "Though I've been known to answer to 'Einstein,' 'maggot', and 'shit stain.'"

Professor O laughed. "Boot Camp must be exactly as I imagine it."

"The movies make it look easy."

"But you persevered. Please. Have a seat."

"Thank you, sir." I sat stiffly, my cap in my hands.

"When do you ship out?"

"Next week. To Fort Benning. Military Occupational Specialty training."

"What division?"

"11B, Infantrymen. My drill sergeant said they're the backbone of the Army."

The professor nodded. "Infantry bears the heaviest burdens of war."

I smiled faintly, imagining myself on a dust-choked road in unbearable heat, fighting a regime that gassed its own people. But I couldn't see beyond the flight with our unit that would take us to Fort Benning, never mind Qatar.

BRING DOWN the Stars

Professor Ondiwuje folded his hands on his desk. His dreadlocks brushed the collar of his navy blue suit. Like Autumn, he was always dressed impeccably. His brown eyes met mine warmly, eyebrows raised.

"The last I heard from you was news of your enlistment and putting your education on hold," he said.

"Had to. Got called up a little faster than anticipated."

"I'd say so." The professor wore a thin-lipped smile. "You never turned in your last assignment, the Object of Devotion poem. I was looking forward to reading it."

"My circumstances changed, sir."

"Quite drastically," he said. "And I'm not *sir*. I'm not your commanding officer, only a poet. Like you."

"I'm not a poet," I said. "Not anymore."

"That's the worst tragedy I've heard all year. Did you never even start my assignment?"

"I started it and can't stop. I've been writing it since you assigned it. Stanza after stanza, crossing them out, erasing them, starting over, again and again and again. I could write it forever."

"Stop writing it," Professor O said, "and give it to her."

I glanced up sharply. "Her?"

"Or him. The person you're in love with." He pursed his lips and cocked his head. "You think a man can look as miserable as you right now for any other reason besides love?"

"I can't give it to her."

"Why not?"

"She doesn't belong to me."

"Ah." Professor O leaned back, his hands resting on his chest now, fingers interlaced. "Unrequited love. The most painful kind."

Once upon a time, I'd tell him it wasn't any such thing. But today, now, on the brink of shipping off to a future I couldn't see, I was honest. With my idol poet. With myself. Out loud.

"Yeah, I love her," I said. "I don't know how it happened, or why, but I do. Something in me connects to something in her. I've felt it since the day we met."

Professor Ondiwuje smiled like a satisfied cat. "That's beautiful."

"Hardly," I said dryly. "She loves my best friend. Because of me."

The professor raised his eyebrows. "How so?"

The old me would've evaded the question, but I'd already admitted out loud I loved Autumn. Everything after that was easy, so I told him everything.

Professor O leaned back in his chair when I was finished. "I see. You gave your gifts to your best friend. Why?"

"Because I love him," I said. "And I want him to be happy."

"What of your happiness? Does it have any role in this drama? Or are you still sitting in the audience, ready to sneak out the back when it's over?"

"It's easier for him to be happy than me," I said. "I didn't want to subject Autumn to my shit. My anger. My stupid baggage that makes it so that I…"

"Live every life but the one you want."

I scrubbed my face with my hands. "I don't know."

"I do. A writer who chooses an economics major. A runner who ignores his gift. A poet's heart now encased in a warrior's armor."

Professor O hitched forward to lean over his desk, arms folded on the mahogany. "Wes, I'm going to ask you a personal question, okay?"

"Okay."

"You ready?"

I snorted a small laugh. "Ready."

"What happened that made you feel you don't deserve anything good for yourself?"

A car screeching away, my mother's curses turning to wailing cries. And me, running down the street. My legs pumping hard and fast, even though I knew I'd never catch him. Even though he was long gone.

"Good feels out of reach," I murmured. "I've had good before and I lost it."

"So now you only reach for that which doesn't hurt to lose."

This introspection was growing painful, like a knife prying into my guts and heart and mind.

The heart hides itself behind the mind.

"You have one life, Wes," Professor O said into my silence. "What you put in it is entirely up to you. I suggest you put in what *you* want. Especially now."

"It's too late," I said.

BRING DOWN the Stars

"Is it? You're sitting right in front of me, flesh and bone, pumping blood and breathing life. That doesn't look like too late to me."

We stood together, and he offered his hand.

"Be safe. My prayers will be with you."

"Thanks."

"Finish the poem. For your own sake. Put your heart on the page and your signature at the bottom."

He gripped my hand tighter, his eyes holding mine intently.

"Own this love, Wes. It's not just hers. It's yours too."

CHAPTER Twenty-Seven

Autumn

Icy rain had fallen the night before and the Uber driver was cautious on the roads. Too cautious for my liking. I held Connor's hand tight and it was all I could do to keep from pressing it between my legs as I kissed his mouth. Ravenous for all of the words he'd written to me over the last ten weeks, wanting to lick, taste, and consume them into the marrow of my bones.

"Where's Ruby?" Connor said hoarsely, once we were inside my apartment.

"Out," I said, leaning back on the slammed-shut door and pulling him against me. "Indefinitely."

"God, baby, I've never seen you like this."

"Need you so bad," I said, tugging at his shirt, then tearing at it.

Connor's mouth crushed mine. I surrendered to his urgency, letting him tear off my dress. Shocking myself by pushing him to his knees and pulling his head between my legs, needing his mouth there. Letting out a Ruby-esque moan as he brought me to a quick, skillful orgasm.

Connor rose shakily to his feet. He picked me up and carried me down the hall. "Yours?" he said at Ruby's bedroom.

"Next one."

He lay me down on my bed and we went at each other, crazed. No words but *yes,* and *fuck* and *so good.* My hands seized and grabbed at him, now all hard, defined muscle and brutal, blind need.

Finally, his body locked up tight and then imploded, and he buried his face in my neck. He panted, heaving gasps that slowly morphed into laughter as he rolled away, forearm across his face.

"Welcome home, soldier," I said, curling into his side.

"Holy *shit,* that felt good."

"I missed you."

"I missed you, too. I missed *this.* Ten weeks is a long time."

"Was it hell?"

"Nah." Connor chuckled. "Well, that damn four-thirty reveille every day was hell. Talk about torture."

I smiled faintly. Words from one of his letters—that I had memorized—came back to me.

There is nothing of you here…and that is harder to endure than any physical pain.

I let them go. He'd had to endure physical and mental exertion I couldn't fathom. Not every part of his ordeal had to do with me, and yet the longing for him to express himself as he had in those letters was there, on the surface of my heart.

"I hate that you have to leave again," I said.

"Me too. But in a weird way, I'm looking forward to it. To doing something meaningful, I mean."

"You are. You will."

I felt him nod. "For the first time, my parents are treating me with respect. My father…the way he looks at me. It's different now. He hugged me. And it's partially thanks to you. *A lot* thanks to you."

"No, it's all you," I said. "You did this."

"I've never been with a girl like you." He cupped my cheek with his hand. "I've never *felt* this way about a girl either. I never thought something …*real* could be mine."

I pressed my lips, then my cheek into his palm. "God, I love hearing this with your own voice."

I swallowed hard and drew in a slow breath, gathering courage, feeling as if I were there again, at the edge of a cliff, ready to jump even if it meant being dashed on the rocks below. The unknown of that jump scared me, not merely for the fear Connor might betray me, but because he was going to war. The rocks under that cliff were a thousand times more jagged and tearing; a million times more unforgiving. And yet…

"Connor?"

"Yeah, babe."

I jumped.

"I'm falling in love with you."

I felt my heartbeat everywhere; in my breath as I lived in that moment with the silence roaring in my ears. The fear of the unknown was vibrant, but I was there, with him, and it was worth everything.

Connor sat up, gently moving me aside. He stared at me, a strange expression in his face—something between nervousness and exhilaration.

"You are?" he whispered.

Tears sprang to my eyes at his naked hope and happiness. I sat up, letting the sheet fall away, and pressed my lips against his shoulder.

"You know I didn't want a relationship," I said. "I wasn't looking for anything after Mark, but I loved how easy-going you were. How you brought me into your circle. But then you started showing me parts of you no one else sees. Those deeper thoughts of your heart. Your poetry. And God, Connor, those letters."

"The letters," he said, and his fingers tightened in mine.

"I fought so hard to protect myself," I said, "but your words broke through. You showed me your soul. I couldn't help but fall for you. With every letter, I fell deeper and deeper."

"You felt all that from…the letters?"

"I first felt it with that poem you wrote about me. Then when we were talking on the phone, when I was in Nebraska. That night… this layer peeled away to reveal your true self. I could feel it. I could feel the real you over the line and it made me feel safe. Then things moved so quickly after Thanksgiving. I thought we'd lost each other. But then the letters started coming. I was *weak* reading them. All that self-protection I built fell away. You were putting your soul in envelopes and mailing it to me. Every word, I became more and more yours."

"Mine," he said, his voice so small against the big frame of his body.

I ran my fingers along his hair, cut short but soft under my skin. "You're handsome and popular and wealthy. I know you worry people see only those parts of you. But I don't. I promise you, if you were poor or everyone hated you, I wouldn't care. I know your soul, Connor, and that's what I love."

"My soul," Connor said slowly, his emerald eyes searching mine. "You're in love…with my soul?"

"Yes," I said, letting the word out into the air between us, naked and fragile. "I am."

We stared a long, silent moment. Connor looked away then. He ran his hands along his head, tugging at hair that wasn't there. Brows furrowed tight over his eyes and mouth drawn down.

Something's wrong.

I gathered the sheet around me, my stomach twisting into knots. "What's the matter?"

"Nothing," he said, still far away. "It's just…" He shook his head abruptly, and a shadow of his beautiful smile returned. "Nothing. It's fine."

"Fine?"

"No, God no. It's more than *fine*." He gathered me into his arms and held me against his chest. "I'm just…a little overwhelmed by everything. Boot Camp was hell, and we're shipping out in a little more than a week. And now this… It's a lot to process."

I stiffened. "I didn't mean to add more to your stress."

"No, no, you're not *stressing* me. No."

"I thought you felt—"

"It's okay," he said, holding me closer.

I waited for him to speak again but only thick, deep silence. When I craned up to look at him in the dimness, his eyes were heavy and his mouth drawn down.

"Connor, what *is* it?"

"Babe, I'm just tired. I haven't had a full night's sleep in months and don't know what to say that…"

"Yes?"

"That you want to hear."

"I want to hear *you*," I said. "Anything you have to say, I want to hear it."

He nodded. "Let me sleep a little. I'll be better once I've had some sleep. Promise."

"All right," I said slowly, and settled against him. "Of course.

You must be exhausted."

Within minutes he was asleep. I lay awake, trying to calm the turmoil in my heart and evade the nagging thought that I'd made a terrible mistake. All the while, Connor's chest under my cheek rose and fell with the steady cadence of his breath.

He's tired, just like he said. That's all.

I finally dozed, waking again in the gray light of early dawn as Connor slipped out from under me. In the dimness, I watched his silhouette draw on his clothes.

I held perfectly still, hardly daring to breathe.

What is happening?

I needed to ask him. To sit up and turn on the light and ask, but I was too afraid of the answer. Too afraid I'd see those rocks come racing up to meet me, and break me apart again.

Connor bent, kissed me softly on the forehead and left.

CHAPTER Twenty-Eight

Weston

I lined up at the starting gate with the other racers. The red-brown track stretched out before me, divided into perfect white lanes. I glanced at my competition, a sneer and a joke ready on my lips.

But it was Connor smiling at me from the lane to my left. On my right, Autumn was beautiful in the morning light. One by one, Ma, Paul, my sisters, Mr. and Mrs. Drake—all took their places, crouching in their street clothes in their lanes as the announcer told us to take our marks.

Set.

The gun went off, and the runners ran. Except me. I fell to the ground, the strength sapped from my body instantaneously. I tried to press my hands to the turf and push up, but my body was made of lead. I could only crane my head to watch the other runners —everyone I cared about most—run ahead and around the curve until I couldn't see them anymore…

I woke with my body heavy and my breath squeezed out of my chest.

Five a.m. and the apartment was empty and silent. Ten weeks

of getting up at 4:30 had been ingrained in me and sleep wasn't coming back. I thought about going out for my ten-mile morning run, but I'd done so much running in Boot Camp, the ritual didn't mean anything to me anymore. Lots of things, I realized with a dull pang, didn't mean anything to me anymore.

You're letting things go.

"I have to," I said to the ceiling. "I'm fucking shipping out for a year. That's all."

The nightmare clung to me as I sat at the dining table with a cup of coffee and the Object of Devotion poem in all its messy, unfinished glory.

Finish it, Professor Ondiwuje whispered. *For your sake. Put your heart on the page and your signature at the bottom.*

He was right. I had to finish it and put it in a drawer with the rest of my writing. Get it out of my system. Get *her* out of my system. Autumn wasn't mine no matter how I'd pretended throughout Boot Camp. The longer I played this impersonation game, the greater the chance she'd be hurt.

The front door banged open and shut, making my pen stutter across the paper.

Too late.

"Jesus, man," I said. "Scare a guy to death, why don't you?"

Connor tossed his keys on the side table, put his hands on his hips and stared at me. His clothes were rumpled, his jaw shadowed with stubble, and I'd never seen his eyes so hard or dark.

I set the pen down. "What?"

"What?" Connor said with mocking imitation. "Yeah, what? As in, what the *fuck*, Wes?"

"What are you talking about?"

"The letters."

I swallowed. "What about them?"

"Don't play stupid. You know goddamn well what. I told you to write about news and weather, and tell Autumn I missed her."

"I did," I said, my throat dry. "I wrote that and made it pretty. I did exactly what you asked for."

Pull the other leg, Einstein, Sarge barked at me, *it's got bells on it.*

Connor shook his head, lips pressed together.

"Dude, what's wrong?"

"Oh nothing," he said with a harsh smile. "Everything's great. My girlfriend's in love with me."

I crossed my arms over my chest, as if I could contain the sudden pain that clenched it. I expected it. I actively worked to make it happen. Yet the reality hurt more than I'd been prepared for.

Let them be happy. That's all that matters.

"Well, that's good, right?" I said, clearing my throat. "Isn't it what you wanted?"

"Yeah," Connor said, his voice hard, but pain swam in his eyes.

"Then what's the problem?"

"The problem is my soul."

"What?"

"She said she loves my soul. But *my* soul…" he said with biting bitterness, his index finger unfolding right at me, "…is *you*."

I blinked. The two quiet words slapped my face, leaving my lips numb, then wrapped warm arms around me, whispering, *she loves you.*

"Connor…"

"She's in love with the 'words of my heart.' The letters. The poems. The goddamn phone call in Nebraska. That wasn't me, man. That was you." His jaw clenched. "It was always you."

"No," I said, shaking my head. "That's not the only thing she loves. She loves how you make her laugh. How you take care of her—"

"Yeah, I make her laugh," he said. "That must be it. That's why she was in bed with me last night, tears in her eyes, saying she's falling for me because I make her *laugh.*"

He crossed to the kitchen and popped a beer. At five in the morning.

You selfish ass, it was too much. You said too much in those letters and fucked everything up…

"I'm so tired of this shit," Connor said after taking a long pull. "So fucking tired of not being enough."

"You are enough," I said, firming my voice, desperate to fix this. "You have what she needs. Things no one else does."

What I could never give her.

"What's that, money? She doesn't give a shit about money."

"Not just money," I said. "Who you are. You make people feel better just by being in your presence. Everyone loves you. She deserves someone who…"

"Who *what*, Wes? Is rich? And popular? Who doesn't have the nickname, Amherst Asshole?"

"Yes," I said, my voice hard. "Exactly."

"So." Connor slid into the chair opposite me. "How long have you been in love with her?"

"I'm not in—"

Connor reared in his seat and for a moment I thought he was going to throw the beer bottle at my head. "Tell me the fucking truth, Wes. Stop lying to me and yourself."

"They're just words," I said. "Fiction. They're—"

"You're telling me you wrote all those letters and it's all bullshit?"

"Connor, man. Listen—"

"She doesn't love me, Wes," Connor said, his voice thick with pain. "She loves you. Your words. Your *soul*. She said so herself. Rich or poor, popular or not, she doesn't care."

"Sure, she says that now," I said, my voice low. "But she would care. Eventually, she would care a lot. What I am…it would wear her down. She's luminous, and my ugliness and my mean streak would do nothing but dim her…"

My mother's words from years ago, that all men were trash—hammered into me, over and over again—came back, along with my worry that I'd hurt any woman I might someday love.

So I vowed not to love anyone

I shook my head and looked to Connor.

"Something's fucking wrong with me. Broken or missing. Whatever it is, you have it."

"Now you're really talking bullshit."

I loosed a frustrated sigh. "You know, man, you need to give yourself a chance."

Connor's eyes widened. "Me? I need to—?"

"The point is," I said quickly, "I'd suck the happiness out of her while trying to figure my shit out. At the end of the day, love letters are just words on a page. You can't live off them."

"No?"

"No."

Connor leveled a gaze at me. "We fucked with her heart. When she finds out, she's going to hate us both."

"She doesn't need to find out."

"You expect me to just go on being with her, knowing you love her?"

"I don't—"

"Wes, for fuck's sake," he cried through his teeth.

"You said it yourself," I said. "She'll hate us. It'll break her heart. You want to do that to her? For what? So I can fuck up whatever's left?"

Connor turned his beer bottle around and around. "I don't want to hurt her."

"So don't." I leaned over the table. "It's too late to tell her, and that's my fault. I'm sorry I…got carried away. So fucking sorry. But we're shipping out in a few days. Deployed to the goddamn front lines for a year or more. That's scary enough for her. We don't need to add to her pain. I took it too far, but I did it for you. And her. To give her everything I can't give her myself."

The best of both of us.

Connor slumped back in his seat. "I should call her." He shot me a look. "Or you should. I don't know what to say."

"Tell her what you feel."

"My best friend is in love with my girlfriend. How exactly, am I supposed to feel about that?" There was no animosity in his tone, only heavy sadness. "Maybe you could write it down for me."

"Connor, just…" I rubbed my eyes. "Forget me. Forget this conversation. I'll get over it. Her. I have nothing with her. You do. Love her back, man. It's so easy."

He shook his head, a wry twist of his usual smile on his lips.

"You know, for a second there, with her tonight, I was happy. No girl's ever said she was in love with me. I've never said it. I've never felt it. I never thought to take things that far because it's not easy. It's fucking hard work. And work was never my thing. It's your thing. You do the work and I reap the benefits." He clinked his beer bottle to my coffee mug. "And I don't know why you do it." He rose to his feet. "I'm going to bed."

"Connor…"

"It's fine, Wes. I'm not going to tell her. Everything's going to change once we step on that plane, anyway."

"Yeah, it will."

You and I are going to change. Maybe irrevocably.

Connor gave me a little salute with his beer bottle and took it with him to his room.

I slumped down at the table, my head in my hands. A few of my poem's words swam into focus while three words screamed across my mind.

She loves you, she loves you, she loves you.

"She loves me."

If I reached out and took that love, it would blow up three lives. Connor signed up to *go to war* to prove he was worthy of love. Autumn gave him her heart and body. I couldn't see past next week, but I knew the truth of right here and now. I was the one who fucked with their hearts, and if I didn't fix it, I'd lose them both.

CHAPTER Twenty-Nine

Autumn

"Hello? Young lady?"

I blinked and whipped my gaze to the customer at the counter. "I'm sorry, what?"

The woman fumed and shook her pastry bag at me. "I wanted a bear claw. This is not a bear claw."

"Oh, I'm so sorry. I'll fix it."

I took the tongs and a small pastry bag to grab the last bear claw in the case.

Three days. They're shipping out in three days.

The bear claw slipped out of my grasp and hit the ground, where it broke into pieces.

"Well, isn't that fantastic," the customer snapped. "That was the last one, wasn't it?"

"I'm sorry," I said. "I'm sorry, I can't…"

I covered my face with my hands, trying to hold back the rising wave of emotion. It crashed down and I bolted, rushing past Edmond to the back room.

"Ma chère?"

In the back, I sank onto an overturned flour bucket, hunched over and hugged my arms, sucking in deep breaths.

"Philippe, take the counter," I heard Edmond say. Then he was crouched down by my feet.

"Ma fille, qu'est-ce qu'il y a?"

"I'm sorry, Edmond. I can't concentrate. I'm a mess."

"You're no mess. Tell me, why the tears?"

"Connor and Wes are shipping out in a few days, for training, and then to the Middle East."

"I know Wes. Mon homme tranquille. Connor is your love, non?"

I literally didn't know how to answer. Since the morning Connor slipped out of my bedroom, we'd hardly spoken. A few texts here and there, telling me he was preparing for deployment, putting me right back to where I had been before he'd left for Basic Training—in the limbo of not knowing where we stood or how he felt. The love I'd given wasn't lost, but stuffed in his back pocket as he walked out of my bedroom. I had no idea if he carried it with him or had thrown it away.

He's scared too, I thought. *You put your heart on the line, but he's risking his life.*

It was a hollow thought, but all I had.

"Yes, Connor's my boyfriend," I said finally.

"A grave situation," Edmond said. "I fear for him, then. And for my quiet man. And for my thoughtful girl who cares for them both."

Waves of fear and love and pain rose up again, trying to drown me. Edmond de Guiche's kindness was a life buoy. I could easily fall into his comforting embrace, clutch at him, cry my eyes out and ride the storm.

Instead, I sucked in a breath and pressed it all down.

"I'm scared for them, and it made me emotional. That's all."

Edmond frowned under his thick black mustache. "That is all? That is everything."

Phil poked his head in from the front. "Mr. de Guiche? Things are getting rough out here."

"Do you need to take the day?" Edmond asked me.

"No, no, I'm fine." I dabbed my eyes on my apron. "I can do this."

I had to do this. I couldn't afford any missed pay.

Before we headed back out, Edmond stopped me and put his

hands on my shoulders.

"You have a thousand hearts' worth of love to give. A thousand tears may fall when one heart breaks. But never cry for shame." He cupped my chin in his thick hand. "Even love lost was well-spent."

I nodded and smiled, but silently I rejected his comfort. Love lost was only that... lost. I'd learned nothing from my failed relationship with Mark, except that I was gullible enough to keep trying. To keep loving, even if it hurt. Edmond would say that was a strength. From where I sat, on an overturned bucket with tear-streaked cheeks and an aching heart, I only felt lost too.

Edmond went home at three, leaving Phil and me to finish the day and close at five. At quarter of, Weston walked in the door.

My heart pounded. It was impossible not to notice Weston's post-Boot Camp physique. He'd been fit before but now, standing there in jeans, a dark shirt, and black jacket, the changes were tangible. Catlike—graceful and lean, but with a new, dark and dangerous beauty.

"Hey," he said.

His expression stony. As usual. Half-scowling under furrowed brows and all at once, I was *pissed*. Angry at Connor's unpredictable silences. Angry at the stupid wars of the world. Angry at farms that fail and hearts that give out. Angry at the tears that won't stop coming. And angry at Weston for looking fucking beautiful and filling me with a confused desire to either slap the scowl off his face or kiss it off...

"Hi," I said, shrugging the last thought away. "Would you like something?"

"I wanted to talk," he said. "If you're free."

"I'm free. We're about to close. Coffee?"

"Not tonight."

He went to his usual table in the corner. I followed, untying my apron. He waited until I sat before sitting, then folded his hands on the table, long fingers laced. I tried to imagine those hands holding a gun. Weston taking careful aim at another human. Sadness and fear welled to the surface again, wrapped in anger at both he and Connor for putting themselves in danger.

"I wanted to see you," Weston said in a low voice. "Talk to you. It's been a long time."

"You must be busy getting ready for deployment."

He nodded. "Lot of shit for me and Connor to pack up."

"Oh really? Packing?" I asked, my lip curling. "That's a full-time, 24/7 job, is it? Is that why Connor's been so quiet?"

"No," Weston said in a low, heavy voice.

I shook my head and let my teary gaze drift to the table between us. "I feel like I'm on a roller coaster I didn't want to ride in the first place. But once I got on, I took the ride. Up, down. High, low. And now I can't get off."

"I get it."

"Do you?" I snapped. I held up my hand before he could answer. "Never mind. I don't want to talk about him right now."

"Understood. I came here to talk to you. How's your dad? And the farm?"

"Dad's better," I said. "Still weak. I don't know if he'll ever be as strong as he was before. Not after a quadruple bypass. And the farm is suffering."

"Tell me."

"Not much to tell. It's the same farm story since time immemorial. Things are tough, the debts pile up, and a bank pounces."

"How much debt?"

"Not an impossible amount, but it's more than we have." I shot him a look. "And that's all I'm going to say."

"And what about your Harvard application?"

"Non-existent." I gave him a tired smile. "I've been a little distracted."

"I'm sorry," Weston said quietly.

"Why are you sorry?"

He shrugged, cracking his knuckles. "As a friend. I'm sorry you're in pain, Autumn."

My vision swam and I swallowed hard. "I lied. I want to talk about him. How is he?"

"Scared," Weston said. "We're not supposed to admit that, but we are."

"It's no excuse to cut me off," I said.

"No, it's not."

BRING DOWN the Stars

"I swear, Weston. It's like the guy who wrote me from Boot Camp is gone. Vanished."

Weston nodded slowly, fingertips worrying between his brows. And said nothing.

"You were with him," I said. "You know him better than anyone. Why would he write to me like that if he wasn't prepared for how it would affect me?"

"I don't think he was thinking that far ahead," Weston said. "Or how it would affect you. He wasn't thinking about whether they were too much or not. Or what you would expect when he got back. He was thinking about himself. And relief. And getting through the day."

"Why?"

Weston thought for a moment. "Basic was hell. All day long, every day, no thought was our own. We had only orders to follow. No opinions. No feelings allowed. Only pushing our bodies to their limits and beyond. Then classes. Then more PT. Total physical and mental exertion like that wrings you out. You can't cry but some days you want to. At the end of the day, we had one hour of personal time to decompress. We poured ourselves out in that one hour."

"You did too?"

He nodded.

"To who?"

Who do you pour yourself into, Weston?

He shrugged. "Different people."

I held his gaze a moment, absorbing this. "But Boot Camp is over and now everything's back to normal?"

"Nothing is normal anymore."

This time, when the tears came, I let them fall.

"And it won't be again, will it? I'm scared about what you two will see or have to do. I'm scared it'll erase Connor's smile. I'm scared of what will happen to me, waiting here for you to come back. But you *will* come back, Weston. Both of you. You have to."

It was on me then. Wave after wave. I covered my face with my hands, drowning in it. A scrape of chair legs and Weston was lifting me to my feet, pulling me against his chest. I buried my face in his shirt, grabbed two tight fists of his jacket. He stroked my hair as I both pushed into the fear and clenched my hands to pull it apart.

"I'm sorry, Autumn," he whispered. "I'm so fucking sorry."

In between the ragged sobs, I inhaled the potent scent of him. Just like the morning when I put on his shirt by mistake, it overwhelmed me. Filling up my nose and throat and chest until all at once, my tears were burnt up on a flush of dry heat that swept through my entire body.

I leaned back in the circle of his arms and looked up, falling into his ocean eyes. His hands rose to cup my face, thumbs brushing along my wet cheekbones.

Just like in the dream.

He held me as if I were the most precious thing he'd ever touched with his calloused hands and scarred knuckles. He swallowed hard and his Adam's apple bobbed over the collar of his black shirt. Then he gently let me go.

"Connor's just as scared," he said. "I'm not excusing him, but believe me when I say it's not his fault."

I nodded, and took a deep breath. Wiped my eyes. "I'm done here. Drive me home?"

"Can't," Weston said. "I sold my piece of shit."

"For a loaf of bread?"

He grinned out of the corner of his mouth. "Something like that. How about a walk?"

So we walked home in the falling twilight. I shivered in the late winter's cold and Weston shrugged out of his jacket and hung it over my shoulders. I closed my eyes at the heady scent of him and his residual body heat in the collar and sleeves. Opened them to gaze at him walking beside me, his hands stuffed in his pockets.

He's beautiful. And he's scared.

I linked my arm in his. "To keep you warm," I told him.

His eyes widened and he slowly stopped walking.

"What?" I said.

His silent gaze roamed over my face, my hair, squinting at the sun setting behind me, taking it all in.

"Nothing," he said. "I just… Nothing."

We resumed walking in comfortable silence. I welcomed it this time. I was out of words. I only wanted to walk with my friend whom I loved.

I do. I love Weston. And I'm losing him, too.

"Connor's family is throwing us a goodbye party," Weston said at my front door. "In two days."

BRING DOWN the Stars

I hugged myself in the chill air, holding my emotions in check. "Thanks for letting me know. I'll try to make it to Connor's party. The one that you are inviting me to."

Weston chuckled. "He *will* call and tell you himself."

I smirked. "I'll take your word for it."

"Will you come?"

"When, and if, he invites me," I said. "I'll say yes."

He smiled a little.

"I'll see you then, Autumn."

"Bye, Weston."

He pressed his lips together and jammed his hands in his pockets. Then he turned and strode away.

Inside my place, I dumped my sweater and purse on the floor and went to my desk and the stack of Connor's letters.

The proverbial moth to the flame, I thought, feeling lost. Like I'd lost myself in a man and this strange relationship with Connor. I should have been drawn straight to my neglected work, but I wanted the letters instead.

"Hello to you too," Ruby said from the couch where she was watching an old Steve Martin rom-com. "How was work?"

"Hey," I said, rifling through envelopes. "Fine."

I scanned the latest letter, the one that made my heart ache with its quiet intensity.

Quiet intensity is exactly how I'd describe Weston Turner.

I blinked at the sudden thought. "Ruby?"

"Yeah?"

I bit my lip, and set the letter down. "Nothing. Never mind. I'm going to lie down a bit."

"Feel okay?"

"Just tired." I went into my room and shut the door, then pulled up my phone.

Are you there? I texted.

I'm here, baby.

Tears came again, as if something deep inside me had sprung a leak.

I need to hear your voice.

No answer for a moment, then my phone lit up with Connor's incoming call.

"Hi," I said, sniffing.

"Are you crying?"

"It's all I ever do lately."

A sigh gusted over the line. "I'm so sorry."

"You're sorry. Weston is sorry. What are you both so sorry for?"

"You talked to him?" His voice curled higher over the words.

"He came to visit me at work. Why?"

A beat. "I don't know what he's sorry about. That we're both knuckleheads who joined the Army?"

I sniffed a laugh. "Don't do that. I'm mad at you."

"I know. Fuck, the last thing I want is to hurt you."

"I'm not talking about joining the Army. I'm scared for you, but the hurt is from your silence, Connor." I blinked back tears. "Why would you write to me like you did in Boot Camp and not expect me to…" I bit back the words, *fall in love with you.* "Have strong feelings for you after?"

"I *wasn't* thinking," he said, sounding almost angry. "I wasn't thinking about anything but myself, to be perfectly honest. Writing to you that way was selfish. Really fucking selfish. And stupid."

"Stupid?" I switched the phone to my other ear. "Do you regret writing them?"

"No. I didn't mean…"

A silence, then a sigh.

"Well?" I demanded. "Were you going to tell me about the party? Were you going to tell me *anything*? Because honestly, Connor, it feels you might skip out without talking to me again and blame it on your deployment."

"I wasn't going to skip out," he said, bitterness infusing his voice. "I just… I'm better on paper, apparently."

"You're good in person too, if you'd just let yourself be."

He made a noncommittal sound. "Wes told you about the party on Tuesday?"

"Yes."

"Will you be there? I want you to be there."

"Do you?"

"Why wouldn't I?"

"I'm so confused right now, Connor, I don't know what to think."

"I know." Now his voice turned gruff. "But I'm scared,

Autumn. I'm not going to lie. Boot Camp was fun and games, but now I'm legit freaking out a little."

"Of course, you must be." I sighed and pulled it together. "I'll be there."

"Thank you, babe," he said. "You're too good for me. Too good for…anyone."

"I don't want anyone," I said. "Just you."

"Just me," he repeated, almost pained.

"Connor?"

"Nothing, babe. See you Tuesday."

CHAPTER Thirty

Autumn

The days dissolved away to Tuesday, the day before Connor and Weston were being deployed. Ruby and I drove to Boston for the goodbye party, which was a semi-formal barbeque in the Drakes' enormous backyard.

"I hope we got the dress code right," Ruby said.

"You look gorgeous. As usual."

Ruby wore jeans and an elegant black blouse that crisscrossed in the back. She straightened her hair, so it curled up at her shoulders and highlighted her eyes only with mascara. She didn't need anything else.

"So besides Connor's family, who's going to be there?" Ruby asked.

"Weston's mother and sisters. A few friends from Connor's old baseball team."

"Baseball players?" Ruby grinned at the windshield. "Sounds promising."

"I want to be you when I grow up."

She glanced over at me and patted my hand.

"Try to have fun, okay? I know it's hard, but you'll get to FaceTime or whatever Army-technological-super-classified-top-secret

BRING DOWN the Stars

method of communication they have over there."

"I know. It's just hard."

"You look fantastic. If that counts for anything."

I wore a purple dress that buttoned down the front and flared at the waist. My hair was tied up in a loose bun and I curled the tendrils that fell down around my face.

I forced a smile.

Ruby pulled up to the curb and looked through her window at the Drake house. "What a cozy little family cottage. Brief me, Goose. I didn't talk with the Drakes much at Boot Camp graduation. Anything I should be prepared for?"

"Mr. Drake changes conversation subjects at the drop of a hat. Just go with it. And Mrs. Drake will ask you to call her Victoria and you won't want to."

"Got it. Let's do this."

A housekeeper answered the door and led us through the house to the backyard. Ruby barely looked at the interior décor. She came from money so she wasn't impressed easily. For all her bawdy irreverence, her manners were impeccable. That and her confidence won over Mr. and Mrs. Drake immediately as we chatted for a few minutes in the kitchen.

"Forgive me, I must mingle," Mrs. Drake said. "Such a pleasure seeing you again, Ruby."

"You too, Victoria."

Ruby shot me a look and I rolled my eyes.

A hired barbecue chef manned three grills, each the size of a small car. Two were crammed with hot dogs, hamburgers, steaks and chicken. The third was all vegetarian fare. Soft drinks and water were laid out on one table, practically untouched, as most of the guests congregated near the open bar.

Weston was nowhere to be seen, but I saw his mother and sisters gabbling together and arguing at one of the six umbrella-covered tables. Connor stood with some baseball buddies, a drink in his hand, talking and laughing. He did a double-take when he saw me, and a strange, nervous smile floated over his lips.

"Hey, baby," he said, coming over. He smelled of gin as he bent to kiss my cheek. "I'm so glad you're here."

"Looks like a nice party," I said.

"Excuse me," Ruby said, slipping away, leaving Connor and

239

me to stand in silence like ex-spouses barely on speaking terms.

"Autumn?"

I glanced up sharply. "Yes?"

Talk to me. Please. Tell me something.

"Look, I... I have something for you. Come on."

He took my hand and guided me back into the house. I followed him down hallways and around corners to an office space. Beautiful, floor-to-ceiling shelves in shiny mahogany lined the walls, every one of them packed tight with books.

"Wait, don't tell me," I said. "You're giving me this library? Just like in *Beauty and the Beast?* I accept."

He laughed as he went to the immense desk in the center of the room. "Not quite. Something better, I hope."

He pulled out an envelope from a drawer, then brought it to me and pressed it into my hand.

"What is this?"

"Open it."

The envelope wasn't sealed. I peeked inside to see a check made out to me. My heart took off and my gaze jumped up to his.

"*Thirty-five thousand* dollars? What ...?"

And then I knew. The envelope trembled in my shaking hands. "Weston told you, didn't he? About the farm?"

He nodded. "It's from both of us, in that sense. Because we both...care about you, Autumn."

I shook my head, tears welling. "I never told him how much we needed."

"Is it enough?"

"It's almost exactly right." I pressed the envelope to his chest. "I can't take this."

Connor caught my hand and held it, so the envelope wouldn't fall. "Yes, you can. Your family needs it."

"It's too much. You have this much?"

Connor bit his cheek. "My father helped."

I sagged. "God, Connor. You told him? You told your parents?" I turned away, my face burning. The envelope fell to the lush, carpeted floor.

His arms came around me from behind to turn me to face him. "Hey. It's nothing to them—"

"It's everything to me!" I cried, tearing out of his grip. "But I can't say no, can I? I have to help my family. I'd be a fool to let my pride stop me, but my parents... They have pride too. And if they knew how I got this..."

I sank down in an overstuffed leather settee with wide brass buttons. Connor retrieved the check from the floor and knelt in front of me.

"We're leaving tomorrow morning," he said. "For God-knows how long. Wes told me about your family's situation, and he didn't—*we* didn't want to leave you alone to cope with it. Not when I can help you."

"This was his idea," I said.

Connor shook his head. "He told me you needed it. I made it happen."

"No, I can't. It's too much. My parents would wonder where I got it and I could never tell them. Never. God, my mother would never speak to me again."

"Why not? For helping them? That's all this is, babe. It's help."

"It's too much."

He pressed the envelope into my hand, and curled my fingers around it. I lifted my tear-stained face.

"What's happening between us, Connor? I'm so confused. I feel like you're two different people. You write me these beautiful letters but when I see you, those words aren't there."

And then I froze. A heavy lead weight dropped into my stomach. Followed by another. Two pieces clicking together. My throat went dry and a million thoughts—a thousand words—suddenly swarmed my brain like white-winged moths. I looked at Connor and my mind tried to conjure him sitting at a table, pen to paper, writing and writing and writing. My name at the top of the page.

I couldn't do it. Connor wasn't there.

But Weston...

Weston Turner materialized at the empty desk in my mind's eye, and it was effortless to picture him there, bent over a notebook, his pen scribbling...

No. Stop. Impossible.

Yet the implications swamped me. A deluge of nauseating suspicion.

"What is it?" Connor asked, his tone wary, his hands stiffening on mine.

I held his gaze hard, searching, thoughts racing through my mind.

It can't be. That's a fucked up thing to do to someone. Catfishing? Like that show? Despicable. Weston would never manipulate me like that. And Connor would never do that and then sleep with me. Never toy with my heart. Why would he?

"You wouldn't... lie to me, would you?" I asked, my voice hardly a whisper. "You wouldn't tell me things that aren't true? Not sentiments like those in the letters?"

I slept with you for a poem.

Connor shook his head from side to side, his lips pressed into a thin line.

"They're all true, Autumn," he said. "Every word in those letters is true."

I nodded slowly. Connor's words were his own. They had to be. Plenty of them came out of his mouth. I'd *heard* them myself. The phone call in Nebraska was a perfect example.

I sucked in a steadying breath. "I just don't know what's happening. Everything feels so tangled up."

Connor blew out his cheeks. "I know you. And I don't know what to do about it."

Mrs. Drake walked into the office then. "Oh, I beg your pardon, I hope I'm not interrupting." Discreetly, she kept her eyes on her son while I wiped the tears from my cheeks. "The guests were starting to ask after you, dear. And Reginald has arrived."

"Be right there, Mom," Connor said.

"Need anything?" she asked him, but I could feel it was directed to me.

"We're good."

She went out and closed the door quietly.

"The famous Reginald," I said.

His eyes were still on the door. "These are my last hours with my friends and family. And you."

"I know. Let's go party."

We both got to our feet. He held the envelope out to me and I took it, tucking the check into my purse, which immediately felt a thousand pounds heavier.

"Thank you," I said, as we walked out. "Even if it stings to accept the money, I'm incredibly grateful."

BRING DOWN the Stars

He smiled, a strange melancholy behind his eyes. "It's what I do."

Out in the backyard, Connor held up his glass. "I'm going to get a refill. Can I bring you something?"

I desperately wanted to get drunk—it wouldn't take much—and get this horrible tangle and tightness out of my stomach. But the last thing I needed was to make a fool of myself in front of the Drakes. It was going to be hard enough looking them in the eye as it was.

"Just a water."

He kissed my cheek again. "Be right back."

But as he approached the bar, a crowd of greetings, hugs, and backslapping surrounded him. He was immediately swallowed up and I knew he wouldn't reemerge for a while. I plucked a water bottle from the cooler near the grill and took it to a corner of the yard. Leaning against the trunk of a dogwood tree, I surveyed the party, not feeling part of it and not caring much. Ruby was talking to some people near the grill. Weston was still nowhere to be seen.

Missing in action, I couldn't help thinking. The damn cap on the bottle wouldn't turn and the plastic was digging into my skin.

"Need some help?"

Weston materialized beside me, looking devastating in jeans and a black dress shirt. He took the bottle and twisted the cap off.

"Aren't you helpful?" I said, snatching the bottle back and taking a fast drink. "Next, you'll be asking Connor to buy me a bottling plant."

Weston smiled at the corner of his mouth. "Seems a bit excessive, don't you think?"

"I told you what I told you in confidence," I said.

"I know," Weston said, his smile falling away. "And I know it's a whole lot of bread—"

"Don't make jokes," I said. "You *know* how hard this is. To be this grateful and this uncomfortable at the same time."

Weston's angular face softened. "We weren't going to leave you to deal with it alone."

"That's what Connor said. But it feels like a payoff. I know that's a terrible way to look at a gift like this, but it's the truth. Like he's guilty and so he's trying to buy me out of being frustrated with him."

Weston's voice was low and heavy. "He wanted to help you. That's all."

Is that all you've done, Weston?

I studied his face—his ocean eyes—as if the answers to my doubts and confusions were written there. The only thing I could grasp was the surety that he'd never hurt me. It didn't seem possible.

"Thank you," I said. "For opening my water bottle."

I watched him, hoping he would get my meaning. I didn't want debt of any kind between us, two scholarship kids.

He smiled and it was like the sun coming out after a cloudy day. "You're welcome."

We stood together, watching the party. Ruby joined Connor's group and had them all laughing within moments. At one of the wrought iron tables, Paul gently wiped a dollop of mustard from the corner of Miranda's mouth. She ceased her arguing with her daughters and smacked a kiss on his lips.

Weston's smile was small and sad as he took it all in. *A goodbye smile*, I thought. And I hated it. Hated every passing second that brought us closer to our goodbye.

I moved closer to him, shoulder to shoulder, the backs our hands brushing.

We stood that way for a long time.

Fueled by an endless supply of food and alcohol, the party didn't end until nearly ten at night. The Army unit supervisor would pick Connor and Weston up at six a.m. to take them to the airport. Only Ruby, Weston's family, and I were staying over at the Drake residence to see them off.

The guests trickled or staggered out, giving Connor tearful or back-slapping hugs goodbye. Miranda cupped her son's face in her hands. "Good night, baby. I'll see you in a coupla hours, okay? For God's sake, someone better wake me if my alarm doesn't go off."

She planted loud kisses on his cheeks and hugged him.

"Okay, good night, Ma," he said.

BRING DOWN the Stars

Paul Winfield shook Weston's hand. "Good night, Wes. See you in a few. I'll make sure Miranda's awake."

The Drakes went up to bed, leaving Ruby, Wes, Connor and me alone.

"Let's go out," Connor said, a slight slur to his words.

"Go out where?" Weston asked.

"This is our last night of freedom," he said. "I don't want it to end yet." His eyes widened. "Hey, let's go to Roxie's."

Weston frowned. "The roadhouse? On Route Ten? That's like an hour from here."

Connor fished out his phone, peering at it blearily. After a few moments, he crowed triumphantly. "It's only a forty-minute drive. Come on, I'll hire a car. It'll be fun." He gave my hand a squeeze. "They have pool tables. I can show you off."

I glanced at Ruby.

She shrugged. "I'm down."

Connor beamed. "Wes?"

"Sure," he said. "Whatever you want."

An hour later, a sedan was taking us west, along a lonely stretch of highway between Amherst and Boston.

"I hear this place is kind of rough," I said, wedged between Connor and Ruby in the back seat while Weston sat up front with the driver.

"Nah, it's great," Connor said. "You'll love it."

CHAPTER Thirty-One

Autumn

The car pulled into the dirt parking lot of Roxie's; a ramshackle, white clapboard building. A single street lamp illuminated the peeling paint and faded red sign. Despite the late hour on a Tuesday night, a few other cars and trucks were in the lot. Country music poured out of the front door.

I thought it strange that the door was left open on such a cold night, until I stepped inside and was sucked into a pocket of smoky heat. In contrast to Yancy's, this joint had one pool table and a sole dartboard, both deserted.

Connor clapped his hands. "Excellent. Wes, you rack 'em. I'll get us beers and shots."

My eyes widened. "Shots?"

"Hell, yeah," he said with a laugh. "You in?"

I bit my lip. Connor deserved to spend his last night before deployment however he wanted, but he was already loaded. Shots and beer would kill my chances to talk to him or be alone with him in a meaningful way.

Then again, sloppy, drunk sex would be the perfect capper on whatever relationship this is.

Screw it. No Drakes were here to judge. Getting drunk was the

BRING DOWN the Stars

way to kill the horrible unease twisting in my gut.

"I'm in," I said.

"You sure about this?" Weston asked me, as the four of us lined up our tequila shots, salt and lime. "Tequila isn't pear cider."

"I got this."

Ruby held up her glass. "To Connor and Weston," she said. "For answering the call of duty."

"Actually," Weston said, "Connor picked up the phone to personally call duty and ask if it needed anything, but your toast works too."

We laughed and downed our shots. I sucked the lime as if my life depended on it, and willed my stomach not to throw the liquor back up. I won the battle and everything suddenly felt warm and loose.

We played pool, laughed, and drank beer between shots. Tequila gave me a rather pleasant, underwater feeling, but I held myself to two slugs and drank plenty of water. Still, the floor kept tilting this way and that under my feet, and I went from hysterical giggling to morbid brooding. No middle ground whatsoever.

Ruby and I sat on stools, watching Connor and Weston play. They talked shit, laughed and ragged on each other mercilessly. Chris Isaac's "Wicked Game" came over the jukebox, and the night finally settled into a mellow warmth.

"Okay, this works for me," Ruby said, as Connor and Wes stripped off their dress shirts, leaving them in jeans and wife-beaters. "Holy God, I think all men should be required to report to Boot Camp if *this* is the result." She nudged my arm. "Look at your man."

I blearily looked up and found Weston.

Oh my God, his arms alone...

That lean physique was honed to perfection. Sweat beaded the tanned skin of his chest and glistened in the hollow of his throat. I followed the cut and defined lines of his shoulder down to his forearm as he bent to take a shot over the pool table.

That's not your man.

The thought sobered me more than it should have.

At two a.m., Roxie's closed and we staggered out to the sedan and the waiting driver. Weston helped Connor who was hardly able to stand. We piled into the car and Connor's head lolled to the window.

The entire ride back, no one spoke. Ruby dozed on my shoulder and Weston faced straight forward in the front seat, not looking back once.

Back at the Drakes, we poured Connor out of the car. He stumbled and swayed up the walk, an arm slung around Weston's shoulders.

"I love you," Connor said. "I do, man. I mean, dude, the fucking *Army*…"

"I know," Weston said, his own eyes bleary. "Come on. Almost there."

We made it to Connor's room—the room he and I were to share. Ruby kissed her fingers and pressed them to my cheek. "G'night, friends. I'll see you in about three hours." She started down the hall to her room, putting her hand out for balance. "I swear to God, there'd better be coffee…"

Weston and I dragged Connor into his room and eased him down on the bed. His mouth hung open, he snored wetly almost instantly.

Weston pulled off Connor's shoes, and then he walked out, unspeaking.

I closed the door and followed him into the suite's small sitting area and sank onto the small couch. A short silence fell. The celebrations were over. My heart clanged in my chest, a steady metronome of fear. Growing louder and louder with each passing second that brought Connor and Weston closer to tomorrow.

"Do you think he'll be okay in the morning?" I asked. "He drank a lot. All day, actually."

"It'll be a long time before he can drink again," Weston said. "He'll dry out in the desert."

"I'm scared for him," I said, pulling my legs under me on the couch.

"I'll watch out for him," Weston said. "I promised I would."

"And who watches out for you?"

"Connor," he said. "The platoon. Myself. I'll be okay."

I raised my eyes to see him looking down at me in a way I'd never seen before. His blue-green eyes soft. His mouth, always a grim line, now slightly parted. His lips…

God, why am I staring at his lips?

"I'm scared for you, too." My voice was small under the thrashing of my blood. I tore my gaze away, but my eyes were drawn right back to him when he spoke.

BRING DOWN the Stars

"You are? Scared for me?"

The tremor of vulnerability in his voice cracked my heart, then his demeanor hardened again and he shook his head. "Don't be."

"How could I not be worried for you both?"

"We'll be fine." He snorted a dry laugh and leaned his hip at the edge of the couch and crossed his arms. "Connor will be more than fine. He lives a charmed life. The other guys will stick to him like glue, so his luck rubs off on them."

"I wonder if he'll have time to write to me."

"Do you want him to?"

"I need his letters to stay close to him. When we're together, he's not the same. I don't get the same feeling from him as I do from his words. I don't feel that electricity."

I felt it now, though. And it was coming from two feet away. The air around Weston was always electric. A crackling force field that kept people away, fueled by his barbed tongue and acid wit. If I reached through it to touch him, no doubt I'd be shocked. It would hurt like hell.

But I want to try...

The thought sent a jolt through me. Why? Why was this happening? Why were my cheeks inflamed and my heart beating hard? I tried to force my alcohol-induced thoughts to go somewhere else, anywhere else but Weston.

"Stop *looking* at me like that," Weston snapped.

I blinked to see him glaring back at me from the edge of the couch. I gripped a cushion for support.

"Sorry, I'm…a little wasted myself."

"I'm going," Weston said. "Night." He strode to the door, but then froze with a hand on the knob. His back to me as he said, "Connor's an idiot for not fucking you one last time before we ship out."

The tone and language made my eyes flare. Weston turned around and his intense stare pinned me to the couch. Another jolt of electricity surged through me. I fought for words in the jumble of thoughts and emotions, soaked in tequila, each one more heated than the last.

"Well, that's crude," I managed. "You're trying to pick a fight with me? Right now?"

"Nah, just being honest," Weston said. "If I had a girl like you and I passed out the night before we'd be separated for months? Maybe longer? I'd curse myself every night while jerking off in my bunk or the latrine. Thinking of what I could've had one last time."

"Why are you saying this...?"

My words trailed away as an image filled my mind: Weston with his eyes closed, his fist curled around himself. Stroking hard to thoughts of me. My face in his head. My name in his mouth. Coming for me.

Slowly, like a cat, he walked over to the couch. He planted his hands on the cushions on either side of me. His gaze moved over my face and lingered on my mouth.

"I'm drunk," Weston said, though his eyes were clear and sharp as always, a fire burning behind the blue-green ocean that no one could see...unless they got as close to him as I was.

I nodded, my lips parted. "Me too," I said. "You should go."

"I will," he said. "Say goodbye to me, Autumn."

"Goodbye, Weston."

For half a heartbeat, we lingered in that moment, then broke it at the same time. I gripped him by the lapels of his shirt and pulled him to me. His hand snaked behind my head and into my hair.

And we kissed.

Hard. Unrelenting.

I kissed Weston.

Something I'd never felt before ripped through me. A heat heavy with words, thoughts and emotions. All unspoken. All of it in Weston's mouth. I could taste him. I bit his lower lip. Licked his upper lip. Sucked on his tongue. Taking and taking, but I couldn't get enough. All the while he fed on me, crazed like a lion at the kill.

What's happening...?

I was falling sideways and backward on the couch, and Weston was sliding onto me, all of his lean, hard weight against me. His mouth crashed into mine, opening and taking my kiss—taking it from my mouth in a delicious sweep of his tongue. Demanding. Almost cruel. Yet beneath that savage kiss, my body loosened like water. I melted in his arms while he lay over me, hard and unyielding.

God, what are we doing...?

The answer broke through the onslaught of Weston's kiss, rose between our rasping breaths and whispered: *Finally.*

This.

BRING DOWN the Stars

Now.
Finally.

His arms slid under me, holding me so close—as close as he could—while his mouth worked over mine with relentless desire. Never breaking for breath, as if he were running the race of his life.

Finally.

My arms snaked around his neck, my fingers sliding into his hair, then down his back. His muscles lean and hard under his shirt. I wanted skin. I wanted heat. I wanted all of him.

Finally.

Kissing him was the completion of something I didn't know had started.

Weston's hands skimmed up my sides, exploring me, touching me intimately for the first time. His thumbs brushed the curves of my breasts and he groaned. He broke away to breathe and pressed his forehead to mine.

"Weston," I whispered against his lips.

He kissed me again, as if he could erase our hesitation with every sweep of his tongue, every bite of his teeth. My eyes fell shut as another wave of heated desire swept through me, leaving me too weak to protest, to find my voice or my conscience.

His mouth trailed down my neck while his hands slipped up my body to cup my breasts. His long fingers undid the top buttons of my dress but too slowly.

"Tear it," I whispered.

Buttons clattered to the floor. My bra clasped in the front and in a heartbeat, Weston had that undone too. He hovered over me, eyes drinking me in. I'd never felt more beautiful in my life. I reached for him, brought his head down to my skin. I moaned as his hands covered both breasts and his mouth went to one nipple. My back arched off the couch to fill his hands. The movement brought our hips together with a hard grind. I felt his erection through his jeans, heavy and thick against the soft material of my dress. Another grind. And another.

Weston let out a small grunt as his mouth crashed back into mine. Our bodies reached and retreated for each other, again and again. Moving as if he were inside me already.

Finally.

He slid one hand down my body to my hip and pulled me tighter to him. My dress fell away as I hooked one leg around his waist and cinched him tight.

"Autumn," he growled into my mouth. "Jesus…"

My hands roamed under his shirt, feeling every slender, perfectly honed muscle. All edges and sharp contours. Not an ounce of fat left after Boot Camp. Only hard sinew, bone and muscle. My fevered imagination recalled his body on the track, slick with sweat, his long legs a blur before stretching to leap over the hurdles. Perfect masculine grace and agility under a bronze sun.

What would it be like to have that body naked on top of me? Those muscles blurring and stretching for me? Thrusting. Beautiful Weston, sweat-slicked and hard, driving into me.

Finally.

My hands were tugging at the button on his jeans, then the zipper. His own hand was between my thighs. Finding me and feeling how wet I was for him…

"Fuck, Autumn, wait… God, wait…"

Weston braced himself over me a moment, a grimace twisting his beautiful features. Then he was on his feet, turning a small, frustrated circle, his breath coming hard.

His sudden absence was colder than the coldest shower. A visceral slap to the face. I sucked in a breath and sat up, as if I'd been submerged in a warm, dark cave, and now was thrust into the naked light of reality.

"Oh God," I whispered. Through tendrils of messy hair, I glanced down at my torn dress and my naked breasts. "What did we do? What did *I* do?"

You cheated. That's what you did.

"Not you," Weston said darkly. He tore a hand through his hair. "Me. I did this. Fuck. I'm sorry. I'm drunk…"

The tequila was still swimming in my blood, but not so much that I could blame it for what I'd done. And I knew damn well Weston wasn't drunk. His eyes were clear and sharp as we regarded each other.

"I don't know what happened," I said, pulling my torn dress closed. "I became what I hate. I did what I swore I'd never do." I lifted my gaze to Weston. "Why…?"

"Why?" he asked. I could see the barrier going back up. Every thorny vine coiled tight around him. Impenetrable. Yet I'd breached it. And instead of being stung…

BRING DOWN the Stars

I was kissed better than I've ever been kissed in my life.

"Because I'm selfish, that's why," Weston said. "Taking what isn't mine. It's all my fault."

"No," I said, taking another deep breath. "I own this, too. I have to take responsibility. It's my fault too. I guess I felt…"

"Lonely," he said. "You were lonely. Connor passed out drunk on the eve of goodbye, and everything you wanted to say to him—all your worry and love—you had no place to put it. So you gave it to me."

"On the eve of goodbye," I murmured.

Poetic choice of words.

The suspicions I'd voiced to Connor swam through my tequila haze, and were refracted stronger in them. Alcohol was my truth serum. I'd told Weston as much.

Weston…?

The image of him writing at a desk came to me swiftly again. Only this time, he set the pen down, stood up and strode toward me, held my face in his hands and kissed me…

I buried my face in my hands. "Oh, God…what is happening? And Connor…"

Connor was in the next room, not fifteen feet away and oblivious. Just as I had been about Mark.

I looked up at Weston. "I cheated on him. That's the bottom line. The only truth…"

"Yeah, well, I cheated on him too," Weston spat. "I'm his best friend. I betrayed him. Because I'm so fucking selfish and I can't stop…"

"Can't stop, what?"

His blue-green eyes raised to meet mine and I saw the answer floating in their ocean depths.

Wanting you.

"I'm drunk and scared to ship out," he said after a moment. "That's why it happened. We don't have to tell him. It would only hurt him. He doesn't…" Weston shook his head, his anger and disgust with himself was palpable. "He doesn't need or deserve this right now. It's my fault."

"I kissed you too—"

"It was my fault and it was wrong and I'm sorry. It won't happen again."

"Weston..."

"It won't happen again," he said and his voice cracked on the last syllable, unleashing something deeper than regret for betraying a friend. Something final that scared me to my core.

A thousand questions and emotions swelled in me, tangling with the confused, heated desire for him. But the barrier was up. Barbed wire now. And behind it, he was unyielding. An ice statue. Beautiful, but immovable. Immutable.

I mustered my shaken dignity. "You're right," I said. "It won't happen again. But it's not up to you to say how I deal with it. I need to tell Connor—"

"Tell him what? That we made a drunken mistake? We can't let him go to war with the one bright spot in his life dimmed."

I blinked in confusion. "What are you talking about, one bright spot?"

"You," Weston said. "You make him happy. You make him proud when all he gets is shit from his parents."

I sagged against the couch, remembering how proud Connor had been at Thanksgiving that I was by his side.

"We can't take that away from him," Weston said. "Not while he's got his finger on the trigger and making life or death decisions. One hesitation, one second of self-doubt and it's over."

He moved toward me and my pulse jumped. His hand rose and my skin tingled in anticipation of his touch, even as guilt coursed through my veins.

"What happened tonight was my fault," he said. "Everything. It's all on me. Not Connor. Don't punish him for my mistakes."

"*Mistakes?*" I said. "I don't—"

He silenced me with his hand on my cheek, and even then, my body responded to his touch and ached for more.

"You can take the guest room," Wes said, his voice softer now, frayed at the edges. His eyes filled with pain. "I'll sleep on the couch here."

I stared at him a moment more, wishing I hadn't drunk a drop of alcohol.

My truth serum...

I couldn't think clearly and the only thing to do was to go. I rose on shaking legs and walked to the door like a sleepwalker, and Weston opened it for me.

BRING DOWN the Stars

"Goodnight, Weston," I said.

"Goodnight, Autumn."

I stepped into the hallway and he shut the door behind me. I fumbled my way through the dark, quiet house to the guest room and its big empty bed. The tears were already flowing. No matter how rocky, up-and-down and confusing things were with Connor, I was his girlfriend. And I cheated on him. I betrayed Connor on the eve of his deployment.

The eve of goodbye.

The shame whipped me to the bone. I was no better than Mark. And yet…

"It wasn't wrong," I whispered against the pillow.

Or rather, it may have been wrong, but it felt perfectly natural. *Inevitable.* As if I'd been waiting for Weston for months.

Finally.

Kissing him was cheating on Connor, but it didn't feel like cheating. It felt like a completion.

What is happening between us? The three of us?

But it was too late to ask.

We said our goodbyes in the gray light of dawn. I felt sluggish and slow; last night's drinking hanging over me like a fog, and what I'd done with Weston feeling like a dream that was both wrong and perfect. Part of me wanted to run away from the porch in shame, and the other wanted to go back to sleep for more.

Weston's mother cried loudly. Connor's mother stifled her tears behind her wrist. Paul shook Weston's hand and was visibly shocked when Weston pulled him in for a hug. They slapped each other's shoulders, then held still a beat. Weston pulled back and said something to Paul. Paul shook his head at first, his expression grim, but Weston was insistent. Finally, Paul nodded and then they shook hands, as if sealing a deal.

"I promise," Paul said.

Connor hugged me and I was petrified, positive he'd sense Weston's lingering presence all over me. When he craned down to kiss me, shame burned my skin.

"Be safe," I whispered.

"I will," he said against my hair.

Ruby took her turn hugging Connor and then Weston. She gave him a pat on the cheek.

"Behave yourself." She smirked. "No, I take that back. Give 'em hell."

He smiled faintly. "Will do."

Then it was only Weston and me. Everyone watching two friends say goodbye.

I moved slowly into his embrace and ringed my arms around his neck.

"Take care of him," I said, my voice cracking. "And you. Take care of you."

And come back to me.

"I will," he said. When he drew back, his eyes were drowning in a blue-green ocean of pain and regret.

When the Army van arrived, my heart didn't break—it tore in half. A vicious rip with sloppy, jagged edges. No defined boundaries, no territory lines indicating which part belonged to which man.

Weston's kisses still burned my swollen lips and I wanted him. I wanted Connor's letters and Weston's conversations. I wanted Connor's poetry and I wanted Weston's electricity that set my blood on fire.

"Come back to me," I whispered, as the Army van drove away with the men I loved.

PART VI
Al-Rai, Syria
June

CHAPTER Thirty-Two

Weston

"Anyone else feel like some shit's about to go down?" Bradbury deadpanned in his nasally, low voice. "No? Just me? Carry on."

We were hunkered down against what was left of the stone structure. This village had been bombed long before we found it, its inhabitants long gone, fleeing as refugees to Turkey. We weren't here for the village, but the road leading out of it to Al-Rai. An escape route from the regimes' forces in Aleppo and northwestern Syria. They wanted to cut off this refugee line. We had one job: keep it open.

Connor sat beside me, our backs to the wall. Bradbury and Erickson crouched kitty-corner. We were all smudged, bloodstained and sweating in our sand-gray camouflage. War was indeed the great equalizer and the antagonism of boot camp was long forgotten. Erickson, Bradbury and I were closer than brothers. Here, under the relentless sun and never-ending stress, I wasn't the Amherst Asshole. I was Iceman, because nothing rattled me. How could it? A man who knows his own fate has nothing left to fear.

As for Connor and me… I didn't have a word for what we were. Something beyond brothers. We were bonded at a molecular level. And in my mind, my one job was to make sure Connor got out of here alive.

BRING DOWN the Stars

I was squad-leader on this mission, with Connor, Jagger, and Erickson under my command. Lieutenant Jeffries was squad-leader of the other half of our platoon, but I'd been promoted in the field to Corporal for "exemplary leadership skills under fire."

Translation: I stuffed all feelings down deep where I couldn't touch them, leaving me precise and unflappable. The horrors we'd seen, the men we'd killed…I pressed them all down or cut them out—*like tonsils*. I'd been the Amherst Asshole. Now I was the Iceman. Cold. Hard. Unfeeling.

Jeffries still outranked me and loved giving orders. I let him. Giving orders wasn't my thing unless it was to keep my men safe. He gave us the 'move up' signal from the other side of the street. The village was at the lip of a flat, wide plain. The terrain ahead was strewn with huge rocks that led into foothills. Intel told us the road ahead was clear, but that was three days ago.

The hair on the back of my neck stood up as the twelve of us crept as quietly as our gear would allow. We moved in a pack toward the last structure in the village, looking to secure it. On Jeffries's order, Bradbury, Mendez and Milton moved farther ahead, and peered over the broken walls of the roofless structure.

Erickson made a hissing sound between his teeth. I raised a fist. My men froze.

Ahead, hostiles crouched behind the red-brown boulders, and the searing whine of an RPG missile tore the air.

"Get down! Get down! Get down!" I bellowed into our headsets.

Connor disobeyed and ran ahead to where the blast had hit.

"Fuck," I muttered.

I dove behind what was left of a smaller house, then leveled my weapon over the jagged edge of what was left of the wall. Our platoon had scattered, but I knew we'd been hit.

"Connor, you asshole…"

I could see him through the haze of kicked up sand, dust, and smoke. He had Bradbury and was dragging him by his vest toward me. I laid down suppressive fire over his head, until he was close enough that I could help him drag Bradbury behind the wall.

Connor fell back on his ass, exhausted, with Bradbury's back against his chest.

"I think he's dead," Connor said, his voice shaking and low. "I think Bradbury's fucking dead, man."

"I ordered you to stay the fuck down," I said.

Shots fired and men's voices shouted. I pushed up from my crouch, took aim over the wall and sprayed the road in front of us. I glanced quickly at Bradbury, then back to my targets, squeezing the trigger of my M4, calm and steady.

"Yeah, he's dead," I said.

A dead body isn't like how it is in the movies. It's like how Stephen King put it in his story "The Body"—the one they made *Stand by Me* out of. Not sleeping. Not unconscious. Dead. The eyes don't always stare perfectly into space, as if the person fell asleep with their eyes open.

Bradbury's eyes were slightly crossed, the whites showing. Blood trickled down his cheek from where a bullet had struck him just under the helmet.

"Fuck," Connor whispered. "Fuck, fuck, fuck."

"Chill out," I said. "And stay *down*."

The sound of gunfire, angry shouts and barking orders were muted under the stifling, oppressive heat. A hostile in white and tan streaked across the terrain in front of me, from boulder to boulder. I squeezed the trigger and he went down.

That was a human being.

No matter how many men I killed—six so far—the thought always filtered into my head. That guy would've killed me if he had the chance. Hell, he was actively *trying* to kill my men when I took him down. He may have been the one who killed Bradbury.

It was still a human being.

The thought always followed a kill. Six times now. I supposed if the thought stopped showing up, I might be in more trouble than I was already.

A few tense minutes later, the 5th Regiment joined up from the east, and the conflict was over.

I lowered my weapon, shouldered it, and jostled Connor.

"Let him go, man. He's gone."

Connor shook his head and clutched Bradbury tighter, his jaw clenched, his lips pressed down and drawn tight.

"He's got a wife," Connor said. "Did you know that? And a baby girl, three months old."

"No, I didn't know," I said and took a sip of water from my

BRING DOWN the Stars

canteen. The men may have been like my brothers, but it was Connor to whom they talked to and confided in.

A medic from the 5th pried Connor's fingers out of Bradbury's armor and pulled the body away. They covered it with a blanket until it was safe for a chopper the body out.

Connor looked at me, fear bright and glassy in his eyes.
Could be one of us next time, he said.
Not you, I answered. *You're going home.*

We turned the burned-out village into our camp. I took first patrol on the south side, then tried to grab an hour or two of sleep. I lay down next to Connor, who was wedged against the wall for cover.

I lay flat, or as flat as I could with my rucksack still strapped to my back. The sky in Syria was unlike anything I'd ever seen in Boston, where the city lights dimmed the star shine. Even Amherst had nothing on the canopy that stretched overhead, impossibly wide, black but strewn with diamonds. I wondered if Autumn ever saw a sky like this in Nebraska.

I hoped she had. I hoped someday she'd see something like this. I wished I could give it to her.

I would bring down the stars for her…

A small smile spread over my lips. I fished under my armor for the small, dirt-smudged notepad and pen I kept there, and wrote down the words before they fled. Not the Object of Devotion poem I'd been writing for months. This was something new. Something that wasn't born of pathetic longing. No objectifying devotion.

Only love.

I slept, and the dream came again.

I lined up at the track. A cool breeze blew over my skin instead of stifling desert heat. I wore my Amherst shorts and running tank. In the lane to my right, Autumn wore the purple from the night of our going away party. It had little white buttons that scattered like popcorn when I tore the dress open. Crazed to touch as much of her as I could before reason and reality rushed back in.

Poised on the track beside me, Autumn was buttoned properly, but her hair was still tousled from my hands. Her lips were red and swollen from my kisses. Her eyes dark and dilated with desire.

On my left, Connor flashed his mega-watt smile, as if nothing were amiss in his world. Beyond him, Ma, Paul, my sisters, and the Drakes took up position. In the far outside lane, Bradbury lay facedown on the ground.

Not sleeping.

Not unconscious.

Dead.

The call came for *set*. We crouched.

The gun went off and I crashed to the track as if a massive hand had flattened me. I felt no pain. I couldn't move, except to reach my arm out to those I loved as they ran away from me.

And then darkness.

I woke up with a gasp, then a strange calmness came over me, along with a deep ache of pain and regret. Pain from missing my people. Regret that the disturbing dream was the last time I would ever see them again.

I'm not coming home from this place.

I reached under my bunk and pulled out the notepad. The rest of the poem I'd begun earlier that night came to me all at once. I wrote without stopping or hesitation, my pen flying across the page, using my thigh as a table. The words no longer hiding behind my diamond mind. No thoughts, only purest emotion. Everything I felt for Autumn from heart to hand. Tears blotched a word or two, but didn't make them unreadable. I let them seep in.

I came to the bottom of the page. The empty space that waited for a signature. My pen hovered, touched down, and I pulled it away.

Connor said I owned Autumn's heart. She loved me, my soul.

And I'm not coming home.

This is all I can give to her.

Take it. It's your love too.

I loved her. My cracked, tarnished heart that was scared to love, loved Autumn Caldwell. My soul sang the words I could never say to her out loud.

The nib of the pen touched down and I wrote my name. My name. Weston. Because that's what she called me, always. Only. I was her Weston, until the day I died. This day, maybe.

I had just finished the 'n' of my name when the first bomb hit.

The concussion rocked the earth and sent debris raining down. Someone in the rear screamed in pain. Was it Erickson? I crammed the paper into my pocket, underneath my body armor and grabbed my weapon. My headset was filled with chatter.

"Incoming hostiles, half-klick south."

BRING DOWN the Stars

"Copy that. We got refugees ahead of them, northbound."

"Not regime, hajis."

"Fuck."

"Go, go, go!"

Connor scrambled to his feet and we shielded our eyes from the explosive bursts to the south. Jagger, our communications officer, shouted into his comm for immediate air strike assistance.

"The north attack earlier was a diversion," I muttered, taking cover with Connor behind a hunk of rubble. "We never looked back."

"They said refugees," Connor said, his face grim, no trace of his trademark smile. I hoped by the time he got out of here, he'd find it again.

Bullets tore the air and exploded plaster chunks tore into flesh and bone. As the sun crept over the eastern horizon, it revealed a train of weary refugees—old men, women and children—running in a panicked clump as gunfire cut the air apart. They'd fled from the south and now the enemy, who knew the terrain better, was mowing them down.

"Fuckers are using them as cover," I muttered. I started to take aim and realized Connor wasn't beside me.

"Connor? *Connor!*"

Then I heard crying.

Somehow, under the barking orders, gunfire, and exploding rubble, I heard a child crying. In the pandemonium of refugees taking cover among us, a single little boy stood apart. Immobile in the chaos, weeping over the body of his dead mother.

Connor was running for him. He didn't see the group of hostiles crouched behind the burned-out shell of a building. But I did.

"Fuck, no! *Connor, stop!*"

I ran after him, getting off a few rounds at the insurgents hiding behind a crumbling wall of scorched stone. Firing made me too slow. I had to save my breath and *run*.

The most important race of my life, with a weapon in my hands, slowing me down. My gear weighed a thousand pounds. It would flatten me to the track like a giant hand, while everyone I loved raced off and disappeared.

I'll never reach him. I'll never reach him. I'm going to lose…

The thoughts pounded in my head with my bellowing breath. Connor was in the open without cover, running straight through

263

gunfire. I ran after, bullets whizzing past me from all sides.

This is it. It's coming.

Connor was nearly to the kid. Plumes of dust and smoke fogged the street in a brown haze. Swirls and eddies billowing. Clouds parting to show an insurgent posed like a bowler about to throw a strike. The pendulum swing of his arm and the grenade rigged from a mortar round flew slow-motion in the dirty air. It rolled and jounced across the rocky soil, its course never veering from its target.

The child.

And Connor.

I channeled everything I had into my legs, forcing them to move faster than they'd ever run before. This was a race for life. Connor's life. I was running the race of his life.

I was nearly there. I could see Connor's eyes fixated on the child and determined to do something right. Something heroic and good that would make his parents—and himself proud. Unaware of the incoming danger. He didn't understand the child was already lost.

I hunched like a linebacker, lowered my shoulders and ran. I was fast. I was going to win this fucking race. Dad's car drove away but not this time. This time, I would catch it…

Connor, still running, reached his left arm out to the boy, shouted at him to *Get down! Get down!*

He was almost to the kid, but I was faster. The fastest. Always.

I won. I fucking won…

I barreled into Connor, knocked him clear off his feet, both of us flying through the air as the grenade exploded. The concussion blasted a crater of dust, dirt, shrapnel and blood.

For a single airborne moment, I only heard the air blowing past my ears. My arms gripped Connor hard. We were floating. We were *flying.*

Connor landed first, striking the ground hard. Our helmets cracked together as I landed on top of him and all the sounds of the world rushed in. Gunfire, explosions, shouts and screams. The rasp of my own sucking breath. Connor lay beneath me, unmoving. Eyes half-open, mouth ajar, his face streaked with blood and grime. Blood poured from his left arm, a piece of metal shrapnel protruding from the elbow joint.

"Connor?" I said, my voice torn and ragged, dust-choked.

He's dead.

BRING DOWN the Stars

I reached my hand that was shaking as if we were in subzero temperatures instead of the merciless desert heat, toward his face.

Fucking God no. Please. Hell no, he can't be dead. This isn't how it's supposed to happen.

I slapped at his cheek. "Connor, man... Come on..."

Another hail of gunfire, like stones pelting around us. I covered Connor's head, shielding him, screaming at him to wake the fuck up and not be dead.

Pain exploded across my back like a string of firecrackers. It slipped under my body armor and my words choked off in a gurgle. Molten bolts of agony pierced my side, my waist, and hip. Bones ground together in my trembling body. My breath grew ragged as I started to hyperventilate.

In a mindless panic, I tried to escape. To crawl away and take Connor with me—*Christ, he wasn't breathing*—but I couldn't move. I couldn't crawl, couldn't stand, couldn't run. I craned my head to look at my legs splayed out behind me. Blood poured from a gunshot wound on the back of my thigh.

But there was no pain.

Nothing.

Below the howling agony that wrapped around my waist, nothing was there.

"Connor... Please."

My vision began to gray out. So dark. The agony was subsiding, growing distant, running ahead down the track and leaving me behind.

I rested my head on Connor's chest, my eyes drifting closed. Stars filtered across the black nothingness. I smiled.

I'd give them all to you, Autumn. My love. For you...

For you, I would
bring down the stars,
wreath their fire
around your neck
like diamonds,
and watch them
pulse
to the beat of your heart

Emma Scott

*For you, I would
capture the candlelight
in the palm of my hand
Give my breath
to give it life
A whisper,
'My love'
So that it may grow
Bright and hot
And burn me*

*For you, I would
drink the salted oceans
Until their depths
Were swallowed
into the depths of me
How deep it is, this life
This love, for you
I cannot touch bottom
I never will*

*For you, I would
mine the stony earth
Until it relinquished
The secrets of time
Cracks in the stone
wrinkles of the Earth
As she turns her face
to another new day
And so I wish to live
Every one of mine
With you*

*For you, I would
be myself
At long last
I would live in my skin
And breathe my words
in my own voice*

BRING DOWN the Stars

Tinged with the accent
Of a child calling to a car
that will never stop
And in the fading echo
Nothing remains but the truth
of me
that is the love
of you

I have loved you with both
Hands tied behind my back
Bound with pen and ink
Paper and words
Sealed with someone else's name
until this moment
in which I am nothing
but a man
who loves a woman.
There is nothing left to say
Except to give
all of my heart
For you

End Book I

SNEAK Peek

Beautiful Hearts Duet book II, *Long Live the Beautiful Hearts* coming soon…

Prologue

Connor

My lungs sucked in air, bringing consciousness and chaos rushing back to me. And pain. A fuck-ton of pain.

My vision was blurred as if I were underwater. I couldn't move, my body pinned down by something heavy on my chest; I could hardly gasp for those first shallow breaths. Gunshots, shouts, and mortar fire sounded distant through the ringing in my ears. My left arm was heavy with a deep, stabbing pain.

I blinked hard, forced myself to focus, and found the anchor that was pressing me down was Wes.

He lay face down on me, his helmet on my chest, unmoving. I couldn't see his eyes, his helmet obscured him. I didn't know if he were alive or dead.

Alive. He has to be alive.

Terror like I'd never known, whipped through me, carrying adrenaline on its currents.

BRING DOWN the Stars

"Wes," I croaked. "*Wes!*"

My gaze darted all over, assessing. A pool of blood, seeping into the sand below him, sent another current of dread racing along my veins. I struggled to sit up, and pain ground steel teeth into me. Trembling as if it were freezing instead of pushing 120 degrees, I turned to see a length of jagged shrapnel lodged under the skin of my forearm, up to my elbow.

"Ah, fuck."

The ugly wrongness of it scared the shit out of me, but I brushed it aside.

Wes.

I took a quick inventory of our situation. We were at the southern edge of the village, most of the structures behind us. The fight was still happening, but had moved eastward; through blasted shells of homes, I saw figures moving in and out amid the smoke and dust.

Wes and I were exposed with no cover. A crater smeared with blood and a little kid's sandal only eight yards away. The memory of running toward the owner of that shoe, to get him behind some cover—to save him—came back to me. I reached for him…and that's all I remembered, but I knew what had happened next.

Wes had chased me down, carried me away from the explosive I didn't see, and saved my ass.

A sob tried to tear out of me, as the other half of the truth battered me. Wes had shielded me with his own body and been shot multiple times as we lay exposed on the dirt street.

And now he's dead.

"Wes," I cried. "God, no…"

Biting back the agony in my arm, I scooted out from under my best friend and gently eased his head to the ground. Wes's eyes were closed, his mouth slightly open. I put two fingers to his throat, and tears stung my eyes to feel his pulse, faint and too slow, but there.

"Thank fuck…" I said on a sigh.

I walked on my knees to inspect his wounds, and a fresh current of fear ripped away the relief. A bullet hole on the back of his thigh had nearly bled him out, dampening his fatigues down to the boot. Around his waist and under his body armor, at least three more gunshot wounds had torn through camo and flesh; a shattered fragment of bone in his hip showing.

269

"God, no, come on, Wes. No..."

I had to force back the nausea and tears of what I was seeing and focus. We were exposed. Ten yards behind me, a pile of rubble was the closest cover. My panic and fear subsided and my training took over.

I crouched on shaking legs, stood over Wes's head, and gripped his rucksack with my right hand to drag him to safety. I gritted my teeth and pulled. He scraped across the gritty sand an inch or two. Too slow. Too heavy.

I sucked in three deep breaths quickly, clenched my jaw and pulled. Gunshots rang out not a dozen yards away, and an explosion showered us with debris. Adrenaline, not strength, got me moving. After a few agonizing moments, I had Wes covered behind the rubble. I fell to my knees beside him.

"You stay with me, Wes, do you hear?" I told him, as I took off my own rucksack. "You fucking stay with me. Don't die on me, or I'll fucking kill you."

I thought I'd vomit from the pain as my rucksack strap brushed my left elbow.

"Medic!" I screamed, as I worked to get my aid kit open. "Help me, please, I need a medic!"

Each platoon had one. I hoped ours—Wilson—wasn't dead, but we'd each been trained in combat lifesaving. I dug into my rucksack and found my CAT. One handed, I fought to get slip the belt-like tourniquet up Wes's right leg, until it was above the wound. I turned the clip around and around, tightening the belt until the clip wouldn't turn any more. The bright red blood stopped flowing out of the ragged hole in his leg. I strapped the clip into place.

"*Medic*," I screamed. "*For fuck's sake, help me! I need a medic!*"

I went to my aid kit again, and grabbed my XSTAT. A lifetime ago, we'd laughingly called them the tampon shots. I tore the package off the over-sized syringe with my teeth, and put the nozzle at the gunshot on Wes's hip. I depressed the plunger and the absorbent sponges filled the gaping wound, and were instantly soaked with blood.

I winced at the sight of his other wounds—a hole in his lower back, another higher, under his body armor. They needed tending but I didn't have the training, and I was fighting for consciousness.

BRING DOWN the Stars

Dizziness and weakness flooded me. My vision grayed out and then came back again. I could do nothing else for him.

I sat on my ass, hard, exhausted. I sucked in a deep breath and put everything I had behind it.

"*Medic!*" I screamed so loud my voice turned ragged at the end. Tears flooded my eyes again. My words turned small against the noise of war. "Jesus Christ, someone help him."

My words sounded so small against the noise of war.

A dull, deep pain throbbed in my arm, as I moved to where Wes's head lay, his cheek on the sand. I weakly slapped at his ashen skin.

"Wake up, Wes," I said hoarsely. "Wake up, right the fuck now. Don't you die, Wes. Please…"

I slumped back against the rubble. There were no more gunshots sounding around us; through the tinny ringing in in my ears, I heard shouts, a woman's cries. I didn't know if we'd won or lost, only that each ticking second was bringing Wes closer to death.

I took his slack hand in mind and held it. My head lolled against the wall of rubble.

"You hold on, okay?" I said. "Listen to me. My voice. Don't go away, Wes. You stay and listen, okay?"

I shut my eyes for a moment, tears squeezed out. Then I sucked in a breath, pushed the grief back

"Remember the time you and I…we were about…fourteen…We ran into Kayla Murphy at the 7-11 after school? She was with some friends, and she smiled at you…You'd had a crush on her forever. You told our buddies about it in Jason Kingsley's rec room later that night. We were sitting around…talking about the girls we liked…and trying to be tough."

I swallowed hard, my throat felt like I'd swallowed glass and sand.

"We were all…boasting about whose ass we wanted to tap, and 'fucking that pussy'…As if we weren't all virgins." I chuckled tiredly. "But not you. You were shooting darts, and you…you had a crush on Kayla Murphy. I remember it…you kept shooting while telling us you wanted to kiss her… You said, 'in the little well of her collarbone, where her heart beats.'"

In my dimming vision, I saw shapes running toward us. Silhouettes of men. Our men.

"All the guys just stared at you," I said, "and you turned around…a dart in your hand, like 'oh fuck, what did I just say?' But instead of taking it back or making a joke… you shrugged and said, 'Yep, that's what I'd do.' And kept shooting those damn darts."

I chuckled, as Wilson, Jeffries and a couple other guys surrounded us. Wilson, the medic, went to work on Wes immediately while Jeffries—his voice distant—told me a chopper was inbound.

I kept talking to Wes and holding his hand.

"The other guys…they had no idea what to make of that. They stared at you then burst out laughing, remember? They thought… you were kidding. I laughed too, but I knew you weren't kidding. You weren't fucking kidding at all, were you, Wes?"

Time wandered away from me and when it came back, Wilson and his team had bandaged Wes's midsection, and were now giving a three-count to turn him over and lay him on his back, on the stretcher.

They'd removed his body armor, and something fell out of the vest pocket. A bent, bloodstained notebook. The chopper arrived; sand and wind and shouts buffeted me, but I reached for the notebook and snatched it just as it flapped on the sand, like a wounded bird about to take off.

Wilson was trying to tend to my arm while telling me to get in the chopper. I ignored him. While they loaded Wes, I flipped the pages of the notebook. Through my hazy vision, I read the poem there, scratched in ink, tearstained, and smudged with blood.

Wes's words.

Wes's tears.

Wes's blood.

At the bottom, his signature. His name, not mine. Like a confession.

"Yes, Wes," I said, tears streaming down my own cheeks. "The truth. This is the truth."

We climbed into the chopper, and more medics worked frantically over my best friend. Saline drip and an oxygen mask, but I saw one shake his head grimly.

Someone helped me buckle in, and tried to treat my arm.

"Leave it," I barked. "Get me a pen."

"A what?" the medic asked over the din of the whirring helicopter blades. "A *pen*?"

I looked over to Wes, his eyes closed, his face a ghastly shade

BRING DOWN the Stars

of white.

"*Give me a goddamn pen,*" I screamed.

The guy left my field of vision, then came back with a ball point. I snatched it out of his hand. I held the notebook against my leg with my left hand—the arm which felt scarily numb—and scratched with a trembling hand on the back of the notebook.

Autumn,
Wes wrote this and everything else. For you.
-C

I tried to write her address, but the pen fell from my fingers. I pressed the notebook against the medic's chest, my eyes falling shut under a wave of dizziness as the chopper lifted off.

"You have to mail this. Mail this…"

"What? Your arm…"

"Fuck my arm, you have to mail this. Autumn…Autumn Caldwell. At Amherst University…Ridell Hall. No…Rhodes…?" My vision grayed out again and this time my eyes wouldn't open. "Fuck, I can't… It's Amherst. The school. You got that? Autumn…"

Then blackness came down.

More from Emma Scott

In Harmony
"I am irrevocably in love with IN HARMONY." —**Katy Regnery,** *New York Times* **Bestselling Author**
"Told through Shakespeare's masterful Hamlet in the era of #metoo, In Harmony is a deeply moving and brutally honest story of survival after shattering, of life after feeling dead inside. If you've ever been a victim of abuse or assault, this book speaks directly to you. This is a 6 STAR and LIFETIME READ!!!--**Karen, Bookalicious Babes Blog**

Amazon: http://amzn.to/2DyByBK

Forever Right Now
You're a tornado, Darlene. I'm swept up.

"Forever Right Now is full of heart and soul--rarely does a book impact me like this one did. Emma Scott has a new forever fan in me." --*New York Times* bestselling author of *Archer's Voice*, **Mia Sheridan**

Amazon: http://amzn.to/2gA9ktr

BRING DOWN the Stars

How to Save a Life (Dreamcatcher #1)
Let's do something really crazy and trust each other.

"You're in for a roller coaster of emotions and a story that will grip you from the beginning to the very end. This is a MUST READ…"—
Book Boyfriend Blog

Amazon: http://amzn.to/2pMgygR
Audible: http://amzn.to/2r20z0R

Full Tilt
I would love you forever, if I only had the chance…

"Full of life, love and glorious feels."—**New York Daily News, Top Ten Hottest Reads of 2016**

Amazon: http://amzn.to/2o1aK1o
Audible: http://amzn.to/2o8A7ST

All In (Full Tilt #2)
Love has no limits…

"A masterpiece!" –AC Book Blog

Amazon: http://amzn.to/2cBvM26
Audible: http://amzn.to/2nUprDQ

Never miss a new release or sale!

Subscribe to Emma's super cute, non-spammy newsletter:
http://bit.ly/2nTGLf6
Follow me on Bookbub: http://bit.ly/2EooYS8
Follow me on Goodreads: http://bit.ly/1Oxcuqn
Follow me on Amazon: http://amzn.to/2FilFA3

Printed in Great Britain
by Amazon